The Hagenspan Chronicles

Book Five

Kenyan's Lamp

Robert W. Tompkins

Kenyan's Lamp

translated from the original tongues by

Robert W. Tompkins

Kenyan's Lamp

Book Five

concerning events which occurred in Hagenspan's long-distant past

In the beginning, a time before time,

when the world first danced to the sunrise song

that Architaedeus sang,

a garden He planted in the sweet virgin earth.

The stars, like jewels in the heavens,

did He lightly hang.

And in that bright and sparkling morn,

He appointed the shining faery folk

to tend the garden of His sowing,

and in the fulness of His knowing,

   He gave the Feielanns.

Once came a time—Deluge was it called—

when the world first trembled before the storm-filled clouds

of Architaedeus' liquid wrath.

Merciful He bade the Feie, innocent of the vile blood of vile man,

to go—swiftly! go—down His

silently ordained path.

So, filling their bursting lungs with sacred air,

they fled through a time that belonged not to them.

Blinding bursts of purest light, purest yearning

for the time—seconds away? aeons?—of their returning

to the Feielanns.

Now the earth's bleak autumn breaks

upon the land once blest, now blest again,

by Architaedeus' kindly grace.

Encroaching man, with tools of iron, trespasses

meadow and hill, forest, rill,

to chase (if they could) the Feie from their place.

But even in this dark'ning day

remains a sanctuary:

The keepers of the garden blest

withdraw, to where they find their rest:

    to the Feielanns.

When, in some distant night, scarlet as blood,

the last of the Feie stares, trembling, at the world

now governed by the lawless laws of men,

her heart will turn and flee across the years—

a comet streaking through a starless sky—

to home—her home—back to her home again.

To die, extinguished like a wisp of smoke;

a spark, a final wink of light ... a dark;

to lie caressed by the mother arms of home,

her tear-stained cheek kist gently by the loam

of the Feielanns.

Chapter One

Alan Poppleton walked slowly through the narrow stone hallways of Beale's Keep, matching his pace to that of the little boy whose hand he held.

"I'm not tired, Uncle Alan," the boy said, rubbing his eyes with his fist. Alan was not really Owan's uncle, but that is what the boy had called Poppleton since he was first able to speak.

"Not tired, eh?" Alan said with a soft smile. "Who was it then, that I saw asleep at the dinner table, almost dropping his head right into his vegetables?"

"That was me. But now I'm awoked."

"Ah—I thought that might have been you. Come along to bed now, and I'll tell you a story."

"A new one?"

"I suppose so."

"One that lasts days and days?"

"Days and days? I'm afraid there aren't too many tales that last that long."

"You don't have to tell it all at once."

Alan chuckled. The few men of Beale's Keep had jointly assumed the duties of fatherhood for Owan (whose natural father was dead), but none more than Alan Poppleton. Alan had known Owan's father and had respected him greatly. He supposed that he loved the little boy, who was fresh and inquisitive and bright. Owan was towheaded and fair of face like *his mother, but had his father's gray, piercing eyes, which stared at Alan insistently now, waiting for his verdict on the story. Alan leaned down and picked the boy up, swinging him through the air. "Come on, slowpoke. If we're going to tell the longest story ever, we'd better get started."*

"What story are you going to tell me?"

"The longest tale my father ever told to me was the story of Kenyan's Lamp. I might be able to stretch that out for a few days."

"Kenyan's Lamp? Ain't that a place?"

"Well, yes. Kenyan's Lamp is the name of a little city way off to the south of here. But a long time ago, Kenyan was a man, and his lamp was—well, you'll see."

Chapter Two

The spray from the waves breaking on the rocks below dissipated to a fine mist up here high above the shore, high up on the stony cliff called Kell's Lookout. Kenyan felt the cool droplets of water on his face and smiled faintly. Some of his happiest moments were spent here, alone, on the top of the craggy cliff with the fresh wind blowing the salty spray up from the surf into the little watchtower that had been fashioned upon the rocks, apparently by the hand of God.

The other guards from Beedlesgate hated their weeks at Kell's Lookout, and often arranged their work details so that they would not have to spend those days alone, but it was never Kenyan that they asked to accompany them, and Kenyan never asked any of them to go with him either.

In the three years that he had served Lord Ester of Fennal, he had not made any real friends, and in fact had been subject to some rather cruel teasing by some of the other younger guards. The older men just looked at him and shook their heads with a frown or a smile, but the young men were merciless in their taunts.

Kenyan was tall and slender. Actually, he was *very* tall, and slender as a scarecrow, and the young guards mocked him by nicknaming him "Ragshag" and "Tatters." His nose was long and pointed, his eyes round and bulging. He had sunken cheeks, and no matter how much he ate, he was unable to add flesh to his frame—and his appetite was almost legendary among the guards. He had black, curly hair that was prematurely thinning on top, and pale, almost colorless gray eyes that gave him the illusion of weakness. He had almost no chin whatsoever, and was unable to grow a beard of any kind, which added to the impression that he was somewhat delicate and feeble-minded.

Nothing of the sort was true—at least, regarding his mind. Kenyan was tenderhearted and sensitive, loving nature, poetry, and music. When fools came to perform at Lord Ester's court, his guffaws and thigh-slappings were loud and genuine, even though his fellow guards elbowed each other and smirked at him. Often when he was not on duty, Kenyan would walk alone for hours, gazing around at the created world with great curiosity and wonder, wearing a perpetually benevolent smile. Sometimes he would sit for hours in a small grove of oaks, doing nothing but patiently watching the subtle ballet of squirrels at play, and listening to the twittering music of the birds as they serenaded him from all sides. With all of the delights he found in the vast expanse of his own thoughts, Kenyan considered himself to be a rich man.

In matters physical, Kenyan was somewhat less prosperous. At swordplay he was awkward and uncertain; in fact, he had never won during practice sessions with his fellows, not even once. He was inexpert with the bow as well, though he practiced often, and with heavier weapons he was virtually useless. He was something of an embarrassment to Lord Ester, but Ester, being a practical man, realized that if he kept Kenyan occupied at watch in the far reaches, that would at least free up one more man for work at the castle who would be otherwise unproductively spent. So Kenyan's turn at distant Kell's Lookout—two days' ride from Beedlesgate—came about somewhat more frequently than that of the other guards.

It did not occur to Kenyan that he might be a lonely man, for he found delight in the wonders and beauties of creation, and did not regard solitude as a punishment to be avoided, but rather as a time of tranquility to be cherished.

Until he saw Lanadine.

✻

Kenyan gazed out across the expanse of the sea to the southwest, seeing nothing but steely blue-gray water melting into the steely blue-gray sky, which rose and returned overhead, giving him the sense that he was enveloped in some kind of a cool, misty cocoon. A tiny speck in the moist hand of God.

If he turned his gaze just a bit to the north, he could see the nearby island of Pembicote, where the fishing boats went out, and where Kenyan had lived as a boy. Pembicote was actually ruled by King Ordric, but the king had left it under the authority of Lord Ester, and the fish that were harvested from the Great Sea off the shores of Pembicote fed all of western Fennal, and added gold to Ester's coffers as well.

Kenyan scanned the horizon across the whole expanse of the sea, seeing nothing extraordinary or out of place. He turned around and looked back across Mondues Baye, to where the villages of Merrick and Fralik lay. He could not actually see the two harbor towns from his position on Kell's Lookout, but he knew where they were positioned, and sometimes he would stare off in their direction, imagining the lives that were led there. Fishermen, merchants, clerics, seamen … so many interesting things to do in the world, and Kenyan was only one man. He smiled wistfully. Nothing to be done for that!

Somewhere off farther to the east—quite a lot farther, Kenyan knew—lay the growing city of Ruric's Keep, which had been founded by King Ordric's father, Ruric the Conciliator, who had received the throne from Hagen himself. It had been Ruric who had united the six counties of Hagenspan with the southern territories known as Sabin's Country and

Sonder, where a different tongue was spoken. After Ruric's death (some years before Kenyan was born), Ordric son of Ruric sat on his father's throne and wore his mantle.

Ruric's Keep intrigued Kenyan. It was said that knights gathered there, men for whom virtue and learning and gentlemanly ways were a code to live by. When he considered the boorish behavior of the guards of Ester, it filled him with no particular resentment … but he did think it would be pleasant to spend some time with men like himself, men who treasured beauty and wisdom instead of brute strength, if such men did in fact exist.

Ruric's Keep intrigued Kenyan. But not perhaps so much as he was intrigued by Lanadine.

Chapter Three

Parry and Creel led their horses up the narrow stone corridor that led to Kell's Lookout, on their way to relieve Kenyan, who had been there by himself for a week.

"Think old Rags will have some supper in the pot for us?" Parry asked.

Creel snorted. "I don't know why they don't just leave him out here all the time."

"Hey, that's an idea. Why don't you suggest that to Lord Ester when we get back to Beedlesgate?"

Creel smirked. "Same reason *you* won't suggest it."

Parry was not by nature a malicious young man, but he was eager to ingratiate himself to Creel, who was slightly older than he was, and ruggedly handsome. Creel had a smug, sardonic attitude, and Parry was really a little intimidated by him, but Creel had few genuine friends—which secretly made him rather sad—so he had taken young Parry under his wing. And Parry, thus held under Creel's wing, had begun to take on some of Creel's scent.

"Rags is a queer bird," the younger guard said, stealing a peek at his companion, "ain't he?"

"Queer as a two-headed chicken what lays square eggs," replied Creel.

Kenyan thought about calling down to the two approaching guards that he could hear every word that they said, but decided against it.

"What do you suppose made him so?"

Creel shrugged. "Just his nature, I guess. I heard his father was a robber, and his mother was a quean, what lost her mind."

Kenyan blanched in horror. His father had been a fisherman, whom the Great Sea had claimed as a prize when Kenyan was still a small boy, and his mother's behavior had always been above reproach, mostly. It hurt him that these stories were being told, if they really were—it's possible that Creel was just lying. Kenyan began gathering his things and stowing them in his pack. He didn't want to remain any longer than necessary after the other two came to relieve him.

A few moments later, Parry called out, "Halloo! Kenyan—we're coming in!"

Struggling not to reveal the stinging bitterness that he felt, Kenyan replied, "Well, come on, then."

Creel and Parry led their mounts into a grassy clearing just below the lookout tower, and Parry said, "Heya, Kenyan. Have a good week?"

"Yes, passable." Kenyan forced a smile onto his homely face, but his eyes held no mirth.

Creel asked, "See anything of Sarbo?"

"No, not this time."

※

Not much was known about Black Sarbo, though much was suspected. It was known that he owned two small, quick sailing vessels that he called nefs, which were always either anchored at the little settlement Sarbo had established, or else out to sea practicing acts of piracy, if the rumors were true. The town that Sarbo had named after himself lay on the western shore of a river that was now known as Sarbo's Run (though it was once called Rynel Esta), whose waters originated in the far north of Hagenspan with the Strait Elles, then divided from that larger river south of Lauren, and emptied into the Great Sea at Mondues Baye.

It was said that he had eighty sailing men, both free and slave, to operate the two boats, and perhaps twice that number that lived permanently in the town of Sarbo, and perhaps that many again that lived in the wilderness surrounding his settlement, hunting, farming, fishing, trading. Of whores and concubines and wives he had over twenty, it was told, and he kept them happy with the treasures he claimed from the sea.

There was an uneasy peace between the people of western Hagenspan and Black Sarbo. While they did not approve of what were most probably lawless acts committed by the sea-bandits, neither did they refuse Sarbo's trade when he came ashore at Merrick, Fralik, and Ester to drink, carouse, and spend. So mothers held their toddlers close to their knees when the men of Sarbo the Black came to their villages, and fathers kept their tongues in their mouths. Since Sarbo practiced no unlawful deeds in Hagenspan itself (for he considered that that would be like unto fouling his own bed), there was no action ever taken against him, no threats made by the local authorities. Just an uneasy peace.

Sarbo himself was a medium-sized man, muscular and boisterous, with a wild tangle of black curls and a braided black beard. He wore no hat, so he was always wind-whipped and tanned, as if he were the embodiment of all the vast wildness of the Great Sea. He had quick, darting black eyes that missed little. One man who had narrowly escaped his wrath whispered that looking into the emptiness of those eyes was like staring into one who had a void where his soul should be. Black Sarbo

9

laughed often and loud, but even those closest to him knew that it was but a short step from Sarbo's amused benevolence to careless acts of cruelty.

※

Lord Ester had instructed his guards at Kell's Lookout to ignite the signal fire whenever they should see the two nefs of Black Sarbo approaching Mondues Baye. Kenyan had wondered about this practice, since nothing was ever done about Sarbo anyway—but his position was not to question, just to obey. At least it wasn't dangerous, even though Kenyan was always alone at Kell's Lookout. There was no way that Sarbo could anchor nearby and make any kind of rapid ascent to the watchtower, even if he should want to—but why would he care anyway?

Parry asked Kenyan, "So, did you see anything this week?"

Kenyan was a little surprised that Parry would attempt conversation with him. "I thought I heard the call of a Blacktailed Godwit, but I couldn't see it anywhere," he stammered.

Parry stared at Kenyan as if he had no idea what he was talking about, and then turned to Creel and grinned incredulously. Creel said dryly, "Anything that weren't a bird?"

"Oh," said Kenyan, embarrassed. "Just fishermen."

"Guess we'll cook us up some victuals," Parry said, still wearing his quizzical smile. "Want to stay and eat with us?"

"No … no, I guess I'd best be starting back for Beedlesgate."

Chapter Four

Lanadine lay back upon the softness of her goose-down cushions with an indulgent smile upon her lovely face. She stretched her arms over her head and arched her back, yawning, sounding a soft sigh as she exhaled.

With whom should she dine tonight? Solonsee, one of her father's guards, had been begging her for several weeks. He was quite handsome, she thought, though perhaps a bit too earnest. There was no one visiting from Ruric's Keep this week, so far as she knew—no young knights at least. Maybe Aoemer, she thought with a coy smile … though it wouldn't do to encourage him too much. He was very forward.

Lanadine knew that she was the most desirable young woman at Beedlesgate, and certainly in the town of Ester, too. Possibly the whole west coast of Hagenspan. Maybe *all* of Hagenspan. *Who knows?* she thought to herself. *Maybe there is no equal to me in all of the world.* She sat up on her bed and looked across the room to her looking glass, and smiled at her reflection. It was a rare moment that a glance at herself in the mirror didn't bring a warm glow of contentment to her belly.

Lanadine had long, gently curling hair that was so black that it was almost blue, and eyes that were so dark that it was nearly impossible to tell where the iris ended and the pupil began. Tall and lithe, she also had long black eyelashes, perfect cheekbones, and luscious rose-petal lips. All of the young men of Beedlesgate longed for her attention, even those who already had perfectly good young women of their own.

Of course, there were also other reasons for the youths to desire Lanadine. She *was* Lord Ester's daughter, and though she was not his principal heir—that would be Estred, her eldest brother—there were still many advantages to marrying into Lord Ester's family. Prestige, wealth, privilege … and the prize of Lanadine herself, of course. So, not only did those young men crave the girl whose hearts were inflamed by mere lust, but also those whose yearnings tended more toward social and political advancement.

Even though Lanadine was peripherally aware of those other reasons to love her, she was supremely confident in her own desirability completely independent of the rewards that her father could offer. She was, after all … Lanadine.

Kenyan rode past the moss-covered stone wall of Beedlesgate, heading toward the entry to the courtyard, then to the stables to drop off his horse, and then the barracks to report to his captain. Maybe, just maybe, if he were very lucky, he might catch a glimpse of Lanadine.

Kenyan had never been interested in females before, at least in anything more than the curious, completely confused sense. But then, one day … Lanadine had smiled at him. He recalled that vision as he rode the last few paces to the castle's gate, wearing a sheepish grin on his homely face. He didn't know why she had smiled at him, and had immediately assumed that she was looking past him, seeing someone beyond him. But no—she had been smiling for *him*.

He had suspected that someone was playing a prank on him, then. But he had courteously bowed and said, "Good morning, m'Lady."

Lanadine had tilted her head, her glorious head, toward him then, and stretched out her hand. Kenyan had actually *touched* her hand! And she had said, "Good morning, sir guard. Are you new here at Ester?"

And he had said humbly, "I am Kenyan, m'Lady. I have served your father for nearly three years."

"Goodness, Kenyan, forgive me!" she had cried with an embarrassed giggle. "We must become more familiar, must we not?"

"Nothing would please me more," Kenyan replied, as the color rose in his face.

She had laughed then, a merry tinkling of bells, and had breezed off to wherever it was that she had to be next, leaving Kenyan standing dumbfounded and delighted.

He wondered why she had noticed him that morning, when for three years she had looked right through him as if he were a pane of glass. Whatever the reason, Kenyan's world had become unsettled that day, and the entrance of something like hope, something like longing, had made his previous pastimes seem dull by comparison. Well, not dull, maybe ... but somehow incomplete.

Fat Henry was guarding the gate as Kenyan walked his horse the final few steps to the castle. Fat Henry was the only guard who was taller than Kenyan, and he was a jovial roisterer who had gotten Kenyan drunk twice—the only two times Kenyan had ever been drunk. He was more good-natured than most of the guards of Beedlesgate, and was even more or less friendly toward Kenyan.

"Heya, Tatters! Back from Kell's?" Henry called.

Kenyan smiled and stopped. They chatted idly about the things that had happened at the castle in the nine days that Kenyan had been gone, and remarked how fine the weather had been. Henry shared some choice gossip about one of the scullery maids, who had been caught outside the guards' quarters after midnight, having apparently mislaid a rather essential part of her attire. "We could use more of that kind of scandal around here!" Fat Henry guffawed, as Kenyan blushed.

Such stories made him think of Lanadine, as if he needed any encouragement, but the thought of Lanadine in a similarly compromised state of undress made his cheeks burn with humiliation.

"What's the matter, Tats? Too spicy for your tender feelings?" Henry slapped him on the shoulder and nearly knocked him to the ground. "Or was it you hoped to have a taste of little Marlina for yourself?"

"Heh, heh," Kenyan chuckled feebly. "I sure would have liked to have seen that," he lied. Trying ineffectively to change the subject, he said, "Seen Lord Ester's daughter anywhere today?"

"Which one?" Fat Henry asked innocently, trying to keep a straight face.

"Well, Lanadine."

Wide-eyed, Henry said in a hushed voice, "Why, she was just past here about an hour before you came, saying, 'When, oh, when will Kenyan get back from Kell's Lookout? My dear heart's about to bust.'"

Kenyan's own heart nearly stopped when he heard those words. "Truly?" he gasped.

"Of course not, you great bloody twit!" Fat Henry roared. "Is your head filled with dead cats, or what? She's Lanadine, and you're ... Kenyan!"

14

Kenyan gave Henry a chinless smile, and said, "Yes, that's … pretty funny, all right. You tweaked me that time." And he walked his horse back to the stables, smiling and shaking his head.

Chapter Five

Aoemer knew that Lanadine was outside the castle with one of her attendants, gathering flowers for tonight's dinner table, and as far as he had heard, she had not yet chosen an escort for the evening.

It was a good thing she didn't know that he was the one who had been trysting with the scullery maid a few nights ago, or propriety would demand that Lanadine should certainly refuse to speak with him again. There was only so much self-control a man could exercise before he had to find an outlet, Aoemer reflected nobly, and sweet little Marlina had been more than willing to help him relieve some of the tension that Lanadine had created in him. Too bad she had been dismissed from Lord Ester's service … she was a fine-looking lass, if a bit stupid.

But Lanadine was the goal. Lanadine, raven-haired and dangerously beautiful—the prettiest girl Aoemer had ever seen—tremendously vain but not stupid, and a daughter of the Lord of Fennal as well. Aoemer knew that he was rather vain himself … but then, when you were as good-looking as he was, what harm was there in being confident? The only other young man at Beedlesgate who was close to as handsome as Aoemer was that idiot Solonsee, who was so pukingly sincere about everything that he would never stand a chance with Lanadine, who loved flattery and presents and gossip.

Aoemer smoothed his hair back with the palms of his hands and strode to the castle gate, thinking to spend a few pleasant moments gabbing with Fat Henry, and pretending not to expect Lanadine's arrival. Then when she came to the gate bearing her burden of blooms, he could bestow his most charming smile upon her and offer to help her carry the flowers back to the dining hall. Surely his charisma and availability and helpfulness would be rewarded with the dinner invitation.

He walked toward the gate, seeing Fat Henry already engaged in conversation with somebody just out of Aoemer's line of sight. Well, whoever it was, they would be happy to have Aoemer added to the conversation; people always were. He prepared a gift, a smile of great generosity, to offer to the person on the other side of Fat Henry, only to have it freeze stiffly on his face when he recognized his rival, the insipid Solonsee. Still, he clapped Henry on the shoulder and said, "Beautiful day, isn't it, gentlemen?"

"Heya, Aoemer," Fat Henry grinned, and Solonsee nodded his way grimly, obviously disappointed to see him there. "What brings you out today?"

"Just enjoying the sun," Aoemer beamed. "What brings *you* out, Sol'?"

Solonsee replied without smiling, "I am hoping to escort Lanadine back to the castle, and I intend to ask her if I might accompany her to dinner tonight."

"Lanadine? Is she out here, too?"

"She—" Solonsee's words were cut short, for Lanadine herself was approaching from the fields with another young woman, and they both carried small bouquets of wildflowers.

"Well, what do you know?" Aoemer said. "Here she comes now. I wonder if she needs help carrying those flowers?"

Solonsee's eyes blazed with a warning. "Why don't you go see if Barner needs you?" he said, referring to their captain. "I think I heard him calling you."

"Why don't you go dive off Kell's Lookout into the Great Sea?" Aoemer replied politely.

"You've been—" Solonsee began angrily, and then bit back his words. Maintaining his composure with difficulty, he said through clenched teeth, "Do not stand between me and Lanadine. You will regret it."

"Well, why don't you take a swing at me right now, and we'll see how much thunder you've got in your maidenly little arms?" Aoemer taunted.

Fat Henry broke in, "Boys, boys—it's my duty to maintain the peace here at the gate, and it just wouldn't be right for two of Lord Ester's guards to break into dance on my watch."

Lanadine saw her two prospective suitors glaring at each other with Fat Henry between them, and deduced that she was the topic of their discussion. She smiled with satisfaction, but suffered a moment's hesitation. She didn't really favor either Solonsee or Aoemer over the other, and she *did* want to keep both of them tied to her string of aspiring swains. To choose one of them over the other for dinner tonight, when both of them were right there with lightning flashing in their eyes, would certainly discourage the one not chosen, and Lanadine wasn't ready to do that, not yet. Better to keep both of them hungry and hopeful.

She thought that perhaps she would ask Fat Henry to be her companion for the evening—*that* would perplex the other two—but then realized that he was probably on guard duty until midnight.

With her cheeks still lifted in a beatific smile, she stepped toward the guards and said, "Good afternoon, gentlemen. What a lovely surprise."

Aoemer stepped forward and bowed his head. "My Lady, if I might help you—"

"May I take your flowers?" Solonsee interrupted, also stepping toward Lanadine.

She laughed lightly and looked past them through the gate. Clomping across the courtyard, raising little puffs of dust where his feet fell, was that gawky guard, the one whose face looked like it had been fashioned by a child from mud. What was his name?

"Oh, Kenyan!" Lanadine called, remembering. "Kenyan!"

Kenyan stopped, stunned, and peered around the courtyard, trying to figure out from whence the voice was calling.

Aoemer, confused and annoyed, called to him, "Out here, Ra— Kenyan. The gate!"

Kenyan saw the three men and two women waving to him from outside the gate, and trotted in their direction, with a mixture of hope and consternation on his face. What on earth could this be?

Lanadine stifled a little laugh as she saw the gangling young man jogging toward them, with his elbows flying out to both sides, looking for all the world like a large featherless chicken.

"M'Lady! How can I serve you?" Kenyan asked breathlessly.

"You've come back from Kell's Lookout, I see! Would you please help me carry these flowers into the dining hall, and then go and clean yourself up so that you can be my companion at dinner this evening?"

Aoemer stood with his mouth agape. *This must be some kind of deception.* Solonsee, who felt certain that he would have been Lanadine's escort tonight if Aoemer had not arrived at the gate, wore a bitter scowl on his handsome face. Fat Henry, who wanted to laugh, limited himself to a broad smile. *Well, what do you know about that?*

Kenyan accepted the flowers from Lanadine, and she looped her hand through his arm with a gentle thank-you. Nodding at her attendant to follow them, she smiled at Aoemer and Solonsee, and said, "Perhaps some other time."

Kenyan nodded at the other guards apologetically, wearing a ridiculously sheepish grin on his homely mug. What a day this was turning out to be!

※

Captain Barner stared at Kenyan incredulously as the latter asked for permission to accompany Lanadine to dinner. "Lanadine has asked you to dine with her?"

"I hardly believe it myself," Kenyan admitted humbly.

"What's that, Cap'?" asked Slater, another one of the young guards.

"Lanadine has apparently asked our Kenyan to be her escort tonight," Barner said, still with wonder in his voice.

Slater shook his head and smiled. "Are you gonna let him go?"

"Well … yes, of course," Barner said. "You won't do anything to shame the guards, will you?"

"I hope not," said Kenyan.

"Lift your arms," Barner commanded, and Kenyan did so. The captain bent toward Kenyan's armpits and sniffed. "Whoo! That won't do," he said, waving his hand in front of his face. "Got any soap?"

"I understand, Cap'. I'll take care of it," Kenyan said.

A few minutes later, having washed, he was back in the barracks, changing into his other tunic, and humming happily, nervously.

Aoemer appeared, leaning in the doorway, wearing a stiff smile. "Well, Rags ... I guess she chose you."

"Aoemer!" Kenyan greeted him. "Did *you* want to eat with Lanadine tonight?"

"Of course. We all do," Aoemer replied, with a wink toward Slater. "But you're the one she chose. Guess there's more to you than we figured."

"I hope so," Kenyan agreed.

"Have you ever been a Lady's escort before?" Aoemer asked helpfully.

Kenyan shook his head. "Never thought I would be."

"Oh, no ... maybe we should tell him about a few things," Aoemer said to Slater.

Slater said eagerly, "Yes! We should, maybe."

"Do you know about the Gentleman's Code for Conduct with Ladies?" Aoemer asked.

"No!" Kenyan said, astonished. "There's a code?"

"Oh, yes," Slater said. "Tells you all about how to behave with a Lady."

"Is there much to learn?" Kenyan said weakly.

"No, not so much," said Aoemer. "Most of it's just common sense and good manners. But there's a few things you need to remember."

"Tell me, please."

"Well, there's really only five major points," Aoemer said, hoping he could think of five things to tell Kenyan. "The first one is— the first one is—"

"Always hold a Lady's chair for her when she sits down, and always stand when she stands," Slater contributed.

"That's not so bad," Kenyan said, nodding. "What's next?"

"Never ask a Lady any questions of a personal nature, which might cause her discomfort," Aoemer recovered.

"Good," Kenyan nodded. "Next?"

"Number Three: If a Lady should ask a gentleman a question, the gentleman should continue to speak on that subject until she requests him to stop, even if he should reveal all that he knows, and more," Slater said, and nearly giggled.

Kenyan looked at him with suspicion, but Aoemer broke in. "Fourth: A gentleman will always ask a Lady for a bite of her food before she proceeds to eat."

"You're tweaking me, aren't you?" Kenyan demanded. "There isn't any code!"

"No, it's so," Aoemer said with as much sincerity as he could muster, and Slater nodded affirmatively. "It's because old King Ruric's wife was nearly poisoned once; that's why the gentleman has a bite of her food first." Slater nodded again.

"I don't know," Kenyan said doubtfully.

"You haven't even heard the best one yet," Aoemer insisted. "Number Five: The Reward."

"Reward?"

"If the Lady is satisfied with your gentlemanly behavior, she must reward you at the end of the evening with a kiss, a kiss on the lips."

Kenyan burst into hearty laughter and slapped his thigh. "Now I know you're telling me stories! *Ha*, ha, ha! A kiss from Lanadine!" He wiped a tear from the corner of his eye.

Aoemer and Slater looked at each other and shook their heads regretfully. "Sad to think that Lanadine asked you to be her escort, and you won't even get the full reward."

"Thank you, boys, for giving me a little laugh. What a couple of jesters you are!"

Slater said, "Rags, if it was funny, we'd be laughing too, wouldn't we? What we told you was the truth."

Captain Barner was just re-entering the barracks, so Kenyan asked Slater, "If there really is a code for gentlemen, then the captain will know about it, right?"

"Why, sure he will," Slater allowed, looking hopefully at Aoemer.

"Captain," Kenyan turned to face Barner, "have you ever heard of a code for gentlemen?"

"A code for gentlemen," Barner repeated, as he stroked his chin. Behind Kenyan's back, Aoemer and Slater were nodding at him vigorously. "Oh, you mean the Gentleman's Code."

"You mean … there is one?" Kenyan said dubiously.

"Well, I don't know that it's rightly written down, but gentlemen know about it," Barner said vaguely.

"What about Rule Number Five?"

"Rule Number Five ... hmmm," he said, and Aoemer and Slater both puckered their lips toward him desperately from behind Kenyan's back, looking something like two gasping, freshly-caught fish. "Oh, yes ... you mean about kissing."

"Yes ... the reward," Kenyan said, and suddenly he was afraid. There really *was* a Gentleman's Code ... and that meant that he really might be required to kiss Lanadine! Surely—surely she knew about those conditions before she invited him to be her dinner guest ... didn't she?

Turning back toward Aoemer, he said feebly, "Does Lanadine know about this?"

Aoemer said, "She does. I have been her escort three times, and have been rewarded with three kisses."

"Two for me, a kiss both times," added Slater.

Barner watched and shook his head—what were they getting poor Tatters into? But he kept his counsel to himself.

"You'd better tell me those rules again," said Kenyan glumly.

Chapter Six

Several minutes before the time Lanadine had specified, Kenyan went to await her arrival at the foyer leading into Beedlesgate's main dining hall. He scratched his eyebrows and rubbed his nose anxiously, and suddenly felt a moment of panic, hoping no boogers were visible in his nostrils. He turned furtively toward a standing suit of armor next to the doorway, and tried in vain to inspect his appearance in the dim reflection provided by the polished metal.

Several of Lord Ester's dinner guests for the evening made their way past Kenyan into the hall, and he felt conspicuously out of place. He had never been invited to the lord's table before, except for a few times when all of the guards were invited as a group. He wasn't even sure Lord Ester knew who he *was*. Now he was going to be on the spot, eating and conversing with Lord Ester, Lady Elandel, and Lanadine. He was going to be spending an hour, maybe more, with Lanadine!

Kenyan had never known a beauty as pure as Lanadine's. Her face was as lovely as the sky, her voice as melodious as the songs of the birds he loved. Her hair was like … like … well, like *something*. It was beautiful, anyway. He scarcely even dared contemplate the loveliness of her figure, so he concentrated instead on the charms of her personality. Although Kenyan had only had two brief conversations with Lanadine, her manners and gentleness and sweetness had been … well, mannerly and gentle and sweet. He chided himself with an inward smile: his fascination with Lanadine had made him dimwitted.

He was amazed that Lanadine would choose him as her dinner companion. Especially when he considered that she knew about Rule Number Five! Was it possible … was it possible that she had seen, somehow, deep into Kenyan's soul and recognized him to be the truest heart that would ever love her? Was it possible … that she would want to share a second dinner with him? Then a third, and a fourth, and a lifetime?

He shook his head with a chuckle. Silliness! He smiled at his reflection in the suit of armor. Well, whatever would happen tomorrow, he suspected that *tonight* would be a night he would never forget. He just hoped, for probably the twentieth time, that he wouldn't do something exceptionally stupid.

"Ah, Kenyan, there you are," Lanadine said, as she approached with her attendant. "That's all right, Millie, Kenyan can see me the rest of the way."

Millie smiled at Kenyan with a slight nod, and departed back where the girls had come from.

"Well … shall we?" Lanadine said with a bright smile.

"It would be my honor, m'Lady," Kenyan replied, holding out his arm toward her, glad he had washed.

She took the proffered arm, and looked past him into the dining hall, craning her neck to see if anyone else might be there, still smiling a little vacantly.

Kenyan, his heart rapidly thumping, chattered nervously, "I thank you for choosing me, m'Lady—you can hardly know how pleased I am." He continued in a confidential tone, "Why, I just learned about the Gentleman's Code today."

Lanadine, not knowing what he was talking about, said politely, "Oh, is that so? How nice for you."

"How nice indeed," Kenyan agreed, offering her what he hoped was an endearing smile.

The pair entered the dining hall, where Lanadine introduced Kenyan to the other guests, who greeted Kenyan with a mixture of amusement and bewilderment. This gangly young man did not seem to be up to Lanadine's usual standards … perhaps he was very wealthy.

After a few moments the Lord Ester and the Lady Elandel entered, and Lanadine presented Kenyan to them. "Father, you know Kenyan, I believe?"

With eyebrows raised, Ester replied, "Yes, we've met, I'm sure." He thought to himself, *My dark-eyed daughter, what are you up to?* but said nothing to betray his thoughts. Lanadine, for her part, seemed as innocent of duplicity as if she were a newborn lamb.

After a few moments of casual small talk, the guests took their seats at Lord Ester's table. Kenyan held Lanadine's chair for her, and she beamed a thank-you to him. Lady Elandel beckoned for the food to be served, and girls came to the table bearing steaming platters of meat. The succulent aromas made Kenyan begin to salivate; during his barren week at Kell's Lookout, he had eaten only dried, salted meat and cold biscuits, and drunk only spring water. His belly blurted a rumble of anticipation, and Kenyan blushed in embarrassment, but Lanadine smiled sympathetically at him, and he felt reassured and grateful.

"May I serve you, m'Lady?" Kenyan asked, and Lanadine, with a surprised arch of her perfectly manicured brow, nodded. Kenyan reached out his fork and speared a slab of venison, which he deposited on Lanadine's plate. Taking his knife, he began carving out a small morsel of the meat.

"You're not going to feed me, too, are you?" Lanadine asked in astonishment.

"Of course not, m'Lady. This one's for me," Kenyan said, and then dropped his voice to a whisper and gave a knowing nod. "The poison."

Lanadine's eyes opened wide in amazement, but she couldn't think of anything to say, so she just watched as Kenyan took a bite of her meat, chewed it thoughtfully, and swallowed. She watched with bemused curiosity as his Adam's apple bobbed up and down with the action of swallowing.

Kenyan said, "Mmm … very tasty. You may proceed, m'Lady, if you wish."

She murmured a bewildered thank-you and took up her own utensils.

Kenyan fell to and began eating heartily, more than making up for his week of privation at the watchtower. The other dinner guests noticed his eager attack on his food; the men smirked at each other, and the women frowned primly. Lanadine observed him eating for several minutes out of the corner of her eye, perplexed, and thought it strange that he didn't try to make conversation with her. Usually her escorts asked her all kinds of questions, hoping to discover ways to flatter her, which she enjoyed greatly.

Thinking that perhaps he needed a little push to get him started, Lanadine asked politely, "So, Kenyan, what do you like to do when you're not on duty?"

Sensing that this was his opportunity to impress her with his knowledge, Kenyan laid down his knife and fork, wiped his fingers on his pantlegs, and said, "If you please, m'Lady, my favorite thing to do in all the world is wander through the woodlands and spy on birds, watching them flit among the trees, and listening to their songs."

Lanadine, whose favorite things to do in all the world were dressing in fine silks and dancing to the music of the fiddles and pipes, said with a nearly imperceptible sigh of resignation, "How very fascinating," and decided to turn and see if the woman seated on her other side had anything interesting to talk about. But before she could turn, Kenyan continued.

He talked about the graceful flight of marsh harriers he had seen circling high overhead, and the bubbling courtship song of the whimbrels he had observed on the shoreline, and she nodded politely, her cheeks frozen in a stilted smile. He told her about a lake that he had discovered inland—nothing more than a large pond, really—where he had been a happy spectator at the shows put on by red-necked grebes and scaups and wigeons. Lanadine's eyes began to glaze over as she listened to the words that meant nothing to her, buffeting her relentlessly like the waves on the beach. She blinked momentarily as Kenyan produced the rising-then-falling whistle that approximated the call of the Greater Wigeon, and she smiled apologetically at her father, who was beginning to wonder just what all this nonsense was about.

Kenyan continued with birdcalls, mimicking the *tsee-ip, tsee-ip* he had heard from the delicate, darting Yellow Wagtails he had recently seen, and Lanadine began to feel a little desperate. She even began to imagine that Kenyan *was* some kind of giant bird … his long, pointed nose rather resembled the bobbing beak of … what? Not a bird. A goblin? The other dinner guests were now listening with amusement, aware of her discomfort and a little pleased by it. Just as Kenyan was beginning to describe his greatest discovery—a solitary Whooper Swan that had once landed at his hidden pond—Lanadine laid her hand gently on his arm and whispered, "Forgive me, Kenyan, but I believe I must retire early tonight."

Kenyan, alarmed, said, "You're not feeling poorly, are you, m'Lady?" He hoped anxiously that he had not failed her with the poison test.

"No," she reassured him, "it's just that your words have filled me with such … filled my mind with such vibrant portraits of nature, that I don't believe I can … contain any more tonight." She smiled thinly at him, not wishing to injure his feelings. He was a very odd man, but certainly gentle and sincere. Still, though, not even the prospect of keeping Aoemer and Solonsee properly balanced was worth another tedious quarter of an hour listening to Kenyan's rambling monologue. "Would you please see me to my rooms?"

"Why, yes, m'Lady, of course," Kenyan stammered. *Rule Number Five!* His hands started to shake, and his heart began hammering noisily in his chest again, or so it felt to Kenyan. "I bid you all good evening," he said as he rose from his seat, his cheeks flaming red, and the other diners returned his farewell. Lanadine smiled numbly at the room, feeling like she was viewing her father's guests from a great distance, and took Kenyan's arm.

They walked together to the outer chamber of Lord Ester's personal suites, beyond which Kenyan was not allowed to proceed. Kenyan was in a state of such bliss as he had never before imagined possible, while Lanadine was in just about as opposite a state as that as she could possibly be. They proceeded in silence, with Kenyan wondering how to gracefully ask for the kiss that Aoemer had promised would be his. Would she just give it to him, or were there words that needed to be spoken first? He should have asked Aoemer! Perhaps it was up to Kenyan to suggest that they might dine together again sometime? No … best not to run too far, too fast.

They arrived at the shadowed vestibule leading to Lanadine's rooms, and she removed her hand from the crook of Kenyan's arm. "Well," she said, "it certainly was an … informative evening."

"Thank you," Kenyan said. "I trust that my company was, ah, acceptable to you?"

"Oh, yes," said Lanadine, wishing for this awkward moment to be over so she could go back to her bedroom and plan. How would Solonsee and Aoemer act tomorrow when they heard about her humiliation of tonight?

"Then, m'Lady … forgive me, but I am inexperienced in these matters." Kenyan looked at her with great tenderness—he had never seen anything so beautiful, so desirable, in all his life, as Lanadine appeared to him now. "Might I ask about Rule Number Five?"

Lanadine, confused again, but not wanting to hear anything about whatever Rule Number Five might be, said, "Oh, yes. I see. Thank you."

"Then, I may proceed?" Kenyan asked, wanting to be absolutely sure.

"Yes, please do," she said, thinking that he was asking her permission to leave.

Kenyan closed his eyes and leaned expectantly toward Lanadine, his face coming uncomfortably close to hers, his fleshy lips puckered. "What—" she said with a start, as she pulled away from him, "what are you doing?"

The next moment seemed to occur in slow motion for Kenyan, who became aware that something was beginning to go terribly wrong. But he was already bending steeply toward Lanadine, and when she jerked backward away from him, he lost his balance and pitched forward into her. Flailing his arms as if he were a red-necked grebe trying to take flight, he fell face first into her chest, experiencing all too briefly that softness that he had not even dared to imagine. Lanadine fell on her rump with a shriek, and Kenyan found himself to his great embarrassment kneeling on the floor with his face in her lap.

"Get up!" Lanadine hissed. "What have you done? Get up!"

Apologizing profusely, Kenyan scrambled to his feet and offered her his hand.

She said angrily, "I'll get *myself* up! Please, just leave!"

Kenyan was heartsick. Much more miserable now than he had been blissful before, he apologized one last time, and left her sitting there on the floor in all of her flashing black rage. As he reached the arch of the doorway, he looked back at her, and thought to himself that she was still the most beautiful thing he had ever seen, all darkness and fury, like a perfect thunderstorm.

"Go!" she shouted.

Utterly defeated, he stepped from within the suddenly claustrophobic walls of the castle into the freshness of the evening. The sky was indigo blue, with white pinpricks of starlight just starting to twinkle, and the coolness of the air was a merciful balm to his blazing cheeks. He didn't want to go back to the barracks now—he *couldn't*—so he headed out of the castle grounds. Maybe a moonlit walk through the fields would help him figure out what had gone so very wrong, and what he could possibly do to rectify it.

As he drew near the gate, Fat Henry called enthusiastically out to him. "Heya, Tatters! How did dinner with Lanadine go?"

Kenyan's lips twisted in the faint shadow of a smile, and he said in a feeble voice, "Fine."

Chapter Seven

Lord Ester sat in council with one of his principal trading partners. The man who sat across the table from him had accumulated vast wealth, and was willing to part with substantial portions of it in order to ensure that favorable conditions for his business continued to exist. He asked for little but that he might be able to carry on his chosen trade unmolested, and enjoy safe passage on the rivers and roads of Fennal. And this Lord Ester was happy to grant, for the man who sat with him had brought Ester wealth unavailable elsewhere in Hagenspan, treasures that even Ordric the King did not possess.

The man across Ester's table laughed, a boisterous, bawdy cackle, and took another draught of the drink he had brought for Ester to try, tossing back his head of black curls as he drained his tankard. The drink was sweet and heady, and he had no name for it, but he was thinking about calling it *rumbullion*, a word from the neighboring islands that made the man think of dancing and fighting and roistering and laughing.

There was a knock on the door to Lord Ester's study, and Ester said to Sarbo the Black (for that was the identity of his guest), "Hide yourself behind that tapestry for a moment, if you will."

Sarbo grunted a grudging acquiescence, rose, and secreted himself behind a heavy drapery that hung in front of a hidden entrance into this study.

"What is it?" Lord Ester called toward the door where the knock had come from.

"If you please, my Lord," said the guard on duty, "your daughter Lanadine requests a moment."

"Hmmp," Lord Ester grumbled. "A moment. Send her in."

Sarbo peeked from behind the tapestry, which was sheltered somewhat by shadows. He had heard that Ester and Elandel had daughters, but he had never seen them. If they looked anything like Elandel, though … he had to have a look.

"Good afternoon, Father," Lanadine said, striding into his study without any hint of formality. "I would like you to punish Kenyan."

"Your birdman from last night?" Ester said with a snort. "And why would you have me punish him?"

"He tried to take liberties with me. It would not be proper for me to tell you how," she said primly. "But he was very fresh."

"Well," Ester said. "Well. And you would have me punish him how?"

Sarbo watched the girl from his hiding place, seeing her long black curls and her fathomless black eyes, and he was filled with desire. *By the devil*, he thought, *she could be my own daughter*. He tried to remember whether he had ever coupled with the Lady Elandel, and decided that he had probably not. He continued to leer as Lanadine bantered saucily with her father. *What a queen she'd make for me! What a delicious tart! I must have her!* He knew he should probably not broach such a subject with the Lord Ester, who, greedy though he might be, would never easily agree to sell his own daughter to Black Sarbo. He stored the thought away in his mind, though—someday, Sarbo would find a way to take Lanadine.

Lord Ester finally agreed with the girl to send Kenyan away for a month at Kell's Lookout, and give him a stern warning that if he should ever offend the lord's family again, he would be turned out of his service entirely. "And flogged," Lanadine insisted.

"And flogged," her father consented. "Send to the barracks, and have him report to me."

"Thank you, Father," Lanadine curtseyed. "You have redeemed the honor of your house, and your name."

"Yes," Lord Ester said with a dry smile.

※

Kenyan had spent the night sleeping fitfully among the trees, suffering the bitter anguish of his soul. He realized now that Aoemer and Slater had deceived him, and understood that somehow, for just one day, he had become their rival for Lanadine's affections. That realization made it easy for him to forgive them for their deception. Yes, they had lied to him … but for the love of Lanadine, Kenyan himself may even have lied.

That was all done now, he knew. There would be no more dinners with Lanadine, no more walking arm in arm; there would be no kiss. Sadly, he thought it again. *There would never be any kiss.*

What to do now? Was he a laughingstock, a buffoon, a fool? Probably. He felt like running away … but where? And how? He still had the vow he had sworn, to serve Lord Ester and Beedlesgate and Fennal and Hagenspan, and he could not run away from that vow. Where would he go?

He wondered why Captain Barner had joined the two young guards in their deception. He had always respected the captain, had always tried his best … even if that wasn't always very good. He thought the captain knew, though … knew that Kenyan had always tried his best, his very best. Even if it wasn't … very good.

Kenyan picked up a fallen twig and began peeling off the bark. It comforted him somewhat, stripping away the rough and shriveled bark, revealing the smooth white wood underneath. He imagined that he was stripping away the foolishness of his own soul, and vowed to himself that whatever it was that lay beneath, he would make as pure as it could possibly be. He rubbed the wood of the twig with his thumbs, until there was no trace of bark left. Sadly admiring his handiwork, he lifted the little stick to his lips, and cherished the sensation of the smoothness against his flesh. He enjoyed the vibrant sense of touch that dwelt in his lips; a touch that would never include Lanadine. But even if he should never kiss Lanadine, he mused, at least he could kiss this little smooth white stick, this twig that represented the purity of his own soul.

He wondered if he should tuck the little talisman in his pocket and keep it … but then he snapped it in two, and tossed it to the ground. Kenyan clambered to his feet, and began dutifully trudging back to Beedlesgate. He had a vow to fulfill.

Tannabal was a guard at the castle who was a little older than most. He had heard rumors of what had transpired last night—who hadn't?—but withheld his judgment until the facts could be made certain. One thing was sure: Poor Kenyan had stuck his foot in it, somehow, and it seemed he was destined to suffer Lanadine's wrath today. That was why Tannabal had never gotten involved with women himself; they were too damned unpredictable. One night they're inviting a fellow to dinner, the next day it's his head they want on the platter.

He saw a lanky form step out from the trees and start to cross the field, and figured that it had to be Kenyan.

Tannabal watched as the younger man approached with dejection spread all over his homely face like gray paint, making his appearance, if possible, even more unappealing than usual. Tannabal frowned in commiseration; Kenyan was no soldier, but it was regrettable to see the poor oaf suffering like this.

"Kenyan," Tannabal nodded to him. "Lord Ester has asked for you to report."

Oh, no. "Are people talking about … last night?" the sad young man asked.

"Some. Not too much."

"What are they, ah, what are they saying?"

"Not too much. Just that Lanadine's mad, though nobody's sure why."

Kenyan nodded. "All right, then." He wondered if he should tidy himself up first before reporting to Lord Ester, and then decided that he should probably respond immediately.

"Buck up, young fellow," Tannabal said kindly, clapping him on the shoulder. "Whatever's going to happen will be over soon."

Kenyan smiled briefly, gratefully, and then began trudging through the courtyard, thinking glumly to himself that it was just yesterday that he had been walking through this same yard, when he had heard the sweet voice of Lanadine calling to him. *Calling him to disaster and humiliation*, he reflected bitterly.

A few moments later, he was ushered into Lord Ester's study by the guard at the door. He began to bend his knees, intending to kneel on the floor before the desk where the lord was seated, but Ester said, "Stand, Kenyan. Stand."

"M'Lord," Kenyan said obediently.

A moment passed as Ester contemplated what to say to this sorry man, this sad excuse for a guard. Ester had actually been rather impressed with Kenyan's knowledge of birds that he had displayed at dinner the night before, but he was also very aware of the youth's limitations with the tools of his profession. There might be a suitable place in the world for this unattractive young man, Ester allowed, but he was having serious doubts about that place being Beedlesgate.

"Well," he said finally.

"M'Lord," Kenyan said again.

Another pause. "You seem to have displeased my daughter," Ester said.

Kenyan had no response to that; he just stood with his pain-filled eyes gazing openly back into Ester's. He thought to himself, *I didn't mean to*, but he didn't speak the words.

Ester stared back at Kenyan, reading the story written on his homely face, recognizing him to be hopelessly honest if a bit foolish, and felt a twinge of compassion. "I will give you a piece of advice," he said. "This is good advice—mark it well."

"Yes, m'Lord," Kenyan said hopefully.

Ester continued to look into Kenyan's eyes. "Never trust a woman." He thought of his own wife Elandel. "Not with your heart, not with your money, not with your secrets. Never, never trust a woman."

Kenyan thought that that was very bitter advice, but it immediately occurred to him that he would probably never get the chance to entrust his heart to a woman anyway ... since she would first have to be entrusted with the uninviting prospect of his face. But he said, "Yes, m'Lord."

"Yes," Lord Ester said, and the moment of camaraderie between them came to an end. "You know that I will have to punish you?"

An involuntary shudder went down Kenyan's spine, but he said again, "Yes, m'Lord."

"It's not so bad as that," Lord Ester said, recognizing Kenyan's fear. "You will serve a month at Kell's Lookout without relief." Kenyan was surprised and grateful—did Ester know that Kenyan scarcely considered that a punishment at all? "But that's not all of it," Ester continued. "If you should offend Lanadine again, you will be flogged and discharged from your position here at Beedlesgate. Do you understand?"

"Yes, m'Lord. Thank you very much," Kenyan said with sincerity.

"Mmm, yes. You are dismissed, then. You may report to Kell's Lookout immediately."

Chapter Eight

Captain Barner pulled Aoemer and Slater aside and said, "Whatever you did to poor old Kenyan last night has caused a bloody ruckus, to be sure. He's been sent back off to Kell's for a month by himself."

Slater, who hated going to Kell's Lookout, said with genuine contrition, "I'm sorry, Cap'. We were just playing with him, but he believed us."

Barner grunted an unsatisfied, "Hmmp," and glared at Aoemer.

"It's his own fault, Cap', for being so damned stupid. He thought he had a fighter's chance with Lanadine—the ugly goon! Him, with his birds and his poems and his politeness," Aoemer spat in derision. "What a half-witted chucklehead."

Barner reprimanded him sharply. "Rags may not have been much good with the blade and the bow, but there's a damn sight worse things in this world than loving birds and poems! Hellfire!" he snapped with disgust.

It was a rare thing for Barner to use strong language, and Aoemer realized that he might have stepped too far. A guilty look darkened his handsome features, and he muttered, "I'm sorry, Captain. Really."

"Well … there's worse things than *that*, too," Barner said gruffly.

Kenyan packed up his clothing and his small collection of little-used weapons. In a few minutes, he'd head over to the cold-room and see how much food he could appropriate for his month at Kell's Lookout. He was hoping for quite a bit, for he was not particularly skillful at procuring his own meat when he was up on the bluff. He thought he might try to snag a couple of laying hens to take along on his trip—then there would at least be eggs, and if worst came to worst … chicken. Of course, carrying two hens for two days on his horse might be problematic.

He left his packs on the edge of his bed and walked over to the stables to find a good horse for the trip. The nag he had taken last time had been bony and swaybacked, and it had hurt Kenyan's pelvic bones to ride her for so long. Of course, he wasn't a particularly good rider, either—most *all* of the horses hurt his bones to ride for two days.

The master of the stables, an old-timer named Bellings, greeted Kenyan with surprise. "What're *you* doin' here, youngster? Just got back from Kell's, I thought, di'n't ye?" Bellings, who chewed on weeds as a matter of recreation—though he claimed the vegetation he masticated had medicinal powers—spat a greenish stream of spittle off to the side of Kenyan's foot.

"I have to go back."

"What happent? Ye forget somethin'?"

"No," Kenyan said ruefully, "I *need* to forget something."

"Ah," Bellings winked, "I get it. Wimmin parblems."

"Uh … yes," Kenyan admitted, and he looked at Bellings guardedly. "You mean, you haven't heard anything?"

"No, I s'pose not." Bellings scratched his head. "There's stuff that I don't hear, workin' here wi' the livestock."

"Well … you probably will."

Bellings chuckled and spurted another stream of green juice across the stable floor. "Who's the lucky gal?"

"It's not like that," Kenyan said, embarrassed. "There was a ... misunderstanding between one of Lord Ester's daughters and me."

"And just what was that misunderstanding?" demanded a familiar female voice from behind Kenyan's back.

Kenyan's heart leaped in his breast, and Bellings quickly excused himself and escaped back to the safety of his stables. Kenyan turned around to face Lanadine, whose black eyes glinted with anger.

"Forgive me, m'Lady—I didn't know you were there," he sputtered.

"I daresay! You are nattering about me with the servants, behind my back!"

"Oh, *no*, m'Lady—"

"You have caused me a great deal of trouble, Kenyan!" she said heatedly, though Kenyan wondered what kind of trouble he could have possibly caused for her. He stole an apologetic glance at Lanadine's maidservant Millie, but her expression was unreadable.

"I am very, very sorry, m'Lady—it was not my intention," he said penitently to Lanadine.

"Well," she said irritably. To Kenyan's eye, she seemed somewhat less beautiful than she had yesterday; there was something about the look in her eyes that suggested cruelty, he thought. Probably just his tortured imagination, though. "Just see that nothing like that ever happens again."

"Oh, it won't," Kenyan agreed enthusiastically.

Lanadine retorted sharply, "And what is *that* supposed to mean?"

"M'Lady?" Kenyan thought he had given an appropriate response, but suddenly sensed that he was treading perilously close to the precipice here, though he had no idea why.

"What is that supposed to mean?" Lanadine repeated.

"I, uh—" Kenyan stammered. "Is there—is there a right answer?"

"The *truth*, if it's not too inconvenient!" The color was beginning to rise in her cheeks.

"Yes, m'Lady."

"Yes, *what*?"

"Um ... just 'yes,' I believe."

"Answer my question!" she yelled, to Kenyan's acute embarrassment. He wished she would keep her voice down, but he knew he was powerless to suggest such a thing. Several other members of the castle's household had started looking toward him, wondering why he was making Lanadine so angry.

"I, ah, I will try not to, ah, offend you again," he said, hoping that it was what she was looking for.

"Offend me?" she demanded. "You tried to *kiss* me! No one has ever kissed me before! That privilege is reserved for the one that I marry!"

Kenyan groaned inwardly. "Forgive me, m'Lady—I was misinformed."

"And what is *that* supposed to mean? Did you think I was a common trollop?" she cried.

Millie, who had been watching with growing sympathy for Kenyan, decided to intervene on his behalf. "Please, Lanadine—he must have been lied to—"

Lanadine turned and hurled the force of her anger toward Millie. "Don't *you* think to rebuke me when I'm disciplining the help!" She reached out and stung Millie with a sharp slap across the cheek.

"M'Lady!" Kenyan protested.

In her fury, Lanadine turned back to Kenyan and slapped him across the face, too. "I am the daughter of Lord Ester! If it pleases me to correct my servants this way, then that is how I shall do it!"

Kenyan cared little for the stinging in his cheek. He just shook his head, almost imperceptibly, sorry to see this woman that he imagined he had loved reduced to such a state. He almost felt pity for her—she may have been the daughter of Lord Ester, but she seemed to have less true nobility in her blood than her own maidservant.

"I don't even want to see your goblin-beaked face turned in my direction again," she snapped.

"No, m'Lady," Kenyan replied, feeling the force of that blow more sharply than he had the physical one.

"If you ever touch me again, I shall have you flogged!"

Millie, who wore her mistress' handprint on her face in red relief, tried again. "Lanadine, please—"

Lanadine reached back her hand, preparing to deal another blow to her attendant, but before she could strike her, she felt her wrist grasped firmly from behind.

Kenyan said apologetically, "Forgive me, m'Lady—but don't beat her again."

Lanadine whirled on him, twisting her wrist from his grasp with a cry of pain. Her black eyes were wild with fury. "*Now* you have done it," she hissed in a low voice. She grabbed her injured wrist, and a bitter tear escaped the corner of her eye. She strode from them toward the castle, presumably to her father.

Millie looked at Kenyan with conflicting emotions playing upon her face. "You poor man," she murmured. "You must run. Run away!"

"I ... can't," Kenyan replied remorsefully. "I have vowed my service to Lord Ester."

"She will have you flogged and turned out anyway," Millie urged. "Please run!"

"I ... can't," Kenyan decided sadly.

Chapter Nine

It was the next morning, and most of Beedlesgate's personnel had gathered in the courtyard as witnesses to Kenyan's punishment. A few were eager to see him chastised for his offense against Lanadine, who was beloved by the castle's household for her great beauty. Even more were just interested in seeing the flogging, for whatever the reason. But many were sympathetic to Kenyan, for Millie had told the tale of the previous day's events and Kenyan's defense of her, and that story had spread rapidly among the servants.

Lord Ester strode to the center of his people, saw Kenyan standing in their midst, and wondered to himself why the man hadn't run away by now. He had been left unguarded in the barracks overnight, and Ester had even quietly instructed Captain Barner not to prevent Kenyan from leaving should he try.

Lanadine walked behind her father, for, as the accuser, it was also her responsibility to witness the punishment for which she had petitioned. She walked in modest dress with eyes downcast, and those who looked upon her (those who were predisposed to believe her side of the story) understood that she was contrite, compassionate—sorry that it had become necessary to punish this ruffian who had mocked her—but the truth was that she was mortified by shame that her humiliation had been made public.

Lord Ester raised his hands, and the murmur of the crowd was silenced.

"Guard Kenyan, you were warned that if you were to offend the Lady Lanadine, you should be flogged, and sent away from this place. Do you agree?"

"If you please, m'Lord—yes, I agree," Kenyan said.

"Do you confess that you have offended Lanadine?" Ester asked.

"If she says she's offended, then, yes, I guess it's so."

"Have you been offended, Lanadine?" Lord Ester asked her.

"Yes, my Lord," she said, so quietly that only those closest to her heard.

"Then, my judgment is certain. Regrettable, but certain." Lord Ester cleared his throat and continued. "Guard Kenyan, you shall receive twelve lashes with the whip—the leather whip, not the rod or the scourge." This was a merciful decision; blows from the leather whip were less painful than the others were. "Then you shall be dismissed from your position in the castle guard. Kenyan, remove your tunic." Turning to Barner, he said, "Captain, please cast lots for the punisher."

Ester referred to the process whereby one of Kenyan's fellow guards would be chosen to deliver the dozen stripes to his back. While the lots were being cast, the center of the courtyard was vacated, and Kenyan stood alone with his back bared, placing his trembling hands against a wooden rail usually used for tethering horses.

Of all of the humiliations Kenyan had suffered in his days at Beedlesgate—the taunts of the young guards, the lack of any true friends, this final embarrassment by Lanadine—this one moment, when he was surrounded by almost all of the personnel of the castle, was the loneliest moment he had ever experienced in his life, lonelier even than when his mother had died. He felt keenly aware that, no matter how hard he tried to live up to the standards that they set, no matter how he tried to fit in, he was irrevocably different from the people who gathered around him. He was Kenyan; they were other. He was ugly; they were not. They belonged … he did not.

The lot fell to Solonsee, the grim young man who was Aoemer's chief rival for Lanadine. He did not smile as he slowly walked over to receive the whip from Captain Barner. He took the weapon in his hand, looked at it solemnly, paused … and handed it back to Barner. Taking off his own shirt, he handed that as well to his captain, and went and stood next to Kenyan in the center of the circle.

"What is this?" Lord Ester asked.

"If you please, my Lord. I will take six of Kenyan's stripes," Solonsee said respectfully.

Only a faint lift of Ester's brow betrayed any emotion on his face. "Very well," he said sternly. "Cast again, Captain Barner."

Kenyan bowed his head and closed his eyes tightly lest a tear escape and run down his cheek. Solonsee's gesture represented the most significant act of friendship he had ever received since his arrival at Beedlesgate three years earlier.

The lots were cast again, and this time the one chosen was Slater, who refused even to go over and retrieve the whip. "My Lord," he said, "it's in my heart to say no to this request. If I need to take some of Kenyan's stripes, too … I will."

Ester measured him with a piercing gaze. "That may not be necessary," he said at last. "Is there *anyone* of the guard who is willing to perform this deed?"

An uncomfortable moment followed with most of the guards unwilling to look either at Ester or at each other, but then Fat Henry said, "I'll do it, Lord."

A quiet murmur went through the assembly. Fat Henry was known to be extremely proficient with the whip. It was said that he could swat

51

flies on fenceposts across the field, flies that the other guards couldn't even see. It was said that he could pick fleas right off a dog's back, though that was probably an exaggeration. Henry walked over to Captain Barner and accepted the leather strap from his hands.

Lanadine raised her narrowed eyes to watch, and a hungry look came over her. Her father had been merciful with the choice of weapons; there might not be any blood. But at least there would be welts, cries of pain, perhaps tears. She was angry with Solonsee for standing next to ugly Kenyan in the courtyard; for a moment she wished she had just chosen Aoemer for dinner two days earlier. But then she remembered—if she had chosen Aoemer, there wouldn't be this spectacle today. So it had all worked out for the best after all.

Fat Henry took a practice swipe with the whip, making a loud *crack!* that echoed through the courtyard, causing several people to jump and then laugh nervously. Then he turned toward the two barebacked men in the center of the circle, and said grimly, "Are you ready, boys?"

Solonsee and Kenyan both nodded, and Fat Henry said softly, "Hold still. Don't jump."

Kenyan wondered what he meant by that, but before he could figure it out, he heard the *whizz* of the leather cord flying through the air, followed by a sharp *crack!* But he only felt a tiny prick of pain, and he jerked, not from the sting, but from surprise. "One," Henry said.

A second later, the snap of the whip sounded again, this time behind Solonsee, who likewise could not resist the impulse to jerk slightly, though it was not certain that the whip had actually made contact with his back. "Two."

Lanadine saw Kenyan and Solonsee jump slightly when the whip made its frightening sound, and though it surprised her somewhat that they did not cry out, it did not immediately occur to her that they were not receiving the blows she had demanded. "Three…. Four."

Lord Ester recognized what was happening, and though he did not entirely approve, he realized that the guards had judged Kenyan to be innocent—a verdict that Ester himself tended to support. He had seen the redness of Lanadine's wrist and her furious tears, but he also knew that his tempestuous, headstrong daughter had a way of manufacturing circumstances to her own advantage. It had always been that way, ever since she was a young child and had first discovered that she was beautiful. "Five." And anyway, Ester reasoned, his sentence was being carried out. "Six." If the blows were not as forceful as might have been anticipated, well, there was no blame in that. Fat Henry glanced across the yard apprehensively to see if Ester had a response to his handiwork; the lord, unsmiling, held his gaze and gave him a small nod. Henry returned the nod, wiped a line of sweat from his brow, and went to work again. "Seven…. Eight."

By this time there was a rumble of discontent audible in the crowd. Those who had come with a lust to see Kenyan's pain felt cheated, and even those whose sentiments were nobler than that weren't really sure what was happening. Lanadine, though, had realized that she was being denied the justice that she supposed was hers, and said, "Stop this!"

Fat Henry's arm had already descended with his next blow, which had flicked against Kenyan's back like the sting of a bee, but did no real damage. Henry pretended he had not heard Lanadine and said, "Nine." He drew his arm back again and sent blow number ten whizzing through the air toward Solonsee, and Lanadine cried in a much louder voice, "Stop!"

Lord Ester turned toward his red-faced, livid daughter, and held up his hand for Henry to halt the flogging. "What is it?" he asked testily.

"Father! The guards are scorning me!" she shouted. "This is a mockery of your justice!"

A dark cloud passed over Ester's face, and he said, "What would you have me do?"

"Make them start over, and this time, really punish them!"

Lord Ester deliberated for just a moment, and then said, "Guard Henry. Have you been giving me less than your best effort at this task?"

"Oh, no, Lord! I've been using all of the skill I got," Henry answered truthfully.

"Yes," Ester replied. "Very impressive, too. Well … there are two stripes yet to be delivered. Deal them out, one apiece, and use a little less skill this time." Henry said, with a discernible trace of regret, "At your command, Lord."

With a grimace, Ester lifted his hand and gave a dismissive wave. Henry did as he was directed, serving Kenyan and Solonsee each a searing welt across the back. Kenyan gasped as the pain shot through his chest like a bolt, which was immediately replaced by a hot throbbing agony along the red stripe on his flesh. Solonsee sucked in his breath with a hiss, and a slight moan passed from his lips as a similar mark was raised on his skin.

A murmur of appreciation rose from the onlookers, except for Lanadine, who still wore a menacing look that nearly spoiled her pretty face. The partially placated crowd began to dissipate, the morning's entertainment concluded.

Kenyan turned to Solonsee and said, "I'm sorry for this … but thank you."

Solonsee looked grimly at Kenyan and replied, "No … *I'm* sorry." Captain Barner and Fat Henry walked over to the two of them, bringing their tunics. "That last one hurt, Henry."

"Sorry, boys," Henry said sheepishly. "I'm good at my work."

Lord Ester stepped over to the little cluster of men, and said, "Kenyan, stop and see me at my study before you leave."

"Yes, m'Lord," Kenyan replied, and he realized sadly that this was the end. He felt that he had shared a significant moment with Solonsee, with Fat Henry, perhaps even with Captain Barner, and that this could maybe have been the beginning of friendship … except that it was over.

"Well, goodbye, fellows," Kenyan said. "I guess I'd better gather up my pack and be pushing on."

Solonsee held out his hand silently and Kenyan grasped it, grateful. Fat Henry said, "Remember us kindly, Tats, like we'll remember you."

Captain Barner looked at Kenyan sadly and cleared his throat. "I feel … I must apologize, Kenyan. If I hadn't let those boys … if I hadn't *helped* them play their trick on you … you would never have suffered this embarrassment today. This pain."

"It's all right, Cap'," Kenyan said appreciatively, "it's all right." A thought occurred to him. "I've had an experience or two because of that, that most people will never get to know. And it wasn't so bad." A smile graced his homely features. "It'll make a fine tale to tell someday, if I can figure out how to make myself look a little less foolish."

"That's the boy," Barner said, clapping him on the arm. "Best wishes to you."

"And you, Captain."

Chapter Ten

Lord Ester folded the note he had written and sealed it with a splooge of wax that he drizzled from a dark red candle. Taking the brass seal that hung on a cord around his neck, he pressed it into the soft wax and held it there until it started to cool. Then he blew on the wax until it hardened, and ran his fingertip lightly over the impression he had made.

His guard stuck his head in the door, announcing that Kenyan had arrived, and Ester waved him in.

"You asked me to report to you, m'Lord."

"Yes." Lord Ester sat at his desk, brooding, tapping his fingers pensively until Kenyan began to feel slightly uncomfortable.

"M'Lord?"

"I am deciding what to do with you, Kenyan."

"I see," Kenyan said softly. He had assumed that he was just going to be turned out … but was there still some way he could serve?

After another short pause, Lord Ester said, "You must leave Beedlesgate, no way around that. I could appoint you to Kell's Lookout permanently, but that would be pointless. You would have no life at all. And I would still have to send people out there anyway, to take food to you. No profit there." Kenyan waited while Lord Ester sorted his thoughts.

"I could just throw you out and have you make your own way. That would be fair enough, I guess. But I can't help but think that you have somehow been the victim of a trap. That these offenses against my daughter were not your fault." He fixed a thoughtful gaze upon Kenyan. "Now, why I should care the least whit about these things, I do not know.

Yet, somehow, it seems that I do." He seemed a little surprised at that thought.

Ester tapped his fingers upon the letter he had written, and came to his decision. "I am sending you to Ruric's Keep. I am making you ... a present. You are my gift to King Ordric."

Ruric's Keep? Kenyan had longed to see the king's city, to meet the knights, to have long conversations about noble themes, to find out if there were others who loved beautiful and delicate things as much as he did. There must be, he reasoned—there were poems, weren't there? *Somebody* must have written them.

Ester continued, "I have written a letter of introduction for you. It will be up to Ordric what he wants to do with you. Of course," he said, "if you choose not to go to Ruric's Keep, that will be entirely up to you. Just go wherever you wish in Hagenspan, and use the letter to blow your nose for all I care. But if you go to the king's city, this letter should provide a means of employment for you, entrance into the king's service. Somewhere. It's up to you."

Ester picked up the sealed square of parchment, tapped it one last time upon his desk, and held it out to Kenyan, who stepped forward and accepted the letter with a respectful thank-you.

"I am not releasing you from your service to me, Kenyan, I think. You didn't run away last night, when you easily could have. And you had no reason to think that your punishment would be so easy for you to bear. That was a happy turn of events, yes, but you had no reason to expect it." He studied Kenyan's face. "From all I've heard, you're a dreadful bowman, and you're more dangerous with a sword to yourself than your enemy. But you showed spirit. Spirit, by staying."

Kenyan did not speak, understanding that the lord was paying him a high compliment. Ester continued, "Lanadine will not always live here at Beedlesgate, perhaps. Who knows? By tomorrow, she may have forgotten all about this. I know she seemed a little cruel today … but she's just a girl, just a silly girl, with her head all filled with ruffles and dancing. Never trust one." He finished his thought. "What I'm saying is this: After some time blows over, if you and Ordric aren't made for each other, come on back to Beedlesgate, and I'll find something for you."

Kenyan bowed low to the ground, and said, "Thank you, m'Lord. Your words are greatly appreciated."

"Yes, yes." Lord Ester had expended many more words on this homely young man than he had ever intended. "You are dismissed."

Kenyan took his letter, and began to leave. Before he reached the door, though, Ester called out, "Tell Bellings I said to outfit you with the best we've got. If you're going to Ruric's Keep, you need to be dressed for the job. You're representing Beedlesgate."

As Kenyan left, the curtain behind Ester was drawn to the side, and a laughing voice said, "Very touching."

"Sarbo. Didn't expect to see you," Ester said.

"Who was that?"

"A hopeless young catastrophe named Kenyan. It's not likely we'll see him in these parts again."

A short time later, Kenyan was leading a very fine reddish-brown gelding to the castle gate. If Bellings the stable-master had not given Kenyan the very best horse available at Beedlesgate, he had not skimped by much. The horse's name was Constant, and Kenyan had always admired him, though he had never so much as taken him for a ride .

Most of the castle's company turned their faces away from Kenyan as he walked to the gate. Some refused to acknowledge him out of a sense of scornful pride, some from an awkward awareness of their own shame. But a few gave him a grudging nod of the head, and a couple wished him good luck.

"Kenyan!" came a cry from behind him, a female voice—but not Lanadine's.

Kenyan turned, surprised, to see Millie walking swiftly toward him.

"Kenyan," she said, panting slightly. "I'm glad I caught you before you left."

He looked at her curiously, not knowing what he could possibly do for her in the scant seconds he had left at Beedlesgate.

"I wanted to give you something," she said, "to say 'thank you.'" Before he could protest, she stood on her tiptoes and kissed him on the cheek. "I know that's not the kiss you wanted," she said, "but it's all I have. Thank you, Kenyan. Thank you for trying to defend me from my mistress."

Kenyan was nearly speechless. "I— I—" he stuttered. "Thank *you*, m'lady," he said at last. "I will always treasure the memory of that kiss."

Millie smiled shyly, and said, "Godspeed, Kenyan. Godspeed."

She turned and walked back toward the castle, with Kenyan staring wonderingly after her. After she had disappeared within those stone walls, Kenyan shook his head with a little smile, and headed past the guard at the gate, who wished him luck. Kenyan waved to him, and turned back again one last time to look at the place that had been his home, mostly, for the past three years. *Well, all things in their season*, he thought. It was the end.

He turned and looked off to the east, to the faint road that would lead his way toward Ruric's Keep, toward all of his future days, and felt a surge of exhilaration.

It was the beginning.

Chapter Eleven

Kenyan woke up the next day with the early morning sunlight glistening like jewels on the dewy grass, and he smiled with contentment. He was no stranger to sleeping out of doors, and he knew that there would be many more such mornings before he arrived at Ruric's Keep.

He rose and stretched, yawning expansively, then stepped away from his little camp and relieved himself against the bushes. He thought he might try saying a prayer—something he rarely did. But this was a new day, a new start, a new life: His first day after Beedlesgate. It might be a good idea to start off by getting on the right side of the Creator. But he couldn't think of anything proper to say, so he just looked up into the brightness of the morning sky, smiled gratefully, and waved.

He had been well provisioned when he left Beedlesgate, at the direction of Lord Ester. Kenyan figured that he probably had enough food for the entire journey to the king's city. But even though he had been blessed with such bounty, he ate just a small, parsimonious breakfast—no reason to take a chance if he had miscalculated how many days the trip might take him. He chatted to Constant as he ate, and decided that he liked the red horse more and more with each passing moment. *What a fine, intelligent beast.*

After breaking his fast and breaking his camp, he hoisted himself on the horse's back and began following the trail that led eastward from Beedlesgate to the town of Sarbo. After he navigated his way across Sarbo's Run, he would ride on for a week or so until he reached the village of Raussi. Then he would cross the invisible border from Fennal into Greening, and perhaps another week or so of travel would bring him to Ruric's Keep. These were things that Kenyan more or less knew by his conversations with the other guards of Beedlesgate, but he did not know them by experience, for he had never been out of the land of Fennal in his life. In fact, he could not remember having ever been anywhere besides Beedlesgate, Kell's Lookout, and the island of his boyhood, Pembicote.

Kenyan was quite nervous about passing through Sarbo's town. He had heard whispers of the man's lawless deeds and merciless cruelty, as had everyone else in Fennal. He toyed with the idea of skirting around the town instead of riding through, but the fact that he carried Lord Ester's letter to the king gave him some small smattering of courage. Surely that would grant him safe passage.

Kak would like to have helped himself to one or two of Sarbo's women while the latter was out of town … but Sarbo always came back so unexpectedly. To be found unadvisedly dipping into one of his honey pots would certainly be cause for the severing of a certain member that Kak was quite fond of—if not outright execution. So Kak contented himself with his own four wives, which was two more than most of Sarbo's men had. Kak was Sarbo the Black's lieutenant, the captain of his second nef, and the voice of authority when Sarbo was gone away on his private business, which was quite frequently the case.

He was feeling a little puckish this evening. Perhaps he should go over to Pelly's and see if he could get a couple of the boys to fight. Just fists, not knives, Kak decided charitably. Yes, perhaps a night of drinking and fighting would be just the fun he was looking for. He slapped one of his wives on her rump to get her to move out of the way, hitched up his leggings, pulled on his boots, and skipped down the steps of his wooden cabin, the home he lived in when he was ashore. "Captain Kak!" greeted the men he encountered, or "Kak the Red!" or "Redbeard Kak!" He greeted them all back with a cheerful punch or wave or shout. He had learned a new word recently—*audacious*—and he wished he could get the men to call him "Audacious Kak," which he thought sounded very impressive. But there weren't many of Sarbo's men who were that imaginative, or for that matter, who knew what "audacious" meant. Since Kak did have a red beard, that was his nickname, no matter how audacious he wished they recognized him to be.

He stomped through the dirty main street of the town that Sarbo had named after himself (to Kak's secret but great disgust), headed for the wood-framed building closest to the harbor where the two nefs were anchored. He glanced at the two ships, their fighting decks rising imposingly above the docks, and felt a quickening in his breast, a longing to return to the sea. But not tonight, not tonight. When Sarbo returned, it would be but a short time before they left their women and headed back out to their wild mistress … but not tonight.

There was a sign on the building that he approached: Pelly's Grog House. Kak ran his tongue around his lips; he was looking forward to getting his bottle from Pelly—one that hadn't been already cut half-and-half with spring water. He had an agreement with Pelly to get his share of Sarbo's *rumbullion* before it was watered down, for Pelly's daughter Biela was Kak's third wife.

Before he reached the Grog House, though, his attention was diverted by a commotion behind him. He heard his name called out, and wheeled to see two of his men leading a horse and rider toward him, one man on either side. But he didn't notice his men so much as he noticed the horse, a very impressive reddish stallion—or maybe it was a gelding; he couldn't tell—upon which sat an extremely silly-looking man. Kak saw the red horse and thought of his own red hair, and knew immediately that they were meant for each other, Redbeard Kak and the striking red horse.

"What've ye brought?" Kak said in a loud voice, as others from the town began to gather, sensing a bit of impending sport.

One-eyed Deke, who refused to wear a patch over his empty socket, called, "We brung ye a vis'tor!"

Kak nodded, smiling grimly, as Kenyan was led forward, stealing a quick glance at the two nefs. He had seen them from time to time from a distance when he had been stationed at Kell's Lookout, but they were much bigger than he had imagined they could have been. His attention was quickly returned to the redbearded man standing before him, though—a man with the unmistakable aura of authority. He wondered if he had misunderstood something, and this could be Black Sarbo?

"Get down, pallie," Kak ordered.

"Yes, m'lord," Kenyan replied, and he dismounted awkwardly. "My name is Kenyan, late of Lord Ester's service, and I am riding for Ruric's Keep."

"That's grand, pallie, that's grand. And ye can call me … Audacious Kak," the red-bearded pirate smiled. "Care to do a little horse-tradin' afore we send ye on yer way?"

"No. No, thank you, indeed," Kenyan replied, and had the uncomfortable sense that it didn't matter what his answer would have been. "I have a letter for the king."

"Really, now? Why'n't ye show it to me, and I'll see if it's fittin' to let ye go on?" The crowd chuckled, an ugly, threatening sound. "For there've been a man or two what tried to come through Sarbo afore, what never made it to their goal. Ye wouldn't want to be one o' those now, would ye?"

Kenyan said nothing, but reached inside his shirt for the folded parchment he had received from Lord Ester. He extended it to Audacious Kak, who stood with his hands on his hips. Kak said, "Can ye read?" Kenyan nodded. Kak continued, "I can read quite a few words meself, but it might be better hearin' it read by the king's own messenger."

Kenyan didn't bother correcting that error. Instead, he broke Lord Ester's wax seal with a heavy sense of regret, and unfolded the crackling dry paper. He scanned the words, which had certainly been intended for King Ordric's eyes alone, and wished he had never seen them.

"Well, read it," Kak commanded.

Shamefacedly, Kenyan began:

> *"Ester, Lord of Fennal, etc., to King Ordric:*
>
> *"I send you a man and a horce. You will no dout have more use for the horce than the man, but if you can find somewhat to occupy him that will serve you, take him with my blessing. He seems to know a grate deal about birds. Other than that, I have found no pracktical use for him.*
>
> *"He is unwelcome at Beedlesgate but has committed no real offence."*

The people of Sarbo laughed uproariously at the message, and Kak could not suppress a smirk of his own. "Is that all of it, pallie?" he said, and Kenyan nodded sadly.

"Well, I guess ye're not goin' to be too harmful to us here, then, are ye?" Kak said gently. Then he nodded to one-eyed Deke, and said, "Check his packs, and see if he has enough to pay the toll." Deke and the other bandit who had escorted Kenyan into the village began removing his belongings from his saddlebags and bedroll. They passed around Kenyan's weapons, his food, even his second tunic, with various townspeople shouting, "That's for me," or "I'll take that."

"Now, Master Birdman, I don't wish ye to think ye'll be leavin' Sarbo emptyhanded," Kak said magnanimously. "We'll feed ye and bed ye tonight, and tomorrow ye can be on yer way. Let's see—" Kak looked around the street, and said, "Peckham! Grab that cat!"

Peckham, a grimy fellow in a torn red shirt, snatched up a skinny cat that looked like a multi-colored patchwork of fur. He brought it and presented it, purring, to Kak.

"Master Birdman! I hereby make ye this very fair and reasonable offer, which I beseech ye to consider very sincerely." He held the sagging piece of purring calico aloft. "This beautiful cat, which will undoubted bring ye many fine hours o' companionship, and keep yer house ever so free o' mice and rats, in exchange for that sorry-lookin' sack o' bones that ye rode in on, what ain't fit for no more'n makin' soap out of it."

The people of Sarbo repeated their menacing gurgle of laughter. Kenyan understood immediately, not so much from the tone in Kak's voice as from the look in his eyes, that he would either accept this offer, or else the next time anyone would see him, his bloated body would be floating face-down in Mondues Baye. He said with resignation, "His name is Constant."

"That's fine, pallie. And yer new cat's name is ... Patch."

The townspeople of Sarbo toasted Kenyan with grog, and gave Kenyan grog to drink as well, and roasted pig to eat. The men sang bawdy songs, mostly about drinking, and drank some more. Several of the women of the village (some of them quite pretty) rushed forward and gave Kenyan kisses on the cheek, and a couple of the older women even pinched him. The men pressed tankards of grog on him until he was quite dizzy and drunk, and, remembering Millie's tender kiss from two days earlier, he began to cry.

"Whassa matter, swabbie?" one of the townsmen said to Kenyan with a friendly slap on the back. "We all thought Old Delicious made ye a fair trade! Gen'rous, even."

One-eyed Deke stared drunkenly at the man, and said, "Who'd ye say?"

"Old Delicious. That's what Kak said his name was. Old Delicious Kak."

From the next table, Audacious Kak shook his head, closed his eyes, and silently grimaced.

The next morning, Kenyan woke up in an uncomfortable position, lying on his back on the moist dirt of the floor, with his feet propped up on a wooden bench. His boots were gone. Apparently he had fallen asleep on the floor of Pelly's Grog House, surrounded by several of the townspeople. But the piercing pain in his grog-filled bladder demanded that he find relief most urgently, even though his head throbbed and he swayed giddily when he tried to stand. One of the men lying on the floor next to him groaned and stirred when Kenyan stepped across his body, but there was no other sound or movement except for a noisy chorus of enthusiastic snoring.

Stepping out onto the main street, Kenyan blinked in the early morning sunlight. There were chickens pecking on the ground, and he could hear the occasional bark of a dog. He wished Kak had traded him a dog instead of that cat, which Kenyan had not seen since the conclusion of the transaction. There were no humans visible yet this morning, though, so Kenyan loosened his trousers and urinated right on the street, peeking back and forth guiltily. It could have been a street on any town in Hagenspan, Kenyan thought, but it was not—he was in the town of Sarbo, and he had no boots and no horse and no food.

He thought maybe he would see if he could find Constant, and try to steal him back. But even as the thought entered his mind, he heard the voice of Audacious Kak. "Leavin' already?"

Kenyan looked around the street, but he couldn't see where the voice was coming from. "Someone has taken my boots."

"Ah, that's a hard one, alright ... but even here in Sarbo we have men what need boots."

Kenyan nodded, and began walking barefoot, toward the east edge of town.

"Hold up, pallie. Ye've forgot yer cat." Kak appeared at Kenyan's elbow, and he did have what appeared to be the same cat from last night. "Ye know, Master Birdman, ye don't need to leave Sarbo, if ye wish to stay."

"Thank you," Kenyan said, but did not stop walking.

"Ye're prob'ly no sailor, but there must be somethin' ye could do."

"Thank you," Kenyan said again. "I was sent to King Ordric, though, by Lord Ester. I should complete that task, if I am able."

Kak studied his homely face, and then nodded approvingly. "Got yer letter?"

Kenyan patted his tunic ineffectually, realizing suddenly that he no longer possessed Lord Ester's letter. He had no idea where it could be, or when he may have lost it.

"That's all right," Kak said. "Ye didn't want that letter, anyway." Slapping Kenyan on the shoulder, he said, "Come on. I'll help ye acrost the river."

Chapter Twelve

There was a legend, already widely told in Kenyan's day, that the great discoverer called Hagen had walked on foot across the whole span of the country that now bore his name. From the western coast to the east, and back again; from the tiny islands south of Sonder all the way to the northern wilds, where there was nothing. Crossing rivers, mountains, passing through forests and plains, it was said that Hagen had met and broken bread with every person living in the land. His exploration of the country had taken over twenty years, but he had endured, endowing the people of Hagen's Span with a sense of continuity, of history, of community. He had been responsible for uniting most of the land, and, even though he had not overtly sought a position of leadership, he had finally become, in effect, Hagenspan's first king.

Kenyan thought about Hagen often, as he walked eastward with his cat Patch. He figured that if Hagen could walk for twenty years, then Kenyan could probably manage the few months it would take him to walk to Ruric's Keep. He hoped he could make it before the snow fell; he didn't mind the cool weather of autumn, but he didn't know if he would ever make it to the king's city at all should there be any snow or ice while he was still in the wilderness. But that was still months away ... he hoped. Truth was, he had lost track of the days, strictly speaking—but it was still hot summertime now, with red and black berries ripe for the picking on bushes bordering the forests along the trail. Kenyan lived on those berries, and nuts and apples and some edible roots he found. He had no weapon for procuring meat, but then, he reflected with a chuckle, even if he had, he probably wouldn't have been able to catch anything. He figured he could eat worms and insects if he got really desperate ... but he wasn't that desperate, not yet. He tore the arms from his tunic, tying off the ends and fashioning them into pouches. When he came upon anything that looked like food, he would gather as much of it as he could find, stuff it into the sleeves of his arm-pouches, and eat from his makeshift storehouse for days.

The cat Patch would disappear for hours at a time, undoubtedly hunting. But when Kenyan would call a halt to each day's march and bed down, it would pop out of the brush at one side of the path or the other and bound across the grass to lie down next to him, purring and rubbing against his face. Kenyan realized after a very short time that he counted the moments he spent stroking the warm little multi-colored bundle of life as the most cherished moments of his day.

That is not to say that Kenyan's days weren't enjoyable in their way. He had more time to devote to studying the birds and wildlife of Hagenspan than he ever had in the past, and he saw (or heard) many species of birds that he had never before observed. In one glorious week of tramping through the inland valleys and woodlands of Fennal (though never straying too far from the path that led to Ruric's Keep), Kenyan saw a Red Kite, many ravens, several Redstarts, and a Pied Flycatcher. He thought once that he heard the call of a Wood Warbler, though he was uncertain about that—whatever it was, he hadn't heard it before. Several days later, he discovered a stream that ran somewhat south of the trail, and he sat for nearly the whole day in rapt silence, watching Goosanders, Kingfishers, Grey Wagtails, and Dippers darting and diving above the water, and in the distance he was sure that he glimpsed two Little Ringed Plovers.

His skin became bronzed by the sun, and his health didn't really seem to suffer at all from his diet of fruits and nuts and water. He made up little songs that he offered to God as gestures of gratitude for sharing His creation with him. In fact, Kenyan could have happily become a hermit, a recluse, and lived out here alone in the wilderness for the rest of his days— just Kenyan and Patch and the birds and God. But, he reasoned, Lord Ester had not released him from his vow of service. And he—Kenyan—had purposed to go to Ruric's Keep and see the king's city. He couldn't imagine how the city could have any glories to surpass those of God's magnificent creation, but Kenyan was nonetheless bound to his sense of duty. His main concern was that—since he had to spend quite a bit of time foraging for food (and just generally looking around)—he wasn't really making very good time getting there.

Four times in the early days of his hike, Kenyan had seen people passing him on the faint road that stretched between Sarbo and the town of Raussi, which was about halfway to Ruric's Keep. The first time it had been two knights (he believed) heading westward, probably toward Beedlesgate. Kenyan had hidden himself behind some trees that time, out of a sense of shame. He was barefoot, and his shirt had no sleeves—how would he explain to *knights* that he was on his way to present himself to the king?

The second and third times he had encountered travelers on the path, they had been heading for Ruric's Keep, Kenyan supposed, and they had been riding hard, a day apart from each other. Even though Kenyan had waved to them and shouted, they had ignored him and kept on riding. He wondered what their business was that was so urgent that they would not stop for a fellow human being, stranded and in need, but he had no way of finding out.

Two days after seeing the last rider racing past him on his way eastward, Kenyan was trudging along the trail with the late afternoon sun sizzling on the backs of his arms, when he crested a little knoll and found, to his great surprise, a small two-wheeled cart by the side of the path. Or at least it *should* have been a two-wheeled cart—at the moment, it was a one-wheeled cart, which was causing its owners great consternation.

A young couple stood beside the wreckage, frustrated and red-faced. All of their worldly goods seemed to be packed on the cart, and the missing wheel lay on its side in the center of the road. Kenyan blushed to notice that the woman was obviously pregnant. A gray and white mule grazed contentedly in the grass beside the road.

"Halloo!" Kenyan greeted them with a wave, suddenly eager for the sound of a human voice.

The woman jumped and tried to hide behind her husband. He shouted desperately toward Kenyan, "Leave us be! We're *tryin'* to leave! Just let us alone, an' ye'll be shut of us forever!"

Kenyan stopped, confused and concerned. "I don't know who you think I am," he called, "but I'm not him."

"Stay back!" the man threatened, and he grabbed a fallen bough and brandished it menacingly.

"Do you need help?" Kenyan asked, and walked toward them. "I'll help you if I can."

The woman peeked out from behind her husband as Kenyan approached, and said softly, "He ain't one of 'em, Jair'. He's a man."

"Who are ye?" the man challenged. "What're ye doin' walkin' on the road all by yerself, with nothin'?"

"I'm just a traveler, who was stripped of his belongings and set afoot by some, ah, bandits," Kenyan said. "I'm coming to you. Don't hit me."

The man did not lower his makeshift weapon, but he allowed Kenyan to approach.

"We *could* use some help," the woman said to her husband.

"Hmmm," he said doubtfully.

"My name's Kenyan. I am headed for Ruric's Keep."

"We used to live there, awhile back," the woman said hesitantly.

Kenyan commented helpfully, "Wheel fall off?"

"Ye're not from the Feielanns?" the man said in a defiant tone.

"I don't think so," Kenyan replied. "I don't know what that is."

"Will ye help us fix our cart?" the woman asked. "My name's Poll, and this is my husband, Jairrus."

"The Feielanns ain't a *what*—it's a *where*," said the man.

"Oh," Kenyan acknowledged. This was a rather confusing conversation. "I'd be happy to try and help you, m'lady," he said to Poll.

"Ye've not met the Arkhanfeie?" Jairrus challenged.

"I've never even heard the word before," Kenyan admitted.

"Well," the man said dubiously, lowering the branch, "I guess ye can help us."

"Looks like we'll have to unload just about everything off your wagon, in order to be able to lift it up and get that wheel back on it," Kenyan figured. "How did it ever fall off?"

"I don't know," Jairrus said sourly. "I'd be willin' to bet that it was one o' them damned limniads."

"Jair'!" the woman said with fear in her voice. "They'll hear ye!"

"I know it," he spat. Turning around in a circle and holding his arms out, he shouted out bitterly to nothing in particular, "If I've offended ye, I beg yer forgiveness. We're *tryin'* to leave!"

"Limniads.... Fairies?" Kenyan asked.

"Yes, the cursed Feielanns are just bustin' with 'em. Limniads and oreads and naiads and dryads too. The whole blasted lot of 'em, each to their own place." Kenyan was amazed. In all of his trampings through nature, he had never seen any fairy folk at all—not that he was able to recognize, anyway. He had eventually been compelled to conclude that fairies were just myth, or that they had become extinct, or that they were of some other land than Hagenspan. "If I help you with your wagon ... will you tell me your story?"

"I'll make ye a bargain," Jairrus grumbled. "If ye help me fix this blamed cart, Polly'll fix ye some dinner. And we'll tell ye our story whilst we work and eat, and ye can tell us yer story, too."

Kenyan's homely face crinkled in a smile ... he was surprised to realize how much he had missed conversation with other humans.

"Is that yer cat?" Poll asked, as Patch stepped gingerly toward the little cluster of activity.

Kenyan nodded, still smiling. The woman bent down and said, "C'mere, Puss," and Patch ran to her and leaped into her lap, already purring.

Chapter Thirteen

Jairrus and Poll had married two years earlier. They were both from large families that lived on the outskirts of Ruric's Keep, and they had no inheritance from their parents, who were very poor except for their wealth of offspring.

Jairrus—a modestly ambitious young man—had wanted to hold land of his own, having no desire to spend his labor on the wishes of another man only to live in a rented flat in the city. He had pled with his young bride, finally convincing her to follow him west and south from Ruric's Keep into the unmapped wilderness, where men sometimes traveled, but none ever remained. That wilderness was wild indeed, and proved to be rich beyond imagination: crystal-flowing streams, verdant grassy meadows, forests filled with old untamed trees and feral beasts. In the mountains at the northern end of the Feielanns (which is how Jairrus came to know this exhilarating wilderness), he imagined that ore and jewels aplenty could be found, and tried in vain to get his bride enthused about exploring the hills with him. But Poll had not cared for that kind of wealth, being satisfied with the riches that could be unearthed from what would doubtlessly be magnificent farmland. The valley south of the mountains lay green and growing, patiently waiting to be claimed.

With great difficulty they forded a small river, driving their mule, Fusty, across with switches. The little cart trailed behind him, bobbing drunkenly in the shallow water, and nearly carried the terrified beast downstream. When they arrived safely at last on the other bank, the mule plopped down on the grass and would scarcely move for two days, no matter how severely they whipped it.

Finally the beast had sufficiently forgotten its ordeal to allow itself to be led from the river, and the young travelers pressed on westward. Poll urged her husband at several spots to stop, put down stakes, and claim the land so she could pull out her spade, turn over the rich dark loam, and begin planting seeds. But there was something about the air that made Jairrus begin to feel uneasy … a stillness, an awareness, a *presence* there, that made him feel as if he and his wife were somehow … intruders.

"The darkness at night was so dark," Jairrus confided to Kenyan. "Black. No stars. Just black. It was fairly spooky, I'll tell ye. Couldn't see yer hand in front o' yer face. Couldn't see nothin' at all. Except for … them."

"Them?" Kenyan asked, but Jairrus grimaced, seemingly unwilling to elucidate.

Poll said softly, "Sometimes, in the dark, we could see 'em. Like ghosts they were … just blurs of light, maybe stoppin' to peek at us for a minute, and then dartin' away, flashin' off to somewheres else I guess."

Kenyan felt a little thrill of fear run down his backbone like a trickle of cold water. First fairies … now ghosts? The Feielanns held some kind of mystery, it seemed—some kind of magic. He thought, a little irrationally, that he would like to see those lands for himself, and wondered what kind of birds lived there. Then he pushed that thought from his mind and forced himself to listen as Jairrus resumed his story.

After seeing the shadowy phantoms, the young couple had argued about returning to Ruric's Keep, almost unwilling to stay in the spirit-inhabited wilds, but even more unwilling to leave the richness of the land they had found. Ultimately, they decided to keep on moving westward, in hopes of crossing the border out of the spirits' domain, and finding land that was still fertile, but free.

Night after night they would see the fleeting glow of the elfin spirits, but other than being unnerved by their spectral visitors, no harm came to them. For more than a week they pushed steadily westward, but then they were confounded when they came to another river—one which flowed much faster and deeper than the one they had successfully crossed before.

"Maybe we should put down our pickets right here," Poll said, and Jairrus was tempted to agree, knowing that there was no way they could force Fusty across the rushing water. But when they woke from an unusually sound sleep the next morning, they found themselves to their utter amazement on the other side of the river—they, their mule, their cart, and all of their belongings. Trembling and teary-eyed, they had no idea how they had gotten there, and were almost too terrified to go on, and said so.

"But you must," said a voice behind them, and they turned to see the softly glowing face of one of the spectres. It took the appearance of a man—but if a man, no ordinary man. The face was noble and calm and dreadful at the same time, like a mighty king who was capable of both great ferocity and great mercy. He was dressed with all the glories of the wild nature they had been traveling through; though Poll could not recall with precision how he was clothed, he seemed to be wearing trees, flowers, moss, grasses, even flowing water. But on his brow he wore a crown of living vines that was encrusted with all of the gemstones Jairrus had lusted for when he imagined the riches of the mountains.

"Who are you?" Jairrus had whispered.

The glowing form replied, "I am the Arkhanfeie. It has cost me much to come back and speak to you today; much of my *aeterpradistum*. I shall not linger here long. You must leave."

"Is this yer land?" Poll asked respectfully.

81

"Long have we tended the gardens of Architaedeus. Our time will be ended soon enough, but not yet."

"Are ye the king o' the ghost folk we been seein'?" she offered.

"We are not ghosts in the way you imagine," the Arkhanfeie said, and it sounded as if he were growing weary. "We are the Feie, and these are the Feielanns." That was the first time Jairrus had heard the word. "I am not king; I am only a prince. Our king is none but Architaedeus Himself."

Jairrus spoke up. "We don't want to take yer lands from ye—just share 'em a bit."

"We wish you no harm," said the Arkhanfeie, closing his eyes. "You must leave." Shimmering brightly, he seemed to dissolve into the air, leaving the two humans baffled and frightened.

"Who is Architaedeus?" Kenyan asked Jairrus.

"We figgered it was their name for God," he replied.

"And what was that other thing that he said? The thing that it cost him a lot of to talk with you?"

"*Aeterpradistum*, he called it, if I caught him right. We don't know what that means."

Kenyan marveled at this story; these were things he had never heard of. He smiled faintly, wondering just how many more things there were in

God's vast world that he had never heard of. "So … this Arkhanfeie asked you to leave … that's why you're going now?"

"Well, actually, that all happened about a year ago. We pushed on away from the river some little ways, but we mostly hung around and tried to start a farm. That's when the tricks started."

Kenyan looked at Jairrus with a question in his eyes, and the other man continued. "Nothin' terrible—not much at first, anyway. But as soon as we put a spade to the soil, it started."

"The night after we dug that dirt for the first time," Poll said, "my spade rusted so bad that I weren't able to use it at all the next day. When I tried it, the blade crumbled into dust right there." Seeing Kenyan's doubtful look, she said, "Ye might not believe me, all right, but I'm the one what dug that dirt with me fingers all spring long, just to plant the handful o' seeds what we brung along with us."

"Some days we'd wake in the mornin' and find that ol' Fusty was clean disappeared away, just like the Feies," Jairrus said. "And then the next mornin' he'd be back, like nothin' had happened. And sometimes our stuff was gone, and then it would come back sometimes, and sometimes it never did."

Poll said, "My crops all grew wrong. Some of 'em grew too fast, and spoilt right on the vine. Some of 'em never growed at all. The longer we stayed—"

"The longer we stayed," her husband interrupted, "the worse it got. We could hear the Feies laughin' at us durin' the night, and they got more and more spiteful. They drove off all the game from anywheres near us, so we had no meat."

Poll said, "And no crops to speak of, though the ground was just as beautiful as you could please. We fin'ly took to eatin' grass and bark before

83

we gave up." She shuddered involuntarily. "One time I'd gathered a bucket o' water for drinkin', and I was just about to dip into it for a sip, when the water itself became one o' them fairies—a naiad, I guess. Gaw, but she was pretty! I was glad Jairrus didn't see her. But she just laughed at me, and disappeared in a flash o' light, and all the water was gone."

Jairrus said bitterly. "We weren't goin' to give up, no way. We was determined to show them Feies that a good honest man and woman wasn't nothin' to be afeared of, nor trifled with. We thought we could outlast 'em in the end, and maybe even be their friends, if they wanted." He looked at Kenyan. "Maybe ye noticed that Polly is … um, that we're expectin' a wee one by and by?" Kenyan nodded, embarrassed.

"Well, that was the end. I expect the Arkhanfeie knew it would be."

Kenyan thought that that was a strange choice of words, and stole a glance at Poll, who blushed with shame.

She said, "We coulda lasted for awhile longer … but a baby, with no food, no water…." She said no more, but shook her head sadly.

"Well, here we are," said Jairrus. "Whatever's been done, 's been done. We been headin' due north, hopin' to find a town or somethin', but then we come upon this road here. Now we're headed westward again, back to civilization anyhow."

"Do you know what the road before you is like?" Kenyan asked, thinking of the town of Sarbo.

"No, not really," Jairrus admitted, "but at least it's a road."

The next morning, the cart repaired, Jairrus and Poll headed on their way again, after sharing breakfast with Kenyan. While the two men had been working on the wheel the night before, Poll had been sewing some pieces of leather together to make Kenyan some crude shoes, which he had received with humble gratitude. As he watched the young couple driving the mule ahead of them, switches in their hands, he felt a twinge of regret. It had been a good night.

He waved at Poll, who had turned and waved her switch at him. Jairrus did not look back.

"Well," he said to his cat Patch with a sigh. "Coming?"

Chapter Fourteen

Kenyan walked on for two more days without seeing anybody. He made mental notes of a couple more species of birds that he observed, but he was not as interested as he had been before. *There might be fairies about!* One of the shoes that Poll had made for him was a little tight and made his toes hurt, so, experiencing a moment of guilty regret, he took them off and began to walk barefoot again. He breathed a sheepish prayer: *God, if there really* are *fairies around, I'd surely like to see them.* But he witnessed nothing unusual—not even at night, though he woke up many times in the darkness and peered around to see if there were any flashes of light that weren't just fireflies.

As he walked he could see the southern reaches of the Sayl Mountains before him in the distance, misty and blue, and he understood that at the place where the road he was following intersected those hills, he could find the town of Raussi. He was starting to think that maybe he should find some kind of employment in Raussi and winter there, and then go on to Ruric's Keep in the spring. But he was somewhat disquieted at the thought of reentering polite society; his recent experiences at Ester and Sarbo had not been very encouraging.

As Kenyan rounded a bend in the road, he was startled to see beside the path a little stone and sod hut with a thatched roof. Chickens pecked among the pebbled dooryard, and two boys chased each other around and between them, slashing at each other with sticks as if they were swords. Kenyan stopped and watched them play for a moment. Then he knelt and slipped his shoes back on, stood up, drew a deep breath, and walked toward the boys.

One of them, the taller one, noticed Kenyan coming their way, and stopped his running. He said a quick something to his brother, who ran into the house, calling, "Ma!" The taller boy stepped to the side of the path, standing between Kenyan and the hut, and brandished his stick protectively.

"Greetings, young fellow," Kenyan said kindly. "I am no threat to you."

"Well, you just keep on walkin', Mister, or else mebbe I'll show myself to be a threat to *you*," the boy said with just a hint of a tremor in his voice.

Kenyan smiled faintly, and said, "Are you the man of the house?"

"No, my pa's out huntin'. But he'll be back quick, so don't go gettin' any idears."

"Who's there, Jace?" called a woman's voice from the hut.

"Just a feller walkin' past, Ma. I'll take care of 'im."

Kenyan asked the boy, "Do you have any chores that need doing? I could probably chop some wood or something for you, in exchange for a meal and a place to lay my head tonight."

"Me'n Jem do our own wood-choppin'. An' there ain't enough food for us to be feedin' every vag that comes trampin' acrost our doorstoop."

"What happent to yer arms?" piped a youthful voice from inside the hut.

"If you mean 'what happened to my shirt,' I had to tear off the sleeves so I could carry food along with me," Kenyan replied toward the doorway. "See? They're full of apples right now." He held up his pouches, which had been slung over his shoulder. "Are you Jem?"

"Why ain'tcha got a horse?" Jem asked, and hopped down from the doorway onto the dirt.

"Get back in the house," Jace commanded.

The woman's voice sounded from within the hut again. "It's all right, Jace. I don't think this feller will hurt us."

"Ma!" the boy complained, his sense of pride bruised.

"That's all right, Jace," his mother said again. "What's your name, Mister?" She appeared in the doorway, a slenderish woman who seemed to be walking with a limp.

"I am Kenyan, m'lady, and I am at your service."

"Thank you, Mister Kenyan. I'm called Ange, when I ain't bein' called Ma."

"I'm pleased to know you," Kenyan replied.

"I'll fix you that meal you asked for … if you'll give me half of your apples."

Kenyan hesitated only a moment. Half of his apples would feed him for several days, and he questioned the wisdom of trading that bounty for one meal. But he glanced at Jem, dirty-faced and scrawny, and thought that perhaps the little family needed the fruit even more than he did. He beckoned to the boy, and said, "Here. Take these to your mother." As Jem skipped over to accept one of Kenyan's arm-pouches, Kenyan asked Ange, "What's dinner, m'lady?"

She blushed faintly, and Kenyan noticed that she was modestly pretty. "We call it 'rumble-bumble.' It's kind of a bean porridge," she said. "That, and apples." Noticing the bemused arch of Kenyan's brow, she said a little defiantly, "We don't have too much, Mister, but you're welcome to share what we got."

"And I thank you, most kindly," Kenyan assured her.

Mollified, Ange said, "Well, I see you ain't got nothin' to catch us some meat. Are you any good at helpin' with the cookin'?"

"I'll do my best."

"Would you rather snap beans, or milk the cow?"

Jace reasserted his manhood here, and said, "I'll milk the cow, Ma, an' you can have this feller snap beans for you, out on the back stoop where I can keep my eye on him."

Smiling apologetically toward Kenyan, Ange said, "If you don't mind snappin' beans...."

"Not at all," Kenyan replied, glad that his appointed task was one in which he wouldn't humiliate himself.

"Well, come on in, then, and you can meet Powder."

Before Kenyan had a chance to wonder who or what Powder was, he felt his cat, who had just arrived, rubbing his patchwork fur against his ankles, and said to Ange, "Is it all right if my cat comes into your house?"

"Yes, I suppose ... Powder will like him."

It took a moment for Kenyan's eyes to adjust to the dimness of the hut's interior, but he noticed again that Ange seemed to be moving with a limp, leaning against her sparse furnishings as she made her way from the front door to the table, upon which sat a small pile of green and yellow and white beans. "There's your beans," she said. "Snap them greens and yellers, so they're about the same size as the whites. After Jace fetches me some milk in here, I'll set that to boilin'. Add the beans, a little salt … rumble-bumble."

"Sounds delicious," Kenyan said, and he meant it.

Ange smiled a shy, grateful smile, and then turned back toward a darker-yet corner of the hut's only room. "Powder, honey. We got a caller."

"Is it my Daddy, Mama?" whispered a pale voice.

"No, honey. But it's a nice man what brung us some apples." Ange beckoned Kenyan to come over to the shadowed corner of the room, and he obeyed.

Lying upon a raised pallet, on what appeared to be a mattress of cornhusks, was a white-haired little girl, younger than Jace and Jem, with cheeks that were sunken, and large pale eyes. "Powder, this is Mister Kenyan."

Kenyan felt a brief stab of dismay as he wondered if the fragile little girl was dying, but he pushed the thought from his mind, swept low to the floor in a deep bow, and said with exaggerated elegance, "I am honored to make your acquaintance, m'lady."

Powder giggled, a staccato burst of gaiety, and said in her wispy voice, "You're funny-looking."

"Yes, that I am—that I am!" Kenyan replied with no trace of regret. "It pleased God to make me with this face and body, and I'm learning to let it please me, too." He smiled broadly at the little white-haired girl. "When

I was just a boy, my mother used to tell me that God makes some of us handsome and some of us smart, and that I should be happy that I got the better portion. It wasn't until I was a bit bigger that I realized I was smart."

Powder giggled again, and said, "You're silly.   I like you, somewhat."

"And I like you, too," Kenyan grinned. "Somewhat."

At that moment, Patch sprang up onto the pallet into Powder's lap, and she said with feeble delight, "Is that your kitty?"

"Well, we've been traveling together a good many days now, but I don't know that I could rightly call him mine," Kenyan said, and he was a bit surprised to hear the words come out of his own mouth. "He pretty much chooses his own path and takes care of himself. But we're friends."

"Can I be his friend, too?" Powder asked hopefully.

"Oh, yes, I believe so. Hear him purring?"

She smiled and nodded her head. She appeared not to be strong enough to gather Patch into her arms, but the cat nestled in the crook of her elbow and let her stroke him.

Kenyan said, "Well, I've got some beans to snap—"

Ange broke in. "I'll do the beans, Mister Kenyan. Why'n't you just stay and talk to Powder for a bit?"

"Would that be all right with you?" Kenyan asked the little girl, and she nodded happily.

※

For the next hour, Kenyan told Powder and her brother Jem about all the birds he had seen on his long summer's walk, describing the colors of their plumage and the different ways they moved through the air. He'd say, "Do you know what the Purple Sandpiper sounds like?" and Jem would shake his head no, his eyes wide with wonder, and then Kenyan would twitter a chirping song and Powder would clap her hands with delight in front of her open mouth, clasping them together like a prayer. The two children sat spellbound as Kenyan unfolded the marvels of his world to them, the marvels that Lanadine had been too bored to hear. It was, perhaps, the happiest, most carefree hour of his young life.

Toward the latter part of Kenyan's monologue, Jace came in from his chores, but he did not join the other children, choosing instead to help his mother around the cookfire. He pretended not to pay attention to Kenyan's discourse, but the hut was so small that Kenyan suspected he had to be listening.

When the meal was finally ready to eat, Ange said, "Sorry to break in on your stories ... but it's on."

Kenyan hesitated. "Where should I be?"

"We gen'rally sit in a circle on the floor around the cookpot and take turns usin' one of the spoons." There were two. "And we take turns spoonin' a bite into Powder when it's food like this, too, 'stead of somethin' you could pick up with your fingers."

"Sometimes I spill," Powder said matter-of-factly.

"Usually," contributed Jem, and Powder nodded.

Kenyan would have liked to sit next to the little white-haired girl and help her with her dinner, but Jace moved assertively to take a place next to her pallet, and Ange took the other position nearest the girl. Jem sat down proudly next to Kenyan. "We're not going to, ah, we're not going to wait for the children's father?" Kenyan asked.

"He might not be back," Ange said simply without looking up, and Jace's forehead wrinkled in a dark scowl.

"He might not be back in time," piped Jem, and nobody had anything else to say about the matter, leaving Kenyan momentarily nonplussed.

After a few moments of tentatively navigating past this awkward commencement, though, dinner became a pleasant affair. The salted bean porridge—the rumble-bumble—was quite delicious, especially to Kenyan, who hadn't had a hot meal since leaving Sarbo. During those moments when a spoon wasn't in his hand, Kenyan shared with the little family some more details of his journey, including most of the story of his adventure in the town of the sea-bandits. He didn't tell Ange about the ladies of Sarbo kissing and pinching him, though.

Jace said sullenly, "If you had a sword, why didn't you fight?"

"Well," Kenyan said, "you have to understand, it was just me, and there was more than twenty of them. And to tell you the truth, I'm really not that good a swordsman."

"But that's how you got Patch?" Powder said in her ethereal voice, thinking it was quite a fair trade after all, and Kenyan nodded with a small smile.

Soon the beans were all gone, and there was only a tiny bit of warm milk left in the bottom of the pot. Ange let Patch lick the pot clean, and Jem passed out one apple to each of the little company. Kenyan, though trying not to stare, let his gaze linger a moment on Ange, and he wondered what the explanation was about her missing husband. He wondered why she walked with that slight limp; he wondered what was wrong with Powder.

Ange, as if sensing the questions hanging murkily in the air, said softly, "The boys' father went huntin', 'bout a week ago. I fear he went south."

South? Kenyan thought, and wondered if he understood what she meant. He said hesitantly, "I just met a couple of people a few days ago who came out of the southern lands. They said ... there are some strange things in the south." Ange nodded briefly. She regretted having spoken.

Kenyan continued, "Some wild things."

Ange shook her head once, quickly, trying to get Kenyan to stop talking for the children's sake, but Jace said, "We know it. Pa always went north before, whenever he went huntin'. He always tole me, 'Safety to the north, Jace. Safety to the north.' I don't know why he'd go south."

Nobody spoke for a few moments; they stared at the hut's earthen floor and watched the dancing shadows cast by the cookfire from across the room. Powder stroked Patch's fur, and Jace said grudgingly, "Sure is a purrin' cat."

Finally Ange patted her hands on her legs and said, "Well." She started to stand up, barely stifling a groan; Kenyan could see that it was painful for her. Reaching a hand out to help her, he was rebuffed by Jace, who said, "We'll do it." And Jem and Jace each took one of their mother's hands, and pulled her to her feet; apparently they had done this many times before.

"Thank you, boys," she said. She picked up the pot from where it rested on Powder's bed, and walked unevenly over to hang it back on its rude wooden peg on the wall above the fireplace. "We just sleep on the floor, Mister Kenyan, 'cept for Powder. You can sleep on the back stoop or the front stoop, whichever you like."

Chapter Fifteen

Jace stepped over the sprawling form of Kenyan, who lay on the ground, partially blocking the back door, snoring resonantly. He felt a surge of distaste as he glanced down at the long, ugly man with his curly black hair and pointed nose. Jace didn't know why he disliked Kenyan, who had been polite to his mother and kind to his brother and sister. But he was anxious for the silly-looking man to pack up his apples and hit the road anyway.

He walked out behind the cowpen and waded into the tall grass where the chickens sometimes laid their eggs. Finding four, he gathered them gently in the front of his tunic and carried them back to the house. Kenyan had awakened, and sat on the back stoop yawning, distractedly scratching his armpit. Jace grunted noncommittally when Kenyan offered him a good-morning, and brushed past him.

"Here's the eggs, Ma," he said, and laid them, wobbly and brown, on the top of the table.

"Only four?" said Ange.

"All I could find."

"Hmm," his mother said. "I guess I could let Mister Kenyan have mine."

"No, Ma! Why?" Jace protested. "You already fed 'im last night."

"Well, we can't let the poor man starve, now, can we?"

Jace stared at her mutely for a moment, and then said crossly, "I'll go out and find another one." He took a step toward the door, but then paused and said, "You're too good, Ma. I could let *him* starve, all right. But I sure wouldn't want *you* to starve for his sake."

"That's my boy," she said with a tender smile.

※

A moment later, Kenyan stuck his head in the back door, and said, "Would it be all right if I came in and said goodbye to Powder before I leave?"

"Come in, Mister Kenyan. Yes, you can talk to Powder. But you can't leave until I feed you breakfast."

"Well, thank you," Kenyan said. "Thank you indeed."

Powder was glad to see him, and said so. "Maybe you don't have to leave? Not right away?"

Kenyan smiled at her, and noticed that Patch was still on the bed with her. Probably he had been there all night. "Well, I'm supposed to go and meet the king," he said lamely. It sounded to Kenyan as if he were trying to make himself seem more important than he really knew himself to be, but that had not been his intention. Still, it was true, more or less, that he was supposed to meet King Ordric. More or less. Lord Ester had told him that he didn't really care if Kenyan went to the king or not, though, hadn't he? "Maybe … if your mother has some chores that I could do, I might stay on a day or two."

"Me'n Jem do our own chores," said Jace, who was just entering the house again, fifth egg in hand. "And Ma does all the indoors work. If you can't hunt," he said without apparent malice, "you ain't no good to us."

98

"No," Kenyan replied, "I suppose not." He smiled an awkward apology to the little white-haired girl. "After breakfast, I'd better be getting on my way."

The dark half-moons under her eyes stood in stark contrast to the pale orbs within their lids, which welled up with quavering pools of tears. "But—" Powder began, her lower lip curled down in an injured pout. She continued in a thready whisper, "What about your kitty?"

Kenyan felt his compassion stir as he looked back at the sad-eyed little girl. He forced a smile onto his homely face and said, "I told you last night that Patch isn't properly *my* cat. If he wants to stay with you … he may." He hoped his faltering smile adequately disguised the surprisingly forceful sense of loss that accompanied this gift, this sacrifice.

In response, Powder reached out and with a mighty effort pulled the cat to her, clutching him to her frail chest. She stared silently up at the tall, homely man who had, with this offering, become her dear friend. Seeing the gratitude in her eyes eased Kenyan's renewed sense of aloneness somewhat, and his smile toward her felt a little less tight on his face. "You two take good care of each other," he said softly.

She said solemnly, "We will, Mister."

During breakfast, most of the conversation was carried by Jem, who told Kenyan with animated enthusiasm about all of the visitors they had had, and all of the chores he had done. Kenyan listened politely, and Ange smiled at her son with maternal approval. Powder ate her egg in silence, feeding small bits of it to her cat. Jace stared at the table, listening, not speaking, expressionless.

When the small meal was concluded, Kenyan thanked the lady of the house profusely, and gathered his arm-pouches. He emptied the remaining apples out onto the little wooden table, and said, "You might as well have these. I can gather more this afternoon."

"Thank you," Ange said, "but you go on and keep two of 'em, just in case you don't find anythin' to eat until later on."

Nodding, Kenyan took a couple of the apples back and rolled them into one of his sleeves, which he slung over his shoulder, the hard weight of the apples thumping him on the back.

He extended his hand to Jem, speaking his name, and the little fellow took the hand, shook it gravely. "Goodbye, Powder," he said, and she waved her fingers at him. "Goodbye, Patch," he said to the cat, who ignored him. "Thank you for your hospitality, Missus," he said to Ange, nodding to her.

"It weren't nothin'," she said, blushing slightly. "We was glad to have you."

Jace stood somewhat apart from the little circle of people saying their farewells, so Kenyan didn't offer his hand to him, but he said, "Goodbye, Jace." The youngster nodded to him, unsmiling. Kenyan's lips twisted upward benevolently, but his gaze was troubled; he wondered what he had done to offend the boy.

"Goodbye, all," he said one last time, waved, and turned to leave.

"Jace," Ange said suddenly, "walk with Mister Kenyan as far as the raspberry bushes in the woods—you know where I mean—and see if there's any still there what the birds ain't got."

"Ma—" the boy protested, but she said firmly, "Go on now."

He glowered at her, but did not disobey. "Come on," he said to Kenyan. Waving again, Kenyan followed Jace out the door, blinking in the brightness of the midmorning.

"It's a long ways. Let's go," Jace said, and immediately began trudging up the road that led toward the east, the mountains, and Raussi. He fell silent again then, and Kenyan fell into place beside him, keeping his pace, not speaking, just wondering.

From time to time Kenyan glanced at Jace, whose brow was furrowed with adolescent frustration, and his face reddened by anger and humiliation maybe, or some other thing inexpressible, but the boy refused to acknowledge his enforced companion.

After walking wordlessly for the space of about an hour, Kenyan saw some raspberry bushes off to the side of the road, and asked, "Is this where we part our ways?"

Jace looked up at him then, and nodded, tight-lipped.

"Goodbye, Jace," Kenyan said tenderly. "Thank you for everything. If I, ah—" he faltered, wondering whether it was an appropriate thing for him to say, then decided to go ahead. "If I see your father, I'll tell him you're missing him, and to hurry home."

Tears sprang unbidden to Jace's eyes, and his chin began to tremble. He fought against them for a moment, but his grief was stronger than he was, and it swiftly conquered him. His slender shoulders shaking, he began to sob. Kenyan didn't know what to do with a crying child, but he awkwardly gathered him into his arms and let him weep, and Jace did not resist, as the searing waves of betrayal, of bereavement poured from his tender soul. Not knowing any words that he could say to comfort him, Kenyan stroked the boy's shoulders and patted his back gently.

101

After quite a long time, Kenyan thought, Jace's sobs began to subside, and after a few more moments, the boy wrested himself from Kenyan's embrace. Rubbing his eyes irritably, Jace said, "This is where I stop," and pointed vaguely in the direction of the raspberries.

"All right," Kenyan nodded, embarrassed at the impotence of his own words. He stuck his hand out toward the red-faced boy, who frowned, but took it anyway. "Goodbye, Jace."

The boy nodded but did not look at Kenyan's face, then he turned and tramped through the tall grass in the direction of the raspberry bushes. Kenyan watched him as he walked away, and wished that there was something he could say, something he could do, but finally he turned too, and started walking eastward. He took one last wistful look back toward Jace, but the boy was out of sight.

Turning again toward the east, he looked at the mountains still in the distance, but not so far now as they had been earlier. He began walking his long walk once more, exhaling a heavy sigh. He missed his cat.

Chapter Sixteen

Two days later, Kenyan was still plodding dispiritedly toward Raussi. He had seen a couple of rooftops from the crown of the last hill he had crested, but then he had descended into a wooded valley, and he could no longer see anything civilized. Still, though, he knew he must be close.

A day ago, he had passed another cottage with smoke wafting comfortably from a chimney, but he had not been greeted and he had not knocked at the door. He knew that the reason he had walked on by had something to do with Jace, but he wasn't sure what it was.

He remembered an impression he had had some time ago, that he would be happy enough to live the rest of his days all alone in the wilderness like a hermit, but he knew now that it wasn't true. Wilderness, yes, but alone—no. It was the loss of the cat Patch that made him aware of this new reality. There was something about having another warm, living, breathing creature to talk to—to *touch*—that made the aloneness less alone, somehow, even if it never spoke a word in reply.

That was why it struck him as a little curious that he had chosen to bypass that roadside cottage a day ago. Here he was now, acknowledging his desire, his hunger for companionship, but when the very thing he longed for had presented itself, he had chosen to timidly walk on by. He wondered why. Maybe it was just—what? *Maybe it was just fear*, he reflected glumly. Maybe this time the husband of the house would be home, and Kenyan wouldn't be welcomed. *Or worse*, he thought, though he didn't know what. Maybe it was just fear, just fear that was stronger than the hunger. *Well*, he mused, *maybe someday the hunger will be stronger than the fear*. He wondered how that would happen. Would something happen to diminish his capacity for fear somehow? Or would his hunger for companionship continue to grow until it was so massive that no weight of fear would be able to surmount it? He hoped for the former, though he had no confidence in that hope.

While he was still thinking these thoughts, he was startled to hear a sudden thunder of hooves materializing from just behind him. Leaping from the path in case the horseman didn't see him in time, he stood and watched as a rider went tearing eastward along the road, not stopping, not even slowing, just like the few other horsemen he had encountered on his long trek.

But as Kenyan stepped back onto the path, the rider ahead pulled back hard on his reins, and wheeled the panting horse around. Kenyan halted, alarmed, wondering what new terror now awaited him. But the rider said in an incredulous voice, "Kenyan?" and slapped the reins against the horse's neck to start him trotting back to where the barefoot young man stood.

It was Solonsee, who had offered to take six of Kenyan's stripes. It was Solonsee, Kenyan's friend. Kenyan started to greet him, all relief and gratitude, but Solonsee interrupted, "I can't stop—I'm on Lord Ester's business. I thought you were dead! Are you still headed for Ruric's Keep?" Upon Kenyan's affirmation, Solonsee said, "Climb up here with me, and I'll buy you a horse in Raussi. You can ride with me."

As they raced the remaining few miles to the village of Raussi, Solonsee quizzed Kenyan on what had become of him in the days since he left Beedlesgate.

"What happened to your shoes?" he asked.

The pell-mell career of the horse's charge made Kenyan's voice vibrate. "They p-pinch my t-toes, so I usually walk w-without them."

"I never saw you walk barefoot at the castle."

"Well, these aren't the same b-boots I had before."

Solonsee thought he understood. "You lost them at Sarbo." He was still driving the horse at a brisk gait, though perhaps not so fast as he had been going before he added Kenyan to the beast's burden. It was all Kenyan could do, though, just to hang on, so he didn't answer directly.

After a moment passed, Kenyan gasped, "Why did you think I was dead?"

"I saw that red horse you were given, in Sarbo. They said you traded it for a cat." In spite of himself, Solonsee smiled a thin little smile. "I thought that meant that they had killed you for the horse. But they said they had sent you on your way in peace." When Kenyan did not respond immediately, Solonsee asked, "*Did* you trade it for a cat?"

Kenyan was fairly certain that he did not want to go into a detailed explanation of his adventure in the town of Sarbo, so, after a moment's pause, he simply said, "Yes."

The horse's hooves thudded their rhythmic pattern on the hardened ground as the trees and bushes dissolved in a blur. Kenyan, on the horse's hindquarters, bounced up and down in agony, his arms wrapped around Solonsee's belly. It was a rare thing for him to ride this fast, and he felt a little queasy. *My beans are getting squashed*, he thought to himself, but he didn't complain aloud. Solonsee asked, "What happened to the cat?"

"I gave him to a little g-girl."

105

"Oh? That must be Powder's cat."

"Yes!" Kenyan exclaimed. "You know Powder?"

"Just saw her this morning, when I stopped to water the horse."

Kenyan digested this information for a queasy moment, and then asked, "Did they mention me?"

"No."

Kenyan didn't know why he should have expected them to mention him anyway, so he didn't comment further. After a moment more, it occurred to him that he didn't know why Solonsee was riding like the wind toward Ruric's Keep, and was shamed that he hadn't thought to ask him. "Might I ask what the L-Lord's business is that you're on?"

"Yes, I suppose it's all right. The fact is," Solonsee said, "Lanadine is gone."

Kenyan felt a renewed surge of nausea, as if he had been punched in the stomach, but he considered that that could have been largely a consequence of his jouncing ride. "Gone?"

"Yes. Lady Elandel is ... distraught. Lord Ester suspects that she has been taken, by Sarbo the Black."

"Sarbo!"

"Yes. Estred her brother is rousing the troops to go and meet Sarbo in his village, and demand his sister's return."

"But ... you just came through the village of Sarbo yourself," Kenyan said, confused.

"Yes. And I would have delivered her myself if I could have. But the ships were gone, the men gone to sea. So I am riding to Ordric to beg the king's help against Black Sarbo should it be needed."

"Oh." Kenyan's mind was jumbled with scattered thoughts and conflicting emotions. "Why did Lord Ester think … that it was Sarbo?"

"He didn't say." If there was more to Solonsee's story that could have been shared, Kenyan didn't have a chance to find out what it was, for the town of Raussi was now rising into view above the road, lying against the foothills of the Sayls on either side of the pass. "I need to part with you here, Rags," Solonsee said, "for I don't believe you can keep up with me on horseback. I'll give you enough gold to outfit you for the rest of your trip, and buy you a hot meal at Penderby's—I'll drop you there. And I'll pay the livery-master and have him pick you out a nag to ride the rest of the way to the king's city." He slowed his flagging horse to an exhausted walk as they entered the marketplace of Raussi, which was just a handful of shops housed in wood-framed buildings. But there were women and children crossing the bare dirt path that constituted Raussi's main street, and Solonsee didn't want to risk running one of them down.

A placard in front of one of the buildings squeaked a lazy complaint against the breeze. Kenyan could not make out the writing on the sign, for it had weathered badly and had not been repainted. But he figured that this must be Penderby's, for Solonsee reined up in front of the door and directed Kenyan to dismount. Solonsee produced a worn leather pouch, shook out a few small wedges of gold, and handed them down to Kenyan. "I'd do more for you if I could," he said apologetically.

"To say 'thank you' would not nearly be enough," Kenyan replied.

The two young men grasped hands for a moment, looking into each other's eyes. Then Solonsee said, "Mayhap we shall meet yet again someday. Farewell, Kenyan."

"I hope so," Kenyan said earnestly. "God go with you, Sol'."

The handsome young man nodded grimly, slapped the reins against his mount's lathered neck, and trotted down the pockmarked street to the livery. A few moments later Solonsee emerged astride a fresh horse, looked up the street to see Kenyan still standing there watching, raised his arm in a mirror of Kenyan's salute, then put his heels to the horse's flanks and was quickly gone from sight.

Kenyan's arm dropped absent-mindedly back to his side as he watched the nothingness fill the spot where Solonsee had been. His friend. Kenyan sighed. Then he determinedly dusted off his leggings and slipped on the boots that Poll had made for him. Hearing the clatter of cookware coming from within the doors of Penderby's, he gave his dusty hands one last clap, and stepped inside.

Chapter Seventeen

Kenyan enjoyed the food at Penderby's, though he wished he had been served by a pretty young maiden instead of the surly gray-haired man who he supposed must have been Penderby himself. He eagerly devoured four huge plates of venison stew that had great tender chunks of carrots and potatoes in the broth, barely pausing to take a breath between swallows. He told Penderby that he had never had better, and the proprietor growled something unintelligible in return.

"My belly must be shrunk," Kenyan said cheerfully. "Time was when I could've downed six plates of that stew before I was filled, but now … I'm about fit to pop."

Penderby replied with an unsmiling snort, and stalked back to his kitchen.

Under his breath, Kenyan murmured, "Not friendly overmuch, are we?" He wondered if there might be any tarts for dessert, but was reluctant to press his host with a question. He considered that maybe a stink from his long days of travel clung to his clothes, and that was why Penderby was unkindly disposed toward him. Lifting his arms furtively, he sniffed his pits, right and left, and thought that they didn't smell too bad. Still dreaming wistfully about a steaming apple tart, he absently patted his tightly stretched belly, and decided that, probably, he had eaten enough already. With an inquisitive arch of his brow, Kenyan glanced around the room to see if any of the other diners were looking at him, and felt a vague sense of disappointment when none of them were; a bit of conversation might have been nice. Scraping his chair noisily, he rose, dropped one of Solonsee's coins on the table, and turned for the door.

Reaching the street, Kenyan paused to look up at the sky. A bright, clear blue canvas was painted with clouds heavy with rain, which wafted swiftly along their easterly course, white and cottony above, but as gray underneath as if they had been dipped in mud. There was a crispness to the air that portended autumn with a sincerity he had not previously noticed. The cool air felt pleasant against the backs of his bare arms, but he realized that it would soon cease to be an enjoyable sensation. "A cloak," he whispered, and wondered where he might find one.

He stood outside Penderby's door for a moment, hoping somebody would come by that he could ask where a cloak could be purchased. He looked up the street and down, but it seemed that this was one of those rare moments when everyone had already got to wherever it was they were going. Except for the wind, Kenyan was the only thing that stirred on the main street of Raussi.

He could go back inside and ask somebody there, he thought— Penderby or one of his patrons. But the notion did not inspire him to any corresponding action. Contorting his homely face into an even homelier grimace, he considered his options, while still secretly hoping for a passerby that he could accost with his question. None appeared, though. The wind gusted again, making the weatherworn plank that hung from Penderby's porch sway drunkenly. "He really should have that repainted," Kenyan said to the emptiness, and the small sound of his own voice disappearing into the whining void of the wind filled him with a kind of melancholy. He nearly turned then and went back into Penderby's, but he didn't. Instead, he made his way down the rickety boards of the porch walkway and toward the livery stable, wondering if Solonsee had already secured a horse for him, or if that was what the gold in his pocket was for.

※

"Come in—come in, out th' wind," a voice cried from within the stable. "An' shet that door, too, fer it's fixin' t' splatter a bit, 'r Tom's a dandy."

Kenyan pulled the door shut, and it was suddenly quite dark in the barn.

"Hang on, I'll strike a flint." Kenyan heard a tapping noise, and then a soft glow appeared, swinging in a flickering arc as the man who had spoken—the livery-master, Kenyan assumed—carried a lantern to the front of the barn.

"My name is Kenyan. I am a friend of Solonsee."

"Don't know no Solonsee. Ye c'n call me Mott." As he drew nearer with the lantern, Kenyan could see Mott's face—or at least as much of his face as there was to see. For from his nose to his belly, he was covered with a tangled gray beard, and on his crown he wore a tasseled cap trimmed with rabbit fur. His nose was flat and dirty, and his eyes were hidden in the shadows of a great bushy brow. His clothing appeared to be brown, or perhaps dark green, and he wore a fur-tipped cape over his tunic. The top of his head came only to Kenyan's waist, for he was a dwarf.

A thrill of excitement fluttered in Kenyan's breast. He had never seen one of these little folk before, and he was a little bit afraid. He dropped to one knee and said, "I am pleased to make your acquaintance, Master Mott."

"Pretty talker, ain't ye?" Mott grumbled, and the way his beard moved, Kenyan thought he might have smiled. "Well, git up. I ain't th' king."

111

"I'm sorry," Kenyan said, scrambling to his feet. "I've never met one of your kind. One of your people. Before."

"What!" Mott cried. "Ye've never met a livery-man afore?"

"No! I mean, yes. No." Kenyan felt the color rising in his cheeks.

"I know what ye mean, ye great silly man. I was jest pullin' yer nose."

"Oh," Kenyan smiled sheepishly. "I didn't mean to offend you."

"Well, that's one point in yer favor, then, ain't it?" the little man rumbled. "What d'ye want with Mott on sech a blust'rous even?"

"Are you sure you don't know Solonsee?" Kenyan repeated hopefully.

"Ye must mean that feller what needed a fast horse for Ruric's Keep."

"Yes! That's him."

"Aye, we've met," Mott conceded. "There! Now that I've answered yer question, ye'll parbly be on yer way?" He held up the lantern to show Kenyan's way back to the door.

"No," Kenyan said, flustered. "There's more."

"Ah, that's grand. A reg'lar conversation, we'll have." He plopped down on a mound of sweet-smelling hay, and said, "Sit yerself down fer a bit, Stretchy."

"All right," Kenyan said cautiously, and took a seat on the floor beside the dwarf. Almost as soon as he had folded his legs underneath him, though, he heard a buzz of contented snoring coming from his companion.

Surprised that he could have fallen asleep so quickly, Kenyan ventured a tentative, "Mott?"

"Ahp!" the little man woke with a startled yelp. "Who's there?"

"It's me—Kenyan."

"So it is!" Mott replied heartily, rearranging his cap. "Have we met?"

"Yes ... I'm Solonsee's friend."

"Don't know no Solonsee." Mott opened and closed his mouth a couple of times, smacking his lips, and Kenyan smiled uncertainly, a feeble grin. "That's arright, Longfeller. I was jest pullin' yer nose."

Kenyan, unsure whether he should be amused or perturbed, decided to stare silently at the floor of the stable.

"I'm sorry, young feller," Mott said softly. "I was jest havin' a spot o' fun wi' ye." When Kenyan did not reply, Mott continued, "There musta been somethin' ye were seekin', when ye come in here?" He nudged Kenyan's shoulder with a stubby fist.

"Well ... I was just wondering ... if you knew of a place where I might buy a cloak."

"A cloak? Why, sure, laddie! I might even have one 'r two layin' around here, what some'un's left behind a time 'r twicet."

"Really? And you'd sell me one?"

"Nay, Stretchy, I'll *give* ye one. Now, would ye be wantin' yer cloak with magic, 'r jest reg'lar?"

"Magic? You have a magic cloak?" Kenyan's eyes grew wide with wonder.

"Well, no, not yet, not rightly. But it's been said that the wee folk have a way wi' magic, wi' spells and sech. If ye was to push a sliver o' gold my way, I'd be happy to work out some words over a bit o' cloth fer ye."

Since Kenyan's experience with Lanadine and the Gentleman's Code for Conduct with Ladies, he had become decidedly more skeptical, so he said, "Well, if you'll just give me a non-magical cloak … perhaps that's what I'll have. Thank you."

"No need t' be hasty!" Mott cried. "How's if I do a little chant fer free over th' robe I given ye, an' then ye can see if it's worth a bit o' gold?"

This proposal struck Kenyan as quite reasonable. "Very well, sir dwarf," he agreed.

The little man stumped over to an empty stall and disappeared within. A moment later, he emerged, clapping the dust and straw off a rude woolen blanket.

"Isn't that a horse-robe?" Kenyan asked suspiciously.

"I'll work a wee clasp onto it, and it'll be jest as fine's a king's gown fer ye. Ye'll see!" Kenyan was almost certain he could make out an impish grin on Mott's shadowed face. "My kind have a way wi' metal-work, if ye ain't heared."

Deciding that, anyway, it was better than the nothing that he currently owned, Kenyan gave a curt nod. And, if there really was a possibility … he certainly would like to own a magic cloak.

The dwarf winked at Kenyan then, and said, "Now be patient wi' me jest a mite." Turning his back to Kenyan, he crouched low over the horse blanket and began mumbling unintelligible words in a low, throaty voice. "Ahp!" he cried, flinging his hands in the air and making Kenyan jump, then he returned to his mumbled incantations, singing his dwarfish spell in a hushed, secretive growl.

Turning at last back to his prospective customer, he said, "There! That was a two-gold-piece bit o' chantin', if ever they was 'un."

"I don't even know what you've done," Kenyan said. "What magic have you worked into the cloth?"

"Right ye are, laddie," Mott agreed, his eyes sparkling in the lantern-light. "Here's what we'll do: ye pay me one piece o' gold fer the work what I already done wi' my chantin', and ye pay me a second piece o' gold oncet ye sees what yer cloak can do."

Kenyan pursed his lips. "All right," he said grudgingly, and worked a smallish bit of gold from his pocket.

"That's what it is!" cried the little man, snatching the coin from Kenyan's fingers, and dancing around in a circling jig, laughing and hurrahing as he danced. After waiting impatiently for a moment, stifling the urge to tap his foot, Kenyan demanded as politely as he was able, "Now show me what the cloak will do."

"Ah, Stretchy, that's what ye want!" Mott replied, and halted his jig in midstride. Laying a stubby finger to the side of his lips for secrecy, the gray-bearded dwarf continued: "I've give ye a mighty spell. From now on t' ferevermore, anyone what wears that cloak will never be able t' be touched by a tongue o' flame. If ye're wearin' that cloak, no fire can ever harm ye, even if it should be th' very fires o' Hell itself!"

"Oh!" Kenyan exclaimed, feeling a fleeting pang of disappointment; he had been hoping for a cloak of invisibility. Still, protection from flames might be handy—who knew what adventures still lay before him? "Will you show me?" he asked, jingling the remaining few coins in his pocket.

"T' be sure!" Mott said. He picked up his lantern from where it rested on the floor, and dashed it against the ground next to the spot where the crumpled horse-robe lay. Immediately, a flame engulfed the blanket and quickly reduced it to a smoldering pile of ashen threads. Unfortunately, the flames also began consuming the pile of hay where Mott had recently sat, and quickly threatened to become an uncontrollable inferno.

Kenyan, terrified, shouted, "Mott!" but the little man had vanished into the shadows from whence he had originally appeared. "Oh, no," Kenyan groaned, and started looking around the stable for something—anything—that might help him extinguish the flames.

He spied a pitchfork and grabbed it, attempting to spread the burning haystack out to someplace where it would find no more fuel to consume, but that only succeeded in igniting most of the rest of the barn—wooden floor, wooden walls, and dry straw everywhere, now licking with greedy yellow tongues of flame.

Suddenly Mott reappeared from the back of the stable, leading a squat brown pony and Solonsee's exhausted mount from earlier. "C'mere, Stretchy! Give a wee man a boost up ont' this pony!"

"Help me put out this fire!" Kenyan shouted.

"Too late fer that. Help me ont' this pony, 'n then come on yerself."

"I won't! I'll help you with the pony, but I can't just run away from this fire."

"Suit yerself. But them Raussi folk are goin' t' be plenty riled wi' ye."

"With me?" Kenyan stammered.

"Aye, once they figger out it's ye what set their town ablaze."

Kenyan opened his mouth, but nothing came out. He stood there, mute and unmoving, a black mannequin framed by the flames, smoking pitchfork clutched uselessly in his hands.

"Come *on*, laddie!"

Without stopping to think further, Kenyan threw the fork to the ground, dashed over to Mott, heaved him up on the pony, and then scrambled up onto the bare back of Solonsee's horse. Grabbing two handsful of mane, he kicked the horse's flanks and pushed open the door to the street.

There were still no townsfolk about in Raussi's cool, twilit evening. An icy blast of wind from the mountains slapped Kenyan across his sweaty, sooty face, making him doubly alert, but still unable to determine what should be done.

"Come *on*, laddie!" Mott snapped again, and urged his pony eastward away from the setting sun. "Fire!" he bellowed in his strange throaty voice, and again, "Fire!"

Kenyan, confused and remorseful, decided to follow Mott.

Chapter Eighteen

"We'd best keep on goin' fer as long as yer horse can still walk," Mott whispered to Kenyan through the rain-spattered darkness.

It was true that Solonsee's horse was starting to show signs of failing, even though the two fugitives from Raussi had prodded their mounts only gently through the dark hours of the night. But even worse than the trembling frailty of the horse between Kenyan's knees was the crushing weight of guilt that seared his shoulders like an iron. *This is the worst thing I've ever done*, he berated himself. He wondered how many buildings might have burned before the people of Raussi had gotten the flames under control. Maybe the fire was still raging! Maybe … maybe people had died. "Mott," he sighed. In a whisper he asked, almost to himself, "Have you no conscience?"

"What's that, laddie?" growled the little man. "My ears is filled up wi' hair."

"Nothing," Kenyan breathed.

"Right," Mott replied, and peered warily at Kenyan from under his bushy eyebrows.

The dawn was starting to break on the eastern horizon, pink and purple smears across the charcoal sky. Mott pointed toward a little stand of trees quite a ways off the main path, and said, "We should make fer that coppice yonder, an' try t' grab a wink 'r two. One of us'll hafta watch th' horses whilst th' other naps, seein' as how we don't have nothin' t' picket 'em with. I'll watch first, if ye want t' sleep."

"I'm not sure I can sleep … not yet," Kenyan said gloomily. "If you can, then do."

A few moments later, the two travelers had secreted themselves behind the little thicket that Mott had indicated, and they were sliding down from their barebacked steeds. Mott squinted at Kenyan's mournful visage, frowned, and said, "Ye mustn't take these things too hard, laddie. A man only has so many tears t' shed in one lifetime, an' he has t' guard 'em precious."

Kenyan looked darkly at the little man and pressed his lips together, holding back the accusing words that would have burst from his tongue.

Mott understood his silence to mean that Kenyan was in grudging agreement with him, so he continued, "It's our natures, ye see? Some folk have got a nature t' get gold, an' some got a nature to lose it. That's jest how we was created. Dwarfs got a nature to covet th' treasures o' stone an' rock. Some say we even come from rock ourselves, back in th' beginnin'. Ye, Stretchy … ye have a nature t' try an' buy a magic cloak fer yerself, when there parbly ain't sech a thing t' be found in all o' Hagenspan."

"But—" Kenyan suddenly realized that however skeptical he had recently become, it was still apparently not skeptical enough.

"Why'n't ye let me take th' first watch?" Mott asked gently. "I'll bet ye're tireder than ye think ye are."

Kenyan exhaled heavily, and it felt as if all of his resistance was dissipated with that sorrowful breath as well. His shoulders slumped; somehow he had the sensation that his chest had grown smaller. But he found to his mild surprise that Mott was correct: he was suddenly exhausted.

"Lay yerself down on that grass," the dwarf directed. "I'll sing ye a little lullaby my own mother usta sing me t' sleep with."

Kenyan felt an unreasonable surge of gratitude for the little man's care. He felt that he wanted to weep … but he guarded his tears as precious. He laid his head on the ground and closed his aching eyes, and felt a wave of vertigo sweep over him, as if the world were spinning around in circles and he was just barely clinging to it. A swirl of red and black colors danced behind his eyelids, and as he drifted toward unconsciousness he heard Mott start to sing in his gruff warbling voice:

> *Gold an' jools, gold an' jools—*
> *ore an' precious stones.*
> *This is what th' dwarf-heart loves,*
> *his meat, his blood, his bones.*
>
> *Gold an' jools, gold an' jools—*
> *precious stones an' ore.*
> *This is what th' dwarf-heart loves,*
> *an' will ferever-more.*

When Kenyan awoke several hours later, Solonsee's horse was gone, Mott's pony was gone … Mott was gone. Before he reached for his pocket, Kenyan knew that the few remaining gold bits that Solonsee had given him were gone as well.

He thought he might curse Mott with a withering oath, but then knew that he wouldn't. It wasn't in his nature to do it.

So now Kenyan was somewhere between Raussi and Ruric's Keep—he knew not where—with no food, no money, no horse, no cloak. He thought for a second that perhaps, as well, he had no hope. Then he noticed, hanging from the gnarled branches of the bush he had slept next to … a gift: Mott's own cape, dusty, brown, and trimmed with rabbit fur. It was too small to make a proper cloak for Kenyan, but at least it would warm his arms against the autumn wind, and cover him a bit while he slept. Once again, Kenyan felt his breast swell with unbidden gratitude to the little gray-bearded stump of a fellow who had dishonored him and robbed him of everything that he had … and had given him his own mantle. For a moment—just a moment—Kenyan wondered if it was a magic cloak.

※

Three misty mornings later, Solonsee was riding back westward from the city of Ruric's Keep, trotting along at a leisurely pace on a fresh mount, and trailing the horse he had borrowed from the livery-master of Raussi behind him. He was still burdened with a gnawing disquiet, but the fact was, his mission for the moment was accomplished. He had seen King Ordric and secured his aid; twenty armed knights would shortly be on their way to Beedlesgate. And there was virtually no way that the nefs of Black Sarbo could have returned up Mondues Baye to the environs of Sarbo's Run yet; oftentimes it was months that passed between Sarbo's visits to his own town.

A shadow of melancholy darkened Solonsee's features, a faint gloom of depression. He had ridden like the wind for the king's city, and to what end? If Lanadine was indeed on Sarbo's boat, then … she was probably lost. And if she had been hidden someplace in the town of Sarbo, Solonsee felt certain that he would have found her … unless she did not wish to be found. And if *that* were true, then she was lost again, even more lost maybe than if Sarbo had stolen her away.

His reverie was interrupted by the appearance of a strange sight at the side of the road. Glistening with a sheen of early-morning dew was a lumpy mound covered with dark fur, which Solonsee thought at first might be a bear … a very thin and bony bear, though. He placed his hand on the haft of his sword, just to be certain of its presence on his thigh.

He puckered his lips and whistled: a shrill call to attention. The thin bear sat up, startled, and Solonsee saw that its face bore no hair, nor did its arms, and he thought that he had seen something like that once before, sometime, and then he remembered where.

"Aren't you Kenyan?" he called through the cottony fog, and the bear called back, humiliated but grateful, "Solonsee?"

"It seems that it's ever my lot to be saving your hide from some disaster or another," Solonsee said with affection, as he rode up to where Kenyan sheepishly waited.

Kenyan could think of no response to that, so he simply said, "Good morning, Sol'."

"Good morning, Rags," Solonsee smiled. "Let's see. Last time I saw you, you had traded Lord Ester's fine red horse for a cat. Now, I suppose, you're going to tell me that you traded all of the gold I gave you for that child-sized scarf you're wearing?"

"Well, no," Kenyan said, embarrassed. "I, uh, I bought some stew."

"That's good," Solonsee said, and his eyes danced with laughter. "You don't seem to have a horse."

"No."

"Didn't you stop at the livery?"

"Yes."

"And didn't Bilkinwreath give you a horse?"

"Who?"

"Bilkinwreath. I think that was his name. The livery-master of Raussi."

"Not Mott?"

"No, I'm sure it wasn't Mott."

"What did he look like?"

"Tall, white-haired fellow. Tall as you, but older." Solonsee looked at Kenyan curiously. "Who's Mott?"

"Somebody I met in Raussi. At the livery. A, uh … a dwarf."

"Really!"

"He said he'd met you."

"Not that *I* know of!"

"Well, that wasn't the only thing he told me that wasn't strictly true."

"I see," Solonsee grinned. "Sell you a cape, did he?" He reached out and fingered the rabbit-fur cloak on Kenyan's shoulders.

"In a manner of speaking," Kenyan said, but did not volunteer the story of his recent failure at the stables of Raussi.

"Nothing more need be said," Solonsee assured him. "But, Rags, here's a thought—if you can be flummoxed so complete out here in the backwoods … how are you ever going to survive the city?"

Kenyan wore a sad look on his hangdog face, but he didn't avoid Solonsee's eyes. "I don't know."

The two companions looked at each other for a moment, then Solonsee mercifully turned to study the horizon. "How about this?" he said at last. "I could ride back to Ruric's Keep with you, if you like … escort you, just to make sure you make it all the way to Ordric's court. If you wish…."

"Don't you need to get back to Beedlesgate?"

"Yes, soon. But I can spare a few more days. If you think—"

"That would be very much appreciated," Kenyan said. "I have an apple, if you're hungry."

Solonsee laughed. "Thank you, my friend."

The next three days passed swiftly for the two travelers. While Solonsee hunted rabbits with his bow, Kenyan gathered autumn nuts that the squirrels had passed over, and small hard apples, pink and yellow with black flecks. As they sat beside the campfire with the succulent smells of roasted meat and roasted nuts making their mouths water, they shared the tales of the paths they had trod in the recent weeks. Solonsee caught Kenyan up on the doings at Beedlesgate since his departure, and Kenyan uneasily admitted his misadventures in Sarbo and in Raussi. Solonsee listened gravely to the story of the fire in the stables, and said, "You were lucky to escape with your skin. The dwarf was right—if the townsfolk had caught you and thought you'd torched their village, they would have demanded your hide." After a brooding moment, he continued, "Too bad for them, though. I don't blame you, Rags … it sounds like that dwarf was up to mischief. I wonder why he saved you? Instead of letting you take his punishment, I mean."

Kenyan had wondered that, too. "I don't know," he said, "but I've shed a bitter tear or two that I just didn't turn the gold over to him all at once, instead of trying to squeeze a bit of magic out of him."

"Well, who was to know? A magic cloak … a man might well wish to have one, if there really is such a thing."

"Mott said there wasn't, after," Kenyan offered.

"Who's to know?" Solonsee continued softly. "There are strange things in this world, things beyond explanation. Perhaps there's still a bit of magic left, too."

"I don't know," Kenyan said. "Maybe."

"There are fewer things in the world now than when it was young, I think … but maybe they're still there, if one was to look for them hard enough."

"You sound like a philosopher."

"No," Solonsee demurred, "I don't think so … no." The pair fell silent, staring at the embers of the fire glowing alternately red then white, then fading to darkness.

Kenyan said, "I know that I was excited about the possibility of seeing one of the fairy folk, if I could … excited and a bit frightened."

"Well, you saw a dwarf. That's more than I've seen! Perhaps this is a magical journey for you after all."

"Perhaps," agreed Kenyan, smiling faintly at the thought.

"But not tomorrow," Solonsee concluded. "Tomorrow, you arrive at the king's city. And the enchantments that you find there are, I think, completely of man's design. Nothing very wild; not like magic. But still very dangerous, if you're not careful."

"I understand."

"I doubt that, Rags," Solonsee said, though not unkindly.

Chapter Nineteen

Kenyan rode through the hard-packed streets of Ruric's Keep with his eyes wide and his negligible chin hanging agape. He had never seen so many people in one place—perhaps *hundreds*—so many that you could hardly pass through the streets without bumping into somebody! Solonsee peered at his companion from the corner of his eye and suppressed an indulgent smile.

The sounds and colors of the king's city bombarded Kenyan's senses: the raucous songs of the vendors in the marketplace in their rainbow-colored robes, bartering fabrics and foods, jewels and tools. All the variegated fruits of the fall were available and on display, for the time of harvest had come, and the farmers and their wives who lived outside the city had come to peddle as well, a mingling of rustic brown in the midst of the gaudy urbanites.

Several times the frustrated horses nearly stepped on children who were darting in and out of the crowd, and once a gap-toothed woman carrying a pumpkin yelled rudely at the two riders when they accidentally jostled her.

"Let's dismount, so we don't trample somebody," Solonsee suggested.

"Yes, let's."

Almost as soon as Kenyan's feet were on the ground, he was accosted by a buxom young woman with dark hair and a round nose, who tumbled into his arms with a shriek and a giggled apology. Kenyan's face turned crimson, and he apologized profusely himself, though he had done nothing amiss. But the woman's soft, plump proximity had him completely flustered, and she was careful to press herself against him several times, apparently unable to regain her balance.

When she finally disentangled herself from Kenyan's awkward arms, she gave him a look of bleak disapproval and flounced away in disappointment. Meanwhile, Solonsee was unable to conceal an indulgent chuckle.

"It's a good thing I was holding the poke, and not you! Elsewise, we'd be beggared by now," Solonsee laughed.

"I don't understand," Kenyan said, baffled.

"That dark-haired lass was a cutpurse, or I'm the queen!"

Kenyan still did not understand. "Cutpurse?"

"Rags, she wasn't feeling around for your manhood," Solonsee grinned. He spoke in a low voice, not wishing to humiliate his friend. "But if you'd had a piece of gold hid anywhere on your body, it'd be tucked safe between her bosoms by now!"

"No!" Kenyan said in astonishment, his jaw slack with disbelief.

"I'm telling you, Rags—we'd better get you to the king straightaway, or there won't be anything but scraps left of you to show him!"

Some short time later, having ploughed as politely as they could through the crowded marketplace, Kenyan and Solonsee came to a kind of a clearing near the street, where a team of workmen were busy constructing a wall of stone and mortar. An impressive man with flowing white whiskers was watching the workers, apparently in charge of the crew. Solonsee made his way directly to the white-haired man and addressed him, Kenyan following at a short distance.

"Sir Pease!" Solonsee was saying. "Does the king hold court today?"

"You're Ester's man, aren't you? Thought you'd headed home." Sir Pease scratched his neck and studied Solonsee and Kenyan. He was not as tall as either of the younger men, but was much broader in the shoulders, and to Kenyan's awestruck eye he appeared almost impossibly strong.

"I had," Solonsee explained, "but another task awaited me, even before I got home. Another of Lord Ester's men—" here he indicated Kenyan "—must have an audience with the king, if it's convenient to His Majesty."

"Well, you're in luck today, lads, if you hurry. King Ordric's hearing all comers today, so long's they register with the bailiff before midday." Sir Pease studied Kenyan with amused curiosity. "You might want to slap on a different shirt ahead of appearing before the king, if you've got one with you."

"I don't," Kenyan gulped. "Will that be a problem?"

"Never know," the old knight said with a twinkle in his eye. "Sometimes the king might give you a shirt out of his own wardrobe— sometimes he'll have your head on a pike. Never can tell, with royals."

Kenyan, ashen-faced, opened his mouth, but no sound came out, so he closed it again.

"Sir Pease, I must ask you to show mercy to my friend here," Solonsee smiled. "He is unacquainted with some of the subtleties of your jesting. Back at Beedlesgate, he was used most unmercifully by some of the guards."

"That so?" Pease said, still appraising Kenyan reflectively. "Hmm."

"I am afraid I'm not very wise, in some ways," Kenyan admitted, ashamed. "You're the first knight I've every met," he added.

"Well, I'm sure you're very impressed," Pease laughed. "Nothing like one of the king's mighty knights to charm the boots off a young lad."

"Yes, sir," Kenyan said. He suddenly felt a sting of self-consciousness over the modest boots that Poll had so generously made for him, and quick on the heels of that discomfiture came a nip of guilt over his humiliation. He felt his face growing warm with impotent anger.

Sir Pease read the thinly veiled frustration on Kenyan's homely face, and quickly apologized. "Don't be getting your fur stroked the wrong way, lad," he said kindly. "I meant you no harm."

"Forgive me," Kenyan said. "My own ill-begotten sense of pride has served to humble me yet again."

Pease slapped Kenyan's shoulder good-naturedly, and said, "That's the lad." Turning back to Solonsee, he asked, "Do you wish to appear with your friend before Ordric, or did you hope to entrust his safety to me?"

Kenyan felt a brief, unreasoning stab of panic. Would Solonsee be parting ways with him now? Kenyan wasn't sure that he was prepared for that yet, though he did not know what still remained that might ready him. He looked at his friend, who was asking him a mute question with his eyes: *Would it be all right if I left you here with Sir Pease?* Kenyan suddenly realized that Solonsee had sacrificed much in order to get him from the spot on the road where he had found him all the way to the king's city. He had given Kenyan gold. He had given him meat. He had been three days headed toward home and had given up that comfortable progress, coming three days back in the wrong direction again. If Solonsee wished to leave him now, and make his way homeward, how could Kenyan possibly deny him that?

"Thank you, Sol'. If you'd be going now, I'm sure I'd be quite secure in Sir Pease's care." Kenyan urged a sincere *thank-you* across the space between them with the earnestness of his gaze, and Solonsee smiled.

"Sir Pease: If you could take care of getting Kenyan on the bailiff's registry, I would like to buy him one last meal before we part ways."

"I can do that."

"Then come along, friend Kenyan, and we'll eat whatever pleases your palate—be it fish, fowl, fruit, or feather!" Solonsee grabbed Kenyan's arm and pulled him back toward the market square. Kenyan smiled happily, feeling foolish but glad.

Chapter Twenty

King Ordric's court was being held outdoors, since the weather was fine for autumn. Also, construction was still being done on some parts of the castle, making the already massive edifice of Ruric's Keep more impressive yet, and the noises of the workmen would have interfered with the king's deliberations. The throne upon which Ordric sat had been carried outside by four servants, and was adorned by carvings of fantastic creatures: dragons and gnomes and lions.

The king himself was easily as striking as his royal chair. Ordric had been a muscular man in his youth, but in his older years had grown quite stout. The appearance he created as he sat on the dais above the milling crowd was that he was a human being of some larger scale than the rest; that he was some kind of grand, benevolent giant. Even more arresting than his oversized proportions, though, was his hair, which was wavy, long, flowing past his shoulders … and pink.

Kenyan stared at the king, his eyes wide, but dared not ask the question. Sir Pease, amused, glanced at his charge, and bent toward him, whispering, "His Majesty's hair was once orange as a pumpkin, though he would have told you it was red as flame. Years ago, though, it began turning a dingy kind of grayish white. Since then he has sought many a different potion to try and dye his locks back to their boyish blush … but this is what he gets!" Pease chuckled, and his own white whiskers tickled Kenyan's ear. "I believe today's hue is the result of crushed strawberries, which may not have given him precisely the color he wishes. But truly, His Majesty smells quite delicious, if you should happen to get close enough to notice!"

In spite of his timidity, Kenyan smiled at the old knight, and hoped that he was not committing some kind of offense against the king in doing so. "When will it be my turn?" he whispered. Ordric had already begun hearing grievances, mostly petty squabbles between merchants.

"When Sir Butters calls your name," Pease said, indicating the bailiff.

Kenyan watched with great curiosity as the king adjudicated the complaints of his subjects. Ordric listened intently as each case was brought before him, then quickly delivered his judgment in a clear, booming voice. Kenyan thought that the king's verdicts were quite sensible, and sometimes wondered that the complainants shouldn't have come to the same conclusions themselves. Still, he was favorably impressed with his first glimpse of royalty. After you got past the pink hair, King Ordric seemed to be a man's man through and through. *Like Lord Ester*, Kenyan reflected. There was something virile and energetic about the two of them, something that seemed to set them apart from common men, or at least that is the sense that impressed itself upon Kenyan.

He realized that the same kind of vitality seemed to exude from Sir Pease, and in a sense, from Solonsee too. These were men who were preordained for honor, or so it seemed to Kenyan. He thought about others that he had known, just for comparison's sake. Aoemer? Kenyan shook his head—no. Fat Henry? A fine, generous boy, but thoroughly common—not noble, Kenyan thought. He wondered why it was that he thought Sir Pease was a greater man than Aoemer or Fat Henry, when he scarcely knew a thing about him. But he felt a confidence, an openness, a sense of honesty and courage, even fearlessness, that seemed to emanate from Sir Pease, even if it was just in Kenyan's imagination. He wondered ... did *all* of the knights possess this quality? Maybe they really *were* the men he had hoped to find: men who valued truth, courage, virtue, wisdom. Kenyan felt something stirring, rising in his chest like hope. He longed to be one of those men, too—a foolish desire, perhaps, but real.

"Kenyan from Ester!" Sir Butters was calling, and Sir Pease nudged Kenyan from his reverie.

"Here I am!" he shouted, waving his bare arm.

"Come down!" the bailiff commanded. "Present yourself."

Kenyan elbowed through the crowded courtyard, and came to the open semicircle in front of the king's platform. Kneeling and bowing low to the ground, he said, "I bring Your Majesty greetings from Ester, Lord of Fennal."

"Rise, Kenyan from Ester," boomed King Ordric. He turned to his bailiff and asked, "We heard a representative from Ester less than a fortnight ago, did we not?"

Sir Butters nodded affirmatively. "Just a week ago, Sire. You approved a troop of soldiers to aid in Ester's complaint against the sea-bandit Sarbo. They have not been sent out yet."

"Is that what brings you to our court today?" inquired the king testily. "Tell Ester to hold his water."

"No, Your Majesty, if you please," Kenyan stammered. "This matter is more personal to me, and less significant to the cause of your esteemed crown."

"Hmm," Ordric considered. "Well, speak on."

"Lord Ester gave me a letter to give to Your Majesty. The tone of it was that he was requesting you to take me into your service, if the thought pleased you."

"I see," the king said, looking with jaded curiosity at the strange, ugly man who stood before him with his knees trembling. "Where is the letter?"

A look of blank dismay was painted upon the craggy pan of Kenyan's face, which was quickly turning the color that King Ordric wished his hair to be. After an audible beat of agonizing silence, Kenyan swallowed and replied, "It was stolen from me by Sarbo's men."

"Sarbo again," the king replied thoughtfully, and then said sharply, "but no letter!"

"No, Your Majesty."

The king patted his thigh absently for a moment, and Kenyan had the impression that he was about to dismiss him. But then Ordric asked, "Well, young man, what would you have us do for you?"

Kenyan, whose frail hope had been failing, was amazed that the king might still entertain his petition. Thinking that an opportunity like this might never present itself again in his lifetime, he decided to risk his remaining shreds of dignity all at once. Standing in the golden rays of the autumn afternoon's sun, with his arms bare and his dwarf's cloak flapping about his shoulders, with no weapon at his side and no gold in his purse, Kenyan the ragged scarecrow asked Ordric, the great King of Hagenspan, "Your Majesty, I would be a knight."

A lilt of laughter rippled through the assembly, and the strawberry-haired king pretended to rub the end of his nose, concealing a smile behind the hand held in front of his ample lips. Kenyan stood still, facing Ordric evenly, aware of the laughter behind him. His neck, ears, and cheeks blazed hot with chagrin, but he held steady.

After a moment, King Ordric said, still wrestling with a small grin, "Friend Kenyan: It is not the habit of your king to grant knighthood to anyone who should happen to ask."

Kenyan had no answer, but stood patiently, unflinching, facing the king. Something of his doggedness gave Ordric a moment's pause; there was something curiously engaging about this ugly young man and his ludicrous request. Instead of merely dismissing his preposterous proposal, the king toyed with the idea for a moment in his royal mind, like a cat worrying a ball of string.

"A quest! We must have a quest," Ordric decided loudly. "If you perform some notable service for the glory of the crown, then, yes! We shall make you a knight. Why not?"

The gathered crowd murmured in surprise, and a few laughed merrily.

"Thank you, Your Majesty," Kenyan said, bowing his head. "What service would you have of me?" He exhaled, and tried to keep from panting; apparently he had been holding his breath.

"We shall see, in due time. For the moment, winter is coming soon, and you look to be singularly ill-equipped to endure a quest such as we have in mind. It is our decree that you shall winter here with the knights, laboring for them as a squire, and then when the springtime comes, you shall have earned the right to be properly outfitted for your journey. Does that answer your desire?"

"Thank you, Majesty," Kenyan replied earnestly.

"Well, whether it does or not, that is our judgment." The king raised his voice to address the assembly. "Have we a knight here who lacks a squire?"

After an uncomfortably silent moment, Sir Pease cleared his throat and said, "Well, Your Highness, I guess it's been awhile since I've trained a squire."

"Well said, Pease." Now that his decision had been made, Ordric seemed impatient to be shut of the matter. "Kenyan, this is Sir Pease. You shall obey him completely until we have determined your quest."

"Yes, Your Majesty."

Ordric dismissed Kenyan with a wave of his pudgy hand, and said, "Next, if you please," to Sir Butters.

As Butters called the next petitioner to stand before the king, Pease grabbed Kenyan's arm and bustled him away back into the crowd. "Well, lad, you've got stones," he said grudgingly. "The king must've been in a good mood."

As they were leaving the courtyard behind, Kenyan could hear Ordric saying to the man now standing before him, "What request do you have of your king?"

"Why, I'd like t' be a knight!"

As the laughter rose around them, Pease hurried Kenyan away, shaking his head.

Chapter Twenty-One

Kenyan was nearly too busy to decide if he was happy. When he tumbled onto his cot at the end of each day, he fell into an exhausted slumber almost immediately, and seldom woke before Sir Pease roused him for breakfast.

Some days, when Pease had nothing in particular planned for Kenyan, he helped the workers building the wall around the castle of Ruric's Keep; sometimes he carried tools and materials for the artisans working within the castle itself. He wasn't very fast or strong, but his labor was steady, consistent, unflagging. Those days were the exception, though, for Pease usually had things for Kenyan to do.

Kenyan was given an old blade, heavy and blunt, in order to practice his swordsmanship. After his first two bouts with other squires (both of whom were quite a bit younger than he), Kenyan was sent to receive remedial instruction in a class with the castle pages, who were beardless youths not even a dozen years old. In an ensuing practice bout with an eight-year-old boy, Kenyan finally tasted victory in a sword battle for the first time in his life, and would have been embarrassed to admit how very happy that triumph made him. His delight was tempered, though, when Sir Pease took him off to one side and said, "Perhaps swordplay is not for you, lad. How are you with the bow?"

So Kenyan practiced archery, drawing the bowstring time after time until his fingers were bloody and sore, and his arms trembling with fatigue. But his accuracy did improve somewhat, and he was pleased with his results, being keenly aware of how poorly he had fared with the bow during his days at Beedlesgate. He even outscored several of the other squires, though he was not close to being one of the best.

And then there was riding. Sir Pease said, "A proper knight must be able to sit a horse," and he drilled Kenyan for an hour and more each day, until it felt as if his body was going to split in two from the constant jouncing up and down upon his tenderest parts. Watching Kenyan try to keep his seat at a gallop, elbows flapping at his sides like the bony wings of a giant stork, was cause for several of the other knights to fall to their knees upon the ground, slapping each other's backs and laughing uncontrollably as tears gushed from their eyes. As Sir Pahlen said to Pease between gasps of mirth, "Best have him ride slow, Pease, or he'll take off with that 'oss and fly it to the moon!" And Sir Pease would smile grimly, gently shaking his snow-white head.

Apart from the daily humiliations of the physical aspects of his training, though, Kenyan spent many hours learning from Sir Pease the ways of King Ordric's chivalry. "As a squire, it is your calling to make the kingdom a better place each day than you found it when you awakened. As a knight, it will be doubly true. Where you find widow, or orphan, or beggar, always do whatever you can to leave their burden a little lighter, their purse a little heavier. It will ever be your duty to encourage the fainthearted, to be a strong arm for the defenseless. To stand arm-in-arm with your brothers who do battle for justice. To protect the virtue of mothers and maids. To always honor your king and your God and the company of the knights."

Kenyan absorbed these things eagerly, earnestly, and put them into such practice as he was able. And he did make slow, painful progress in his training with arms, once even defeating a fellow squire at swordplay, when the other slipped on the icy yard and fell on his rump, dropping his blade. But privately Sir Pease confided to the king, "I don't know if the lad is cut to be a knight, Highness."

Ordric, who had occasionally observed Kenyan's lessons from his balcony perch, replied distractedly, "It's true that he ofttimes appears more

140

the fool than the fools who are paid to do so. But he has a certain tenacity about him that appeals to us. We have seen him pricked by a blade, lain flat on his back, and grinning like an imbecile as if it were only his due to be so abused. And then, we have seen him stand back to his feet, and try yet again. And yet again." Ordric turned and fixed Pease with a hawklike gaze. "Is there nothing about the youth that is ... special?"

Sir Pease felt that part of Kenyan's slowness to develop was attributable to his own fading skills as a tutor, and blushed with vexation. "The lad seems to know a good deal about the ways of the woodlands." Suspecting somehow that this comment was not quite complimentary enough, he added, "He's a wonder at mimicking the songs of birds."

"That is little enough to recommend him," King Ordric remarked dourly. "Perhaps we could find some other occupation for him. An instructor for the children? Perhaps. Can he read? Can he do sums?" The king sighed loudly. "But ... a knight?"

The two men sat in silence for a moment, and then Sir Pease tentatively voiced an idea he had been thinking about for some days. "Your Majesty mentioned a quest for the lad?"

"Yes." Ordric waited impatiently for Pease to continue.

"Perhaps ... if Your Majesty were to give young Kenyan a quest that was so difficult he could not possibly complete it ... then you would be spared the humiliation of naming him among your chosen nobles." Pease was a bit ashamed to have spoken the thought aloud—it seemed disloyal to Kenyan, whom he rather liked—but he had another notion. "And, if the task was so difficult that he could not possibly complete it, but somehow he *did* ...then there would be no dishonor in his being a knight, for the very arm of God must be with him."

Ordric pondered this, the grim line of his mouth drawn tight, the only sound breaking the silence being the tapping of his index finger upon the arm of his chair. "We ... shall consider it."

It was an uncommonly warm day for midwinter, and Kenyan was at liberty in Ruric's Keep, and in his pocket he carried two small gold coins that Sir Pease had given him. Pease, who did appreciate the dogged faithfulness with which Kenyan attended him, had told him to take this day and this gold, and to spend them each on whatever pleased his heart. This was a blessing that Kenyan had never experienced before, and he was a little overwhelmed at his prospects. He had been given free time before when he had been a guard at Beedlesgate, but he had never had gold!

He walked through the streets of the city, looking around with interest at everything there was to see. He noted with gentle amusement that everything looked a little more intriguing when there was actually the chance that he could *purchase* something if he was struck by the proper whim.

Boys ran and splashed in puddles that had been created by the melting snow. With a melancholy pang, Kenyan remembered Jace and Jem, and wondered what had become of them. Vendors cried out their well-practiced calls, advertising whatever it was they had to trade, be it meat or cloth or tool. Kenyan strolled past a dentist, who was working with some pliers in the mouth of a man who sat on a barrel next to the street, surrounded by curious onlookers, tears streaming down his cheeks and moaning audibly. With a cry of success, the dentist gave a vigorous jerk on the unfortunate sufferer, and then held a black and bloody tooth aloft for the appreciative crowd to see. An involuntary shudder coursed up Kenyan's spine.

He turned a corner, and saw an old woman sitting next to a building like a sack of rags, her head bound with an old cloth that covered her eyes, a small basket in front of her fashioned from dried bark. Periodically, she raised her voice to cry, "Pity! Pity fer th' poor an' th' blind!"

As he drew near, he saw some of the urchins who had been plashing in the puddles jostling each other playfully, and pushing one of their number forward toward the blind woman. The one selected by his mates tiptoed up to the ragged old beggar, scooping up a handful of pebbles as he came, and said, "Here you go, Mum." He plinked the pebbles into her little basket, as she said, "Bless ye, lad!" clasping her hands together in front of her sooty, whiskered face.

The boys ran away, laughing, as Kenyan shot them a dark look that they didn't notice. He walked up to the shabby old crone, and knelt next to her, involuntarily flinching at the unpalatable odor rising from her rags. "Hello, old mother," he said softly. "I have a piece of gold I'd like to give to you, but I wish you'd take it from my hand, instead of having me toss it in your bowl." He was concerned that the boys might come back and, under the pretense of presenting some more alms to the old woman, take whatever might be of value in her basket.

"Bless ye, young sir," she said, turning her wrinkled face toward the sound of Kenyan's voice. She smiled beatifically, revealing three crooked, yellow teeth. "I'll say a prayer to th' gods fer ye. An' ye'll have a reward, ye will, fer the gods listens to me."

"Thank you, old mother," Kenyan said sincerely as he pressed one of his gold pieces into her palm. *Only morning, and half my gold gone already*, he thought with a smile. *I hope Sir Pease doesn't ask how I spent it*.

He wandered the streets of Ruric's Keep for another hour, but found that he was becoming bored and frustrated. The hawking of the vendors sounded increasingly less like a plea to trade, and more like an angry harangue. The constant jostle and press of the crowd was unpleasant; Kenyan was discomfited by the noise and the smell and the closeness of so many other humans. He thought back wistfully to the free time he had enjoyed at Beedlesgate, alone in his grove of oaks surrounded by the birds and squirrels, and thought that perhaps he might try to leave the city and see if he could find someplace like that. But street after street led nowhere but to another street or alley or dead end, and Kenyan soon realized that the morning had already turned to afternoon, and that he did not have time enough left to leave the city and return before nightfall, even if that's all that he did.

As the afternoon began to wane, gray clouds arrived and blotted out the sun, returning the earth to its proper seasonal chill. Thinking that maybe he'd just have a cup of hot tea someplace before returning to the castle, Kenyan tried to remember if he'd seen any place in his travels today that would be likely to offer that humble pleasure. He hoped that, when he found it, there might be a pretty serving girl there who might bless him with a smile. *That* would be a good day.

Kenyan looked up at the horizon, such as he could see it, and turned round in a circle until he found the fluttering banners of the castle. He started making his way in that general direction, and soon found that he was back on the street where he had given the alms to the old beggar-woman. Wondering idly if she was still about, he glanced around trying to see her, but she appeared to be gone. He hoped that, wherever she was, she was warm, her belly full, and that she might have grandchildren playing at her feet.

Kenyan had tried mostly to avoid meeting the eyes of his fellow citizens during the afternoon, but the crowd was thinning out now due to the nipping reminder of winter in the air, and the fact that most people had accomplished enough business for the day. He glanced from face to face, wondering how different their lives were from his own, and wondering if they were more or less happy than he was.

He quickly noticed the tear-washed face of a homely, stout woman who had broad stripes of gray hair where it must have once been brown. Her features were red and creased, and her lower lip trembled, as if she might burst into tears again at any moment. For a second he thought he might pass her by, but then he remembered Pease's injunction—*Where you find widow, or orphan, or beggar, always do whatever you can to leave their burden a little lighter*—and before he could think about it twice, he found himself asking her, "What troubles you, mother?"

"Are ye a knight, sir?" she asked him anxiously.

"Not yet, but I hope to be, one day."

"P'raps ye'll do," she said. "I come to market this morn wi' three pieces o' silver what my husband give me fer the buyin' of our victuals." Kenyan nodded. "Well, I drapped 'em in the street, lickety scoot, an' before I could stoop to pick 'em up, that butcher-man what sells dogs an' goats an' chickens fer meat snatched 'em up his own self. I seen him doin' it wi' my own eye!"

"He wouldn't give them back to you?" Kenyan asked.

"He said they was *his*, an' if I'd lost any silver, it must not o' been these pieces, what was his!" She grabbed Kenyan's arm. "Come wi' me now, an' make him give me back my coins!"

"I don't believe I have the authority to do that," Kenyan said hesitantly.

"Well—" the woman seemed about to hurl some kind of insulting retort toward the ineffectual would-be knight, but then her shoulders slumped, and she said instead, "I expect that's so. It'd jest be his words agin mine, an' who's to say which one's tellin' true? It's me, though," she concluded resentfully, and then sorrow swept over her red, puckered face again. "Guess I'll jest hafta go on back to my husband an' take the beatin' what's comin' to me."

"Wait," Kenyan said, and mentally he said goodbye to the cup of hot tea and the pretty young serving girl of his imagination, "I may not be able to make the butcher give you back the coins you lost, but I can do this." He produced his remaining gold piece and handed it to her.

"Oh!" she cried, clapping her hands together once, and dancing a celebratory little step before Kenyan in the street. "Bless ye, sir!" she said as she took the coin from his hand. "Bend down here, now, an' let me kiss ye!" As Kenyan complied, blushing, she took his face between her hands and gave him a loud smack on each cheek, to the merry laughter of the remaining townspeople who had overheard their exchange.

An hour later, when Sir Pease found him hungrily attacking his dinner at the castle, the old knight asked him, "Did you enjoy your day, lad?"

"Well, yes," Kenyan decided. "Yes, I did."

"And what did those two gold pieces buy for you this day?" he said with a twinkle in his eye.

Kenyan weighed his response for a moment and then said, "Well, one piece bought me the prayers of a blind beggar." Pease nodded approvingly. "And the other one bought me two kisses on the cheek, from a woman who was even homelier than me, if that's possible."

Pease laughed, and slapped Kenyan's shoulder. "Well, then, it was money well spent, wouldn't you say?"

Kenyan grinned, nodded, and turned his attention back to his dinner.

One day as spring was approaching, King Ordric was again holding court at Ruric's Keep (though indoors), and Sir Butters was again the acting bailiff. The supplicants waited in the alcove outside the hall of the king's great throne until they were called, so there was no general clamor as there had been when Kenyan had had his case heard by the king. Each party, upon being called by Butters, entered the throne room to present his petition before the king alone, with the exception of the ever-present bailiff.

Ordric—whose hair was an orange-gold today instead of pink—listened throughout the afternoon to the complaints of his people, some petty, some great, mostly petty. A peasant's hen had been killed by another peasant's dog. A fisherman claimed one of his rivals was maliciously snipping his nets. One of the knights requested a furlough to tend to his ailing parents. A widow complained that her neighbor was stealing eggs and replacing them with stones. When the fine thread of his patience had been stretched nearly to its breaking point, he groaned, "How long shall we suffer these people, these bumpkins, these underwits? Sir Butters! Send the rest away, and have them come back some other time."

"Begging your pardon, Majesty, but there's only one left," Butters hesitated. "Would you have me send him away?"

Ordric's plump chest swelled and then sank with a great sigh. "If there is but one ... we shall hear him."

Sir Butters stepped to the alcove, blinking at the scroll he had inscribed with this day's appointments, and tried to make out his own handwriting. "Gumn—? Gumnbote?" he inquired tentatively.

The only man left in the hallway looked around from side to side, and then said happily, "Well, I guess that must be me, then, ain't it?"

Sir Butters sniffed, with a look on his face that faintly suggested disdain. "This way, please."

"Right you are," Gumnbote said cheerfully, following close behind the bailiff.

The king was yawning broadly as the two men entered the throne room, and was eager to be done with his wearying functions for the day. "You have requested an audience with your king," Ordric began. "How shall we serve you?" he said, with barely concealed boredom.

"Well, Your Kingship," Gumnbote began, "I thought that mebbe you'd seen me about somewheres."

"Not that we recall," said the king with some reservation.

"I was afraid o' that," Gumnbote said with disappointment. "I can't seem to find meself anywheres."

"What do you mean?" Ordric felt a pulse of alarm beginning to throb in his temple. "You're right there."

"That's what it looks like, I know," said the strange man, and King Ordric peered at him with more interest. "But I'm lost, sure as I'm standin' here, and I can't find meself at all."

Sir Butters demanded roughly, "You've been tippling the strong drink, hain't ye?"

Gumnbote said solemnly, "I promise on my mother's grave, should she happen to have passed, that I ain't drunk nothin' stronger than fairy-water for two full moons, and I ain't even sure I've drank that."

"Fairy-water!" blurted the bailiff. "What are you saying?"

"I am certain," said Gumnbote, "that I don't know." He then proceeded to sit down on the floor of the king's hall, falling fast asleep almost immediately, and nothing the bailiff tried would rouse him at all. Finally the king told Butters to drape a blanket over the sleeping man, and post a guard to alert him as soon as Gumnbote awakened.

Chapter Twenty-Two

"Kenyan," Sir Pease said, shaking his shoulder gently and repeating his name. "Wake up, lad."

Kenyan opened one bleary eye and croaked, "Am I late?"

"Nay, lad, but it's early," Pease replied. "It's time for you to be up, though, and dress yourself proper. The king has called for you."

"The king?" Kenyan blinked his eyes rapidly, trying to banish the lingering sleep. "Have I done something wrong?"

"I don't think so," Pease whispered. "I believe His Majesty has decided upon your quest."

"Quest," Kenyan repeated, as if he did not understand the word, but then he realized what Sir Pease was saying, and felt a stab of panic. "I'm not ready."

"You might not be ready to fight a dragon or a troll," Pease agreed, "but I think what the king has chosen may suit you alright, if you keep your wits about you."

"What is it?" Kenyan asked.

"It wouldn't be right for me to tell you that, before the king has his say. But if you'll get yourself out of that bed, you'll find out soon enough, and proper."

A short time later, Pease and Kenyan were ushered into the king's private dining room by Sir Butters. The king was already seated, and there was also a sandy-haired wedge of a man who was dressed in little more than tatters, much as Kenyan had been clothed when he arrived at Ruric's

Keep. The stranger was eating a large breakfast with single-minded purpose, as if he had not eaten in some time and might not expect to again for awhile.

Kenyan was unsure whether he should be concerned with this new man or not, but was fairly certain that he should address himself to the king. "Your Majesty," he said, bowing.

"Yes, yes. Kenyan." Ordric seemed more than usually distracted, but Kenyan was used to people taking scant notice of his presence; he felt honored that the king even remembered his name. "We want you to hear what this man has to say."

The stranger spoke. "While I'm tellin' my tale, Your Kingship, would it be alright if you had your cook whip up another batch of this yeller stuff for me?" he asked, and Pease and Kenyan were both startled at his impudence.

"You mean the eggs?" Sir Butters asked.

"Aye. Eggs. I knew that," the ragged man nodded.

Ordric waved Butters off toward the kitchen, and the bailiff complied.

"This fellow is known to us only as Gumnbote," the king introduced. "He has a story to tell. Please," he said to the man, "tell us again what you told us last night, and leave nothing out."

"As you say." Gumnbote paused, raising a hand to his mouth to conceal a satisfied belch. "There! That food was fine, just fine, Your Kingship." He turned to Pease and Kenyan, and began: "There really ain't too much to tell, at least not so's I remember. I s'pose there may be a great lot to tell, at that, but I ain't the one to tell it, for I don't seem to know my own brain no mores."

Kenyan was curious as to how much of a tale this odd man could tell, since he apparently didn't even seem to know it himself, but he felt that it wasn't his place to ask questions just yet, not in the presence of the king himself.

Gumnbote continued, "Fact is, I expect my name's not really Gumnbote at all. When the egg-man asked me yesterday, I just said the first thing what popped into my head. It coulda been Bleek or Parsnip for all I knowed, but I opened up my mouth, and what come out but Gumnbote? And it's a fine big name, with two parts, Gumn and Bote, and it don't seem to mean nothin' else, so's it might as well mean Me."

At that moment, Sir Butters—Gumnbote's "egg-man"—came back into the chamber bearing a steaming platter of his new namesake, so the narrative was once again delayed as Gumnbote fell to.

After he had swallowed down his first couple of mouthsful, Gumnbote said, "I don't mean to keep your lordships waitin'. I'll talk while I eat, if that ain't too unpolite."

King Ordric said, with admirable self-restraint, "Please."

"Well, it all started some time ago. I don't rightly know how long. Coulda been years, coulda been months, but I do figger that it's at least months. I woke up in total blackness, one day, and even though I was just as old as I am today, almost, it was as if I was never borned afore at all. For I knew nothin' of where I ever been, nor where I was, nor even *who* I was. All I knowed was, that I *was*, but it was dark, mighty dark. I came to think, maybe I was in Hell, but it was a sight colder than I should've expected.

"Some things I remembered. I knowed I was a man and not a woman. But I di'n't know if I was a son, nor a brother, nor a husband, nor a father. Other things, too, I did remember, which you'll figger out as you listen, but many things I forgot, if I ever knowed 'em at all.

"At first I was afeared to move around, for wheresoever I'd look, there weren't nothin' but dark. Well, sometimes I'd see little dancin' lights, off to the distance, but I didn't know if I was really seein' 'em, or if I was just off my nut.

"I don't know how long I lived like that, just goin' dotty in the darkness. Ever' once in awhiles, I'd reach down and pluck some grass and eat it. And I'd suck the dew off the grass in the mornin's so I didn't starve o' thirst. At least I think it was the mornin's, for they was just as black as the dead o' night to me."

He paused to fill his mouth again, chew, swallow, then wipe his lips with the back of a threadbare sleeve.

"And sometimes when I'd see the little dancin' lights, I'd hear 'em laughin'," he continued. "Sometimes the lights would grow a little bigger, like some'un was carryin' a candlestick closer to me, but then they'd just blink out and be gone. And sometimes it was just dark, fearful dark. And the laughter, it sounded sometimes like a runnin' brook nearby, sometimes it sounded like the wind whistlin' betwixt the trees. But it was laughter—or so I believe.

"Now it sounds like I was there in the dark for ages and ages, maybe, but honest, I don't know. I slept, and I woke, and I slept and I woke. Maybe it was time after time in the same day … maybe it was days and days and days. I don't rightly know, I guess.

"After awhile I decided that I needed to move on. I di'n't know if I'd fall offen a cliff, or drownd in a river, or what. But I couldn't stay any longer in the dark, what with that mockin' laughter in my ears, and the only thing to see bein' the little white lights off to the distance. I needed to see

154

colors again—the blue o' the sky, the green o' the grass—though to be fair, I don't know how I even knowed what blue and green even was. But I did.

"So I picked a direction and started walkin'. And again, if I'da walked in circles, I coulda walked on forever and never got noplace, but it was better than sittin' on the ground in the dark and not doin' nothin'. I started off and I tried to hold a straight line, and I kept on walkin', and when I fell to sleep, I prayed that I could keep on goin' in the same direction tomorrow.

"Well, after a few days o' walkin' like that, if they was days, one o' the dancin' lights started comin' toward me, growin' bigger and bigger like I told you about. And this time it didn't blink out, but it kept on comin' toward me until it liked to blind me, and it was comin' fast—faster'n a deer could run. I was scared, so scared I'da pissed my drawers if I had any water in me."

He stopped and rubbed the whiskers on his chin for a moment, apparently deep in thought. "Who knows? Maybe my name *is* Gumnbote. Who knows?" he said softly. "Not me."

King Ordric cleared his throat, and said, "Would you please tell the others about the light?"

"Sorry! Forgot meself again," Gumnbote replied agreeably. "It was the Arkhanfeie."

Kenyan's heart leaped in his chest at the sound of that word, which he had heard only once before: in the tale that Jairrus and Poll had told him about the fairylands. He felt his palms begin to sweat, and his breath seemed too shallow in his breast.

Gumnbote continued, "Once my eyes was able to see in the light, I could make him out. It was like his skin was *made* o' light." His voice dropped so low that the others in the room strained to make it out, almost as if he were talking to himself. "And he was beautiful, too, as beautiful's a woman, but still strong like a man. Maybe he weren't neither. But he seemed like a man—a lovely, powerful man."

He chuckled once, a staccato burst of self-conscious embarrassment. "I'm just as much a man as any of you boys are, so don't be thinkin' I ain't right. You'da thought he was lovely too."

Before he was able to stop himself, Kenyan blurted out, "How was he clothed?"

"Well, that's somethin', ain't it? I couldn't tell you if he was dressed in nothin' at all, or if he was dressed in everythin' in the world. For a bit, I thought he was wearin' water, and for a bit, I thought he coulda been a tree, he was so green. But on his brow, he wore a twisty kind of crown that was covered with every manner of precious jewel I ever even imagined. It musta been worth most o' the king's treasure."

Ordric addressed Kenyan, and there was the slightest hint of suspicion in his voice, "Do you know something about this Arkhanfeie?"

Kenyan said cautiously, "I have heard the name spoken before. Apparently … he is the ruler of, ah, the fairy folk living in Hagenspan."

"Aye, that's it," agreed Gumnbote.

The king seemed to stiffen, but maintained his composure. "We are Ordric the King, son of Ruric the Conciliator, and there is no part of Hagenspan that falls outside our sway. If there is another who names himself a king in Hagenspan, we have not heard it!"

"No, Your Majesty," Kenyan quickly agreed.

This haughty attitude of King Ordric's was largely posturing, and he knew it. While Ordric was certainly the king of the *men* of Hagenspan, he was well aware that there were still other, older peoples, who did not necessarily bow the knee to Ruric's Keep. The sprites and kobolds of the northern wastes, the trolls of the northeast, the dwarfs wherever they happened to be—Ordric knew that they bore him no allegiance. The dragons, of course—it was whispered that there were at least six of them stalking the wastes—they certainly were beyond Ordric's command. For it to be revealed now to the king that there really were fairy folk living somewhere within his borders came as no great surprise to him, and in fact, he had heard rumors of the Arkhanfeie before. It had been long understood that there were things wilder than nature living in the wilderness.

"Please continue your story," Ordric said after a forbidding moment's pause.

"Yes, Your Kingship." Gumnbote glanced quickly at Kenyan, as if annoyed that his narrative had been interrupted. "Let's see ... the Arkhanfeie. Well, he spoke to me. He said, 'I have sent the darkness the surrounds you, and I have sent the darkness that is within you.' Or somethin' like that. All I can think is, I musta done somethin' powerful wrong to have some'un like the Arkhanfeie mad at me. But anyway, he told me that since it was in my heart to walk, he was allowin' me to leave, and he told me to do that. Leave. And don't come back. And, well ... that's about all of my tale."

"How did you come to be here?" asked Sir Pease.

"I don't know. After the Arkhanfeie finished talkin', he winked out. Just disappeared, quick as you like. But he musta caused the darkness to be a little less dark, in one direction anyways, and so I walked that way. It was like walkin' through a field of gray for awhile after that, and I drank some gray water and ate some gray grass, and heared some gray laughter still, but I kept on walkin' toward where it was brighter. And after awhile, there started to be colors again, peekin' out o' the gray, and then I found some apples layin' on the ground, and I never tasted nor saw anythin' so sweet in all my life. Maybe." He shook his head sadly. "Maybe I seen great and noble things before, what I've clean forgot, but I don't remember 'em. For it's in my heart that I left part of who I *am* back there in the Arkhanfeie's land, and I ache to know just who it is that I was.

"But anyway, here I am now. This is where I ended up after I finished walkin'."

The room fell silent, and Kenyan gradually became aware of other sounds: the clatter of the kitchen, shouts from the courtyard, the buzzing of a fly. He began wondering uneasily why the king had invited him to hear Gumnbote's story, and how this could possibly relate to his own impending quest.

As if reading Kenyan's thought, King Ordric stirred in his chair and said, "Kenyan, squire of Sir Pease, we have previously judged that you should be named a knight in Hagenspan upon completion of a quest to be determined at the proper time." Kenyan raised his eyes and saw the king regarding him with measured curiosity. "This is that time."

"Yes, Your Majesty."

"A knighthood is not to be conferred lightly, and this quest will not be insignificant."

"No, Your Majesty." Kenyan waited pensively for the king to elucidate, and tried once to swallow, but found that his mouth was too dry.

"Your task shall have three parts:

"One. To travel back to your homeland of Fennal and secure another letter from Lord Ester, to replace the one that you failed to present last autumn." Kenyan exhaled softly. *That didn't sound too hard*, he thought.

"Two. The route that you shall travel shall be through the land where Gumnbote lost himself. And, to demonstrate your worthiness to be called a knight, you shall help Gumnbote recover what he lost."

Kenyan felt his neck growing warm with alarm; he had no idea how to help Gumnbote recover … what? Himself? He wanted to ask, *Will Gumnbote be going with me?* but waited to hear the king's final stipulation.

"Three. To prove that you will defend the crown of Hagenspan with all vigor, and subdue any threat to the sovereignty of Ruric's Keep, you shall obtain one jewel from the Arkhanfeie's crown, in token of his submission to the reign of this Ordric, your King."

The blood drained from Kenyan's face, and an involuntary shudder ran up his spine. He felt his stomach lurch, as if he were going to be sick, and wondered if he could possibly refuse the king's quest. Maybe he didn't need to be a knight so very badly after all.

"Do not come to us again until your quest is complete. We are Ordric the King, and we have spoken."

Kenyan heard his voice saying, "Yes, Your Majesty," and wondered how he was keeping from giggling like an idiot. Then he felt Sir Pease take his arm and lead him from the room.

Chapter Twenty-Three

"I thought you said the quest was something I could *do*!" Kenyan complained to Sir Pease.

"Well, lad, I didn't say it would be easy." Pease twisted his bearded face in a fatherly smile toward his frustrated companion. "Calm your fears. This is the road that's laid out for you, and it's just up to you to walk it. One step at a time, keep your heart true, and see what happens."

"But … a jewel from the Arkhanfeie's crown?" Kenyan repeated helplessly.

"I must say, I was surprised to hear that," Sir Pease admitted. "I knew he intended to send you back to the wilderness that Gumnbote came from, but that bit about the jewel caught me napping." The two men were walking to the king's armory in order to outfit Kenyan for his journey. "A word of advice: Don't try to take the jewel by force. Ask him for one."

"Do you think that will work?"

"No, probably not. But I've seen you try to fight. *That* wouldn't work, and that's a certainty."

Kenyan smiled ruefully, and Pease slapped his back and laughed. Kenyan chuckled too, but his cheer quickly abated. A jewel from the Arkhanfeie's crown.

※

Bendell, the master of King Ordric's armory, was a short, fat man who had long white hairs growing out of his ears, and his manner reminded Kenyan somewhat of the dwarf Mott. The rumor of Kenyan's quest had spread swiftly throughout Ruric's Keep, and Bendell had figured that he would be coming for equipment. "So, you'll be wantin' a sword, aye?" he grumbled, squinting up at the tall young man, and continuing to move his mouth after his words were ended, as if he were chewing some invisible cud.

Kenyan looked at Sir Pease and remembered what he had said about not trying to take the jewel from the fairy king by force. "No, I believe not. Perhaps just a staff."

"A staff!" Bendell sputtered. "Why, you don't need me for that! Just go an' whack a stout branch offen the nearest tree!"

"I had in mind something more ... ceremonial, perhaps."

Sir Pease appraised Kenyan with a look, and said, "You intend to make a *trade* with the Arkhanfeie." He smiled a little vacantly. "I wonder if it will work?"

"I don't know," Kenyan admitted. "But he seems to love the things of wood and meadow and stream, according to what I've been told. Which isn't much, of course. But maybe a wooden staff would please him." He frowned and tilted his head as if in thought. "Maybe a staff that has been carved ... would offend him, not please him." He grimaced, dismissing his ruminations. "I expect there's no possible good that would come of me carrying a sword, though!" Turning his attention back to the armory-master, Kenyan asked, "Do you have such a staff?"

"Wait here," the little man groused peevishly, and he disappeared into another room.

Kenyan and Pease made small talk as they waited for Bendell. From the other chamber they could hear a clattering of wooden objects, a scraping of heavy items across a dusty floor, and the muttered oaths of the little man. A few times they heard a thump, and then a muffled shout, almost like the startled bark of an angry dog. Finally the armory-master returned, red-faced and sweating, with his cap knocked askew.

"It's a happy thing for you, lad, that you've found favor with me," Bendell snarled, and Kenyan wondered what it would be like for those who had *not* found favor with him. "Here! I think this'll do." He thrust a parcel into Kenyan's hands, something hard and lumpy, but covered by a velvety wrap.

"May I open it?" Kenyan asked tentatively.

"Of course!" Bendell shouted, and Kenyan feared that the little man was about to snatch the package back out of his hands. He hastily unwrapped the heavy stick, and looked at it without comprehension. It looked like … a branch. Gnarled and knotted, it didn't appear to have been worked at all by any craftsman. He wondered why a knobby stick would be wrapped in velvet.

"I don't understand," Kenyan said. "What is it?"

Bendell pressed his lips tightly shut, and his face grew bright red until he fairly glowed with anger. His lips trembled as he fought to control his temper, but he did indeed master that emotion, and said with some difficulty, "There's a tale to be told about that staff, but I ain't no storyteller. Do you want it or not?"

"Yes, thank you," Kenyan said, re-wrapping his prize and thinking to himself, *Another mystery.*

"Well chosen," said Sir Pease softly. His eyes gleamed wistfully as he watched Kenyan hide the staff within the folds of the fabric. "How did you come to be in possession of an elfin rune-stick?" he asked Bendell.

"So, there's at least *one* person in the kingdom who has regard for the old days," the squat man spat, and chewed furiously. "The idiot steward of Ordric's treasure-room was goin' to throw it *out*, for God's sake!" A growl began to grow in his throat, and he snapped it off with an angry bark, again sounding remarkably like a disturbed dog.

"There have been no elves here since before Hagen himself, or so I understood," Pease said thoughtfully.

"Almost. Hagen met some. They gave gifts." Kenyan and Pease waited for him to continue, but Bendell seemed disinclined to tell any more of what he knew, if in fact he did know more. His gaze became distant, and he smacked his mouth thoughtfully, as if he were going to say something else, and then did not.

"Well, thank you," Kenyan said apologetically. "I didn't understand the significance of the gift you chose."

"Hmmp!" Bendell growled, and glowered at Kenyan from beneath a beetled brow. "Sure you don't want a sword too?"

"Thank you," Kenyan said, hoping he sounded respectful, "but no."

"Well, there you are, then!" Without another word, the little man stomped off to other rooms, his own domain.

Sir Pease and Kenyan stared after him for a moment, and then looked at each other. With a bemused lift of his flowing white eyebrows, Pease concluded, "Well, there you are, then!"

※

Gumnbote was waiting at the king's livery stable when Kenyan and Pease arrived. He was accompanied by Sir Butters, who had been given the task of watching over him until his departure with Kenyan. "Where ya been? I was 'most afeared that you may've got as lost as *me*," Gumnbote said, with a quirky smile crinkling his features.

Kenyan's thoughts were clouded by a lingering grim foreboding about the enormity of his impending quest, so he did not return Gumnbote's smile. But Sir Pease and Sir Butters, who had no such worries, chuckled lightly.

"There, lad, no call for worry," Pease said softly when he saw the dark look on Kenyan's face. "Come aside for a bit," he beckoned, and Kenyan obeyed. They strode to the side of the stable and leaned against the fence of a corral that was attached to the building. Kenyan expressionlessly watched the horses being worked there by the stable-hands, took a deep breath, and exhaled a long sigh.

Pease regarded the homely young man thoughtfully, and then spoke. "You're anxious, yes? Fearful, even. You worry that you'll fail in your quest for the king. Am I right?"

Kenyan stared back at his mentor for a moment, reluctant to admit yet again his uncertainty, his frailty, but then he nodded once in the affirmative.

"I'll speak plain, for we won't speak again for some time, if we ever do," Pease continued intently. "Kenyan, my boy, it must be clear to you that, ah, God hasn't, ah, blest you with the most extraordinary set of natural gifts that He ever gave a man." If Pease was waiting for an acknowledgement from Kenyan, the only one he got was a slight reddening of the youth's craggy cheeks. "But it does seem, though, that you have been … greatly favored with—for lack of a better word— *luck*."

At that Kenyan gave a silent snort. *Luck?* Scenes from his life flashed through Kenyan's mind in an instant: his father's death, and his mother's, his embarrassment with Lanadine, his humiliation at the town of Sarbo. He felt anything but lucky! Pease recognized the wounded anger in the eyes of his young charge, and smiled at him tenderly.

"Look at it this way, lad: After your mother died, you were penniless and adrift, or so I understand. And yet Lord Ester took you in. Lord Ester! A man not known for his generosity, if I may say so. And when eventually you fell out of favor at Beedlesgate, what did Ester do? Did he send you away in disgrace? No! He gave you a letter of introduction for the king himself!

"When you lost your way among thieves and were wandering alone in the wilderness, did you end up eaten by the wild beasts? Thrown in the stockade as an arsonist? Garroted by Sarbo's ill band? No! Every time things looked bleakest for you, it seems, God sent your stout friend Solonsee to carry you a bit further along the path!

"Now you have lived as a guest of King Ordric for almost half a year, eating his meat and warmed by his fires. He has given you an impossible task, which you shall almost certainly fail to complete." Sir Pease laid his heavy old hand upon Kenyan's shoulder. "Now's the time you should expect great things, young Kenyan! For it seems that every time you fail … you prosper. And the more foolishly you fall, the more spectacularly you soar."

He gazed into Kenyan's eyes, as if willing him to believe. "I admit that 'luck' is a poor word for it. The very favor of God, more like. But if there *is* such a thing as luck, well, then … you've got it, lad."

Kenyan smiled sheepishly in spite of his trepidation. "I don't know...."

"Think of it, boy: How many young men your age are there in Hagenspan? Might there be hundreds? Perhaps even a thousand? And how many of them, do you suppose, would trade everything that they have to be in your boots today?" Pease sighed wistfully. "It almost makes me wish that I were young again myself, that I might tag along and see what adventures you'll meet."

Before Kenyan had a chance to ask Sir Pease to *please* come along with him, the old knight said, "But, no. This road is yours to walk, not mine." He clapped his hand on Kenyan's neck. "Expect great things, boy!"

※

"What! Is it summer already?" Gumnbote asked as he and Sir Butters were joined again by Pease and Kenyan, and this time Kenyan offered him a tentative smile.

"I guess we'd better finish with our provisions and then be on our way," he said, and glanced at Pease, who nodded encouragement at him.

"A pair of fine strong horses, maybe? A black one, and a white-an'-gray dappled?" Gumnbote said, with as much eagerness kindled in his eyes as Kenyan had observed in the short time he had known him.

"I'm thinking, maybe ... a cart," Kenyan replied.

"Why, sure, a cart, and a mule or whatnot so's to pull it," Gumnbote agreed.

"I'm thinking … a cart. A cart, and no mule, and no horses." After an awkward moment's hesitation, Kenyan smiled apologetically at Gumnbote, who looked even more perplexed than usual.

Sir Pease said cautiously, "That's a mighty long walk, lad."

Kenyan sighed, and said, "I don't know if I'm right or wrong. I don't know." His gray eyes shone, and his cheeks crinkled in a frustrated frown. "But—I think—anything that looks like ostentation or a show of force against the Arkhanfeie might be received with asperity. Whereas something that looks like humility to the Arkhanfeie may be received, perhaps, with kindness, or tolerance, or … grace, perhaps. I don't know."

"Yes, I see your point," Pease nodded. "But it will be a long walk." He took a deep breath and patted his belly, turning his face toward the springtime sun in a silent prayer. His great bushy brow arched, his forehead wrinkled, and his eyes smiled benevolently. "Well, this is *your* quest, lad. If the Almighty had desired your destruction, He probably would have accomplished that already. Trust your heart."

Kenyan nodded his thanks, as Gumnbote muttered plaintively, "A mighty long walk."

Chapter Twenty-Four

Over the course of the next three weeks, Kenyan grew to know Gumnbote quite well, or at least as well as somebody could know someone who wasn't exactly sure who he was himself. Several times each day, Gumnbote would say something like, "It surely is a sad thing, not knowin' nothin'," or "Be glad you at least know who you are," or sometimes just sigh out a long, audible groan which said the same thing without words.

The pair of travelers trudged along side-by-side through the long hours of each long day, each of them bearing one arm of the cart that bumped along behind them, bearing the entirety of their meager provisions for the quest. They would talk long through the mornings, and then plod silently through the hot afternoons with sweat running down the sides of their faces, until they made weary camp at dusk. By the second morning of their journey, Kenyan and Gumnbote were both nursing painful blisters on their hands, but after a few more days had passed, they were both satisfyingly callused.

Early in the trip, they endured the mocking laughter of townspeople who watched them as they lumbered past. "What a fine, pretty pair of jackasses you two are!" jeered one fat woman who spied them from her doorway. "A-pullin' your cart like a couple of donkey-men!"

"Thankee, thankee kind," replied Gumnbote between drops of sweat. "And what a fine, pretty pair o' girls *you* two are, too," he said generously.

"Well!" she huffed, and shook her apron crossly at them before turning and stomping back to her kitchen.

Two other times before they left the outskirts of the partly civilized lands immediately beyond Ruric's Keep, they were pelted by pebbles and pinecones thrown by small, laughing boys. The first time that happened, the pair of travelers grimaced sidelong at each other and kept on walking, as the debris rained down upon them, pebbles pinging painfully off their shoulders. But the second time, after getting *thwack*ed in the side of the head by a pinecone, Gumnbote dropped his arm of the cart and ran growling toward the boys, who fled back to the safety of their homes, trailing shrieks of terror behind them. As Gumnbote returned to his burden, rubbing his head and chuckling merrily, Kenyan said wryly, "You probably shouldn't have done that."

"Nope," Gumnbote agreed cheerfully. "And on we go."

It was not long before they left the road, left civilization altogether, and began heading through the fields, through the wild plains, toward the dark, distant forests … toward the Feielanns. Once in awhile they came across spots where a wagon wheel had at one time carved a rut into the ground, and Kenyan wondered if they were following the same path that Jairrus and Poll had taken when they had left Ruric's Keep in search of their elusive fortune. He found himself wondering about old King Hagen, too … had Hagen met the Arkhanfeie, during the many years of his sojourning?

Kenyan glanced at Gumnbote, who was apparently lost in thoughts of his own, and said, "Is this the way that you came from? When you came to the king's city?"

His companion grunted. "Don't rightly know." The afternoon sun was shining brightly on Gumnbote's red, perspiring face. "It was darker." It was harder pulling the supply wagon now that they had left the road. "And a good bit cooler, too." They dragged the cart a few weary, lurching steps more.

"Want to stop for the day?" Kenyan panted.

"You're the chief," Gumnbote said, but he didn't seem disinclined to stop.

"Let's." The cart pitched forward to a halt, and both men groaned as they dropped their handles to the ground. Kenyan arched his aching back, turning his face toward the sky, his eyes closed, hoping to catch the breath of a breeze across his cheeks.

"Maybe it was a mistake bringing the cart," Kenyan mused aloud. "Maybe we should have just carried packs."

In a low voice, Gumnbote replied, "A couple o' strong horses wouldn't have hurt my feelin's none." He sat down on the ground, and then stretched out with a dreamy look on his face. "I do love the look of a dappled horse."

Kenyan had an idea. "Do you think that maybe, in your old life before, you had a dappled horse?"

"Hmm." Gumnbote stared thoughtfully at the wisp of a cloud that was forming in the azure sky above him. "I guess I don't know if I ever had a horse or not." Another contemplative moment passed, and then he said softly, "But if I ever had one, I hope it was a dappled."

※

As Gumnbote built a pyramid of kindling and began striking flint for a campfire, Kenyan drew the staff Bendell had given him from the corner of the cart where it had been stowed. Unwrapping the velvety folds of fabric, he held the wooden staff gingerly in his hands and inspected it closely. He had done this several times along the way, trying to discern some pattern of writing or design or ornamentation or *something* about the stick that would distinguish it from any other piece of a branch that had blown down out of a tree, but he was unable to do so.

The wood was craggy and gnarled, but smooth and shining, as if it had been rubbed by the oils of a hundred hands. Whorls and twists spiraled around the shaft of wood, but if those markings represented some kind of language, it was past Kenyan's knowledge. One end of the stick was wider than the other; Kenyan figured that probably the broader end was the top, if it mattered. On this larger end, there was a smooth round knob, such as might be found on the crest of a walking stick. Kenyan traced his finger across the knob, and was surprised at how cool and fresh the old wood felt to his fingertip.

"What was it your friend called that stick?" Gumnbote asked.

"Pease? He said it was a rune-stick, an elfin rune-stick."

"What's that mean?"

Kenyan stared at the rod without speaking for a moment, and then admitted, "I don't know."

"Nope," Gumnbote agreed. Then he continued, "But it's from the elfs. That's pretty grand, ain't it?"

"Yes, I suppose it is." Kenyan extended the staff to Gumnbote, so that he could examine it if he wished, but Gumnbote declined with a shake

172

of his head. "I met a dwarf once," Kenyan said, almost defensively, and felt foolish for having said it.

"Oh?" Gumnbote said politely. "Ain't that ... somethin'." Sensing something of his companion's dissatisfaction in the ensuing silence, he said, "Did you want to tell me about it?"

"No, I guess not," Kenyan replied. "I'll start putting some dinner together for us."

Gumnbote nodded dreamily, and wondered if *he* had ever met a dwarf.

Sometime in the dark hours past midnight, Kenyan was awakened by the rhythmic rasp of Gumnbote's snoring. He tried to will himself back to sleep through the irritation of the mingled burrs and snorts, but found himself more and more vexed, as if every fresh burst of sound were a personal affront to his own nerves. He pressed his eyes more tightly shut, and rolled over on his other side.

Groggily trying to suppress his sense of irritation with his companion, he eventually felt himself drifting back off toward sleep—but suddenly he was once more aware of ... *something*. The darkness, which had wrapped itself around the travelers like a blanket, suddenly seemed less intense, less dark. From behind Kenyan's closed eyelids, he became acutely aware of a brightness in front of his face—or, if not a brightness, at least a lessening in the darkness. His first impression was that it must be nearing the dawn, and he must be facing the sunrise, but he realized almost instantly that that was not the source of the light. At the same moment, he became certain of a *presence* near him: not Gumnbote, but another *someone*. That realization caused an unreasoning stab of fear to jolt through his chest, and he quickly decided not to open his eyes. Chiding himself for a fool—just because he couldn't see the someone didn't mean the someone couldn't see *him*—he decided to open his eyes just a crack, and see if he could identify the source of the brightness.

Kenyan's eyes fluttered briefly; he found that it wasn't as easy to open his eyes just a crack (and actually *see* anything) as he had thought it would be. Forcing himself to take the risk—whatever that might be—he opened his eyes all the way.

Hovering in front of his own face was the face of another, staring intently back at him, almost as if he were gazing at his own reflection in a pool by faintest moonlight. But the face that Kenyan saw was one of such exquisite, poignant beauty as to steal his very breath from his lips. The beauty was somehow *other* than natural human beauty, but if Kenyan had to guess, he would have said it was female. The eyes that stared into his were filled with curiosity, with wonder, perhaps clouded by a shade of timidity, and the face that framed the eyes seemed to glow softly; as if the unnatural light that Kenyan had sensed came from the skin itself.

These impressions were made upon Kenyan in an instant, for as soon as the beautiful eyes realized that Kenyan had awakened, the face was gone, in a flash of searing light. Kenyan uttered a kind of startled yelp, then, gasping in dread, in shock, found that he could no longer see anything at all except for a cold, pure white. He batted his eyes blindly for a few moments, fairly shuddering with terror, until a comforting blackness began to form around the stars again, and he began to hear Gumnbote's snoring again over the beating of his own heart.

He cast his blanket off and struggled to sit up. Looking around, still blinking away the gray fog that lingered in his eyes, he spied far off to the west a sudden flash of white light—just a sparkle, a twinkle. Perhaps ... just a firefly.

No, Kenyan thought. *No*. He exhaled slowly through his mouth, drew in another cautious breath, released that one too. He prayed silently, as his heart continued to throb painfully in his chest. *God, whether I live or die now is in Your hands. But I thank You for this. This blessing.*

Kenyan strained to see if he could see any more distant flashes of light but there were none. *Still, though!* he told himself, as a tear of gratitude formed in the corner of each eye, *I have seen a fairy!*

Chapter Twenty-Five

Réchetthaerielle had journeyed far to see the men. She had seen men before, of course—just a few—but rarely up close. During the five millennia or so that she had been the keeper of Maedwe Feorr, men had occasionally crossed through her domain. But she had mostly avoided them, hiding herself among the flowing grasses of her protectorate, becoming one with the grasses … becoming invisible, becoming grass, until she sensed that the men were far away … that they were gone—that long ago perhaps, they had passed out of her province.

She was curious about men, of course, curious but wary. The Arkhanfeie himself had commanded her that she should hide, and so she had.

But she knew that one day all the world—even her own beloved Maedwe Feorr—would belong to men, for thus had Architaedeus ordained. And if Blessed Architaedeus, the One Who was wise above all, had determined that the earth would one day be ruled by mankind … could men then be evil? Could they be cruel? Would they not love her land, even as Réchetthaerielle herself did love? Would they not cherish her flowers and her grasses and her earth, even as Réchetthaerielle did cherish?

The Arkhanfeie thought not. He was stern and severe, even more severe than the elves, who had departed from the land. The elves, before they left, had met the man-king, and had given gifts, and had received gifts. Then they had gone, leaving the Feielanns to be cared for by the Feie alone.

Perhaps it was loneliness that made the Arkhanfeie so grave, Réchetthaerielle reflected. For an age and an age again, Réchetthaerielle had been lonely too … perhaps that was why she had gone to look at the men. Gone even beyond the border of Maedwe Feorr, which she should not have done. She had heard accounts of dire punishments meted out to others who had left their proper domain, and she blanched at the thought that she too might be deserving of similar castigation. She rehearsed her own plea silently in her heart: *I only left for a moment, just to see the men. Maedwe Feorr was in no danger, and I dashed right back.* Somehow her denial sounded hollow in her own ears, though, and she hoped she would not be required to speak it.

She had seen one of those men before: the stocky, fair-haired one. The Arkhanfeie would not be pleased to see that he had returned to the Feielanns. The Arkhanfeie had judged the man according to his own justice, and sentenced him to darkness, for it was in his power to do so. But then, after just a short span of the earth's turnings, his heart turned as well, and he had extended that man mercy—mercy as if from Architaedeus Himself—and granted him light, and granted him leave. Why was it that the man would return to the Feielanns now? Réchetthaerielle trembled, acknowledging that there were things indeed that she did not understand of the ways of men.

But the other man … Réchetthaerielle was even more troubled by him.

From time to time in ages gone by, Réchetthaerielle had come upon men as they slept, and she had gazed at their dark faces, and beyond into their dark souls. She had smelled the foul reek of their perspiration, and had smelled the rank stench of their greed, the cold stink of their fear. With impish delight, she had stolen their caps, exposing their funny rounded ears, and had vanished into the darkness before they awoke only to hear her elated, lilting laughter lingering behind her.

The men she had teased had had souls of *murnanmermaerus*, she knew. Greed made them ugly, ugly beneath their skin, ugly deep into their bones. Occasionally she had seen souls that had a flicker of light in them, like a fire not yet fully kindled, and she wondered if at last someone was coming to claim Maedwe Feorr from her hand, and she would flee from them and weep for part of an age, weep for the losing of the land she had not lost. But the world went on as it always had, and the men would pass from her realm, and she endured. Often in recent days, when men entered the Feielanns (which happened but seldom), she let them pass altogether without a glance into their souls, for fear that she would see one with a glimmer of *pouaeimus*—of beauty, of light—and that she would either be destroyed or diminished.

But this new man, the one with the dark curling hair—black as the loam beneath the golden meadow—when Réchetthaerielle had gazed beyond his eyes into his soul, she had seen a brightness, a winsomeness, that was as if he had been kissed by Blessed Architaedeus Himself. She stared at him in wonder: wondering at this fine, clear soul, wondering also that she was not frightened as she thought she should be. And he had opened his eyes, and he had *seen* her!

He had seen her ... Réchetthaerielle had never before been seen by a man. She felt that she had somehow been violated ... but also somehow validated. She felt that her own nymphlin soul was not, any more, entirely her own. But even though there was a curious sense of loss that troubled her and caused a shadow to cloud the brightness of her face, there was also an even-more curious sense of *found*, that made her heart flutter like a bird.

She thought, with this mingled sense of joy and fear, that this might be the man ... the man that she could entrust with the precious treasure of Maedwe Feorr. But she also realized that she did not possess the wisdom to make such a choice. *I am probably wrong*, she thought. *I must ask the Arkhanfeie.* She thought again about the dark-haired man. *Sometime soon.*

179

※

Kenyan woke to the clatter and sizzle of Gumnbote making breakfast, and he was surprised that he had not awakened first. There had not been many mornings in the past three weeks that had seen Gumnbote get up without Kenyan's slightly exasperated assistance.

"Hey, there you are," Gumnbote said approvingly as he saw his companion sit up and stretch.

"Thanks for putting breakfast on," Kenyan said. "Smells good."

"Well, you were sleepin' so peaceful," Gumnbote explained.

"Yes. I don't remember when I've slept so well," Kenyan replied. He stood up, made a manageable bundle of his blanket, and then walked a few paces away so he could relieve himself.

Suddenly he remembered: *he had seen a fairy*. A shiver ran up his spine, and he looked around nervously. Where was she now?

He finished his business quickly, hoping he had not revealed himself disrespectfully, and strode back to camp. Remembering Jairrus' and Poll's stories of the fairies' mischief, he checked through his belongings to see if anything was missing. Nothing seemed out of place. He squeezed the velvet wrap to make sure the rune-stick was still safe; it was.

"Whatcha lookin' for?" Gumnbote queried.

Kenyan jumped, startled. He looked at Gumnbote blankly, unsure if he should tell him about the fairy or not. "Nothing," he said.

Gumnbote looked at him curiously, and repeated, "Nothing. Did you find it?"

Kenyan chuckled nervously and said, "No."

"Well, I shouldn't wonder," Gumnbote agreed. "It's probably right where you left it." He held out a plate toward Kenyan. "I'll help you look after breakfast, if it's important."

Kenyan smiled, feeling a little guilty, and said, "Thank you, Gummy."

That afternoon, Kenyan and Gumnbote crossed the border into Maedwe Feorr, though there was no sign to mark it, and the only person who knew it was the unseen Réchetthaerielle. She slipped silently from stalk to stem to shoot, straining to steal snatches of their conversation.

The stocky man with the straw-colored hair was saying, as if he didn't remember that he had just said it moments ago, "It sure is a sadness, not knowin'."

His companion, who was wondering about fairies as he walked and looking about the meadow with great care, said distractedly (but not unkindly), "I feel bad about your sadness, Gummy."

"Thankee," Gumnbote said. "It does help somewhat, just not bein' alone."

"I'm glad to be here with you," Kenyan said, and realized to his surprise that it was really true. He *was* glad to be here in the terrifying wilderness, glad to be here with Gumnbote. "I hope we can find an answer to your mystery soon, and you won't have the sadness of not knowing any more." He hoped—he prayed—that he would be able to lead Gumnbote to his answer ... but he also realized that he might never accomplish that nebulous goal. And if he did not, then neither would he be a knight in Hagenspan ... though out here in the wild meadow, with the possibility of fairies lurking behind every sunbathed rock or windblown leaf, it didn't seem to matter to him quite so much whether he ever became a knight or not.

"What's the saddest thing that ever happent to you?" Gumnbote asked.

Kenyan had shared many of his humiliations as they had trudged along the trail, but there was one thing he had never spoken of that still caused his heart pain, though he was years removed from it. "Why do you ask that?" he asked gently.

"No reason," Gumnbote replied. "Just makin' conversation."

They walked in silence for a few moments. Réchetthaerielle's ears twitched as she strained to hear the dark man's words, urging herself, willing herself to hear. She wondered what would make such a man sad. She knew what would make *her* sad—the thought of losing Maedwe Feorr almost made her sob even now.

Kenyan cleared his throat, and hesitantly began. "One time when I was a boy, the fishermen of Pembicote came to my mother's door and told her that my father would not be coming home anymore. That was hard, but that wasn't the saddest I ever was.

"After that day, it was my mother and me, through every season, through every trial, through everything. My mother was always there for me, always there with me. Her name was Abagale. When other children would tease me because of my ugliness or my awkwardness, she was always there to take me in her arms and let me know I was loved.

"We were very poor, but we did not starve. I know now that she was no more beautiful or noble than a hundred other women, but she was my mother, and I adored her. I have no idea how she provided for us, but she did, and here I am now.

"One day a few years ago, she began complaining of pains in her belly. There was no way I could afford a physician. I didn't know how to make her comfortable—whether she needed herbs or leeches or balms or chrisms. But I made her such soothing teas as I was able to make, and she drank, and smiled, though I could see she was in terrible pain. In mornings I would go and ask the women of my village what to do for her, and in the afternoons I would come back and try what they had told me, but nothing helped.

"After awhile she stopped eating altogether. But even though she did not eat, her belly grew as round as a gourd." Kenyan's throat began to constrict, and his voice became tight and small. "Her very face changed its countenance ... so I would not have been able to even know that it was she ... except for the love that shone from her eyes."

He stopped, laid down his arm of the cart, and choked, "Pardon me, my friend." Kneeling to the earth, he held his head in his hands and wept for some time. Réchetthaerielle stared at the dark-haired man in pity, great tears welling up in her own tender eyes. She understood few of the words the man had spoken, but she could tell that he had experienced a great sorrow. She was not entirely certain, for instance, what a "mother" was, but she understood that the dark-haired man had loved it greatly, and had somehow lost it.

After a few minutes had passed, Kenyan rubbed his eyes on his sleeve, blew his nose, coughed and spat. "Forgive me," he said to Gumnbote, who replied, "No need."

Kenyan looked at his companion through his red-rimmed eyes, and said, "She died, of course." Gumnbote nodded solemnly. "That's what started me on my way to the mainland, to see if Lord Ester would take me in and let me learn a trade. I knew nothing but a bit of fishing, a bit of gardening, but he made me a guard in his house, for a time anyway. You've heard most of the rest."

Kenyan looked off to the west, seeing something distant beyond what his eyes could perceive. He drew in a deep, shuddering breath, and released it. "When I think of my mother now, I can no longer recall her face, the way I knew it as a child. I can only see the misshapen mask that she wore during the days just prior to her death. That ... is a source of great sadness to me. But still I remember ... that one time in my life, I loved, and was loved." His chest heaved. "And that now, she is gone, beyond my reach. I still mourn today." Fresh tears appeared in his eyes, and he stared down at the ground again, blew his nose again.

Gumnbote laid his hand on his friend's shoulder penitently. "I'm sorry I asked you about this. I was just testin' you, I expect. I just wanted to know, when you said that you felt bad about my sadness, if you'd ever knowed enough sadness yourself so that you could really understand. I guess you have."

Kenyan shook his head, still facing the earth. "You don't need to apologize. My mother used to say that God saves every one of our tears in His bottle." He chuckled sardonically. "I never knew what God wanted with our tears, but it comforted me when I was a child." He turned his weary eyes toward Gumnbote, and smiled a tired smile. "Funny. It seems that it comforts me still."

Gumnbote smiled grimly at Kenyan, and asked, "Do you want to go on further today, or do you want to make camp here?"

"I guess we're not in any great hurry today, are we?" Kenyan replied softly. "Let's stop, and make a hot meal, and find a soft spot to sleep."

It was long after dark when Réchetthaerielle decided to steal up and look at the dark man again, the dark man with the bright soul. She had mourned for him throughout the early watches of the night, mourned that he had lost his mother, though she felt blessed that he had watered the soil of Maedwe Feorr with the tears of his eyes. She was briefly tempted to fly hastily through those hours, and diminish the ache of her sympathetic mourning. But, compelled by the curious affection she felt for this dark, bright man, she chose to linger in the moments and taste fully the bitter draught of his sorrow.

Kenyan was lying patiently upon the earth, eyes closed, listening to Gumnbote snore. Since they had retired early tonight, he was sleeping lightly. Besides, he was clinging eagerly to the faint hope that another fairy might come, that he might get another chance to see one. A gray thread of fear dulled his enthusiasm somewhat: What if it were the Arkhanfeie? Still, he thought ... that's why he had come on this quest, wasn't it?

After a time, Kenyan felt himself beginning to doze ... a moment more, and he realized abstractedly that he was asleep and beginning to dream. A moment more—or perhaps it was an hour—passed in an instant, and then he felt the soft glow of moonlight upon his face, and suddenly was alert again ... and he realized that he was not alone.

As calmly as he possibly could, he opened his eyes. To his great delight, he found that he beheld the same radiantly glowing face that he had seen the night before, staring back at him in rapt wonder. She started, an involuntary spasm of fear, but stayed for just a moment. Kenyan dared not speak, dared not rise up, lest he scare the girl away again, but he just silently gazed into her eyes.

Réchetthaerielle did not know why she didn't flee, why she didn't hide. She opened her mouth and drew in a shallow, tremulous breath. She allowed the man to look at her openly, and she blushed faintly, the faint yellow-green of springtime. Knowing that somehow she had been forever changed, she urged her soul into a white burst of *vitapradistum* and disappeared from Kenyan's sight.

Kenyan, alone again but for Gumnbote snoring peacefully at his back, waited patiently for the snow-white blindness to fade to gray, fade to black, and wondered at what he had seen. His heart sang for joy within his chest, and he marveled at how very lovely the girl—the fairy—had seemed to his eyes. She seemed so young, so innocent, so skittish, so wary, so wild. He wondered if he would see her again, and fervently hoped so. He wondered if, next time, he might try to speak to her.

When Kenyan awoke the next morning, he found four perfect peaches lying on the earth near his head. Gumnbote saw the gift that had been left for his companion, and asked, bewildered, "Where on earth do you think *they* come from? There's no peach trees anywhere within eyeshot! And how'd they get to be ripe already?"

Kenyan shook his head, smiling bashfully, his heart dancing yet. He handed a peach to his friend.

Chapter Twenty-Six

"So, you seen a fairy," Gumnbote said testily.

Kenyan nodded.

Gumnbote snorted faintly, not bothering to mask his disdain. "Beautiful, was it?"

Kenyan nodded again.

"Well, I admit, you prob'ly seen somethin', all right. But I don't bear no particular love for their kind, what with them stealin' my mem'ries and all."

Kenyan looked at his friend tolerantly, not wishing to openly disagree with him. He understood that Gumnbote had suffered at the hands of the Arkhanfeie, but he found it hard to believe that the beautiful girl he had seen glowing with moonlight could have had anything to do with robbing Gumnbote's memories. The two travelers had journeyed two more days toward the west, and Kenyan had not seen the girl again, though both mornings when he had awakened, there had been small gifts of fresh, perfectly-ripened fruit. He felt a sort of anxious sorrow that she had not appeared again, though; he longed to see her, to speak to her if he dared. Shaking his head and smiling sadly, he remembered his humiliation with Lanadine, and wondered why he thought this would end differently.

"What?" said Gumnbote suspiciously.

"What what?" Kenyan asked. "What do you mean?"

"You was smilin'," Gumnbote accused. "You ain't playin' false with me, are you?"

Kenyan regarded his companion solemnly, and chose his words with care. "For my part, you have nothing to fear. I swear, I will try as hard as I possibly can to keep you safe, and to help you find whatever is left of that which you have lost."

Gumnbote, only partially appeased, grumbled, "Seems to me that you're gettin', well, kinda *fond* o' the fairies. You've seen 'em, an' they ain't streck you blind. Hell, they even bring you *food*! Kinda makes me, well, afraid—a little bit—that you're goin' to be on their side, when it comes down to it."

"Oh, no, I shouldn't think so," Kenyan said uncomfortably. "You and I—we're the same kind. And besides, I promised King Ordric that I would help you." Gumnbote humphed a disgruntled acknowledgement, and the two fell silent for a bit. And Kenyan thought—not for the first time—troubled thoughts about his companion.

What if Gumnbote was actually a bad man? The thought had lurked at the outer fringes of Kenyan's consciousness for some days. The Arkhanfeie, though cold and stern, did not seem to be bad ... at least according to Kenyan's information, which was admittedly scant. But what if the Arkhanfeie had actually pronounced a sound judgment against Gumnbote, and the latter's memory loss was only his just desserts for some crime committed against the people of the Feielanns? Since Gumnbote didn't even know himself anymore, he could have previously been almost *any*one, Kenyan thought with a shudder. For all Kenyan knew, he could be Black Sarbo himself! Kenyan stole a guilty glance at his companion's sandy hair and ruddy complexion, and thought that he was probably not Black Sarbo ... but maybe he had been some other bad man.

Then again ... Gumnbote did not seem like a bad man. Confused, yes. Testy sometimes, yes, but then, who wouldn't be? He could just as easily be Ange's lost husband—Jace's lost father. Even if he still didn't seem to be able to remember anything about it.

Once, a couple of weeks earlier, the idea had first come to Kenyan that perhaps Gumnbote was Ange's missing husband, and his heart had leaped at the thought, and he had felt that it must be true. So he had asked, "Gummy, does the name *Ange* mean anything to you?"

"Why, no, I don't b'lieve so," he said, scratching his chin and looking perplexed. He said the name again, trying it out on his tongue. "Ange." He looked at Kenyan. "Who is it?"

"Just a woman who ... lost a man. I thought maybe it could've been you."

"Hmm," Gumnbote said, interested. "Ange." He trudged on for a few more paces, hauling the bumping cart across the rolling plain, lost in his own thoughts. "Nope. If I knowed her oncet, I can't remember her now."

After that day, Kenyan had told Gummy several more times about his encounter with the little family, but every time he told the tale, it was as if Gumnbote were hearing it for the first time. Kenyan urged prayers heavenward for Ange and for Jace and Jem and Powder ... praying that the children's father would return safely, whoever he was. Wherever he was. And he hoped that it was not Gumnbote, who did not know them, and who Kenyan was leading back to the dangerous Feielanns, where his memories had been stolen away in the first place.

Kenyan was jarred from his reverie by Gumnbote saying, "Whatcha thinkin' now?" He sounded conciliatory, as if atoning for his suspicions of a moment earlier by his present polite inquisitiveness.

"I was just thinking about Ange and her children again, and maybe saying a little prayer for them."

"Ange ... that sounds familiar."

※

Réchetthaerielle had hastened to the western border of her realm, seeking to barter with her friends. She bore flowers in her arms, the colorful blooms of Maedwe Feorr's springtime—she called them Golden Starfire and Blue-as-Sky—which were much beloved by Baeriboelle, one of the naiads of Ripar Flowan. Halting at the banks of the river, she lifted her voice to sing a melodic summons to her sisters, the three limniads of Maedwe Na. The Three were not Réchetthaerielle's sisters by birth, for such is not the origin of limniads. But they were sisters in purpose, being appointed by Architaedeus' decree to mind the gardens allotted to them.

The rippling waters of Ripar Flowan glistened in the mid-morning sun, and Réchetthaerielle squinted at the brightness of the reflected light. A swirl appeared before her in the glistening water, which then rose up in a slender column, then swelled to take the form of a maiden, though nearly as clear as liquid glass. Baeriboelle the naiad sang out in her burbling, laughing, cry: "Réche, my sister! So soon am I blessed by your presence again!"

Réchetthaerielle smiled gently, and said, "I am the one blessed, dear Baeri." Without expending any more time on conversation, she immediately began her transaction. "I have brought petals of blue and gold to scatter in your pool, the colors and fragrances of their crushing to give you delight."

"Thank you, sweetheart," Baeriboelle gushed, laughing merrily. She flung her hands toward the sky, causing the water to fall in a rainbowed curtain all around her friend. "I must find a gift for you! What desires your heart?"

"If it is not too much to ask," Réchetthaerielle said as she knelt to lay her delicately perfumed petals upon the water, "I would have four small plums from Graf Norduren." Graf Norduren was an orchard in the northernmost reaches of the Feielanns, quite beyond the reach of Maedwe Feorr, whose borders Réchetthaerielle was not permitted to leave. She felt a quick guilty pang of conscience, remembering that she had, in fact, left her own place just days ago in order to see the men.

"Fruit again!" Baeriboelle cried. "My sister, what a hunger you have acquired for fruit! It was just days ago, wasn't it, that I brought you the pears?"

"It was yesterday," Réchetthaerielle admitted.

"So it was!" Baeri giggled. "Well, Réche, for my love of you, you shall have them! Will you wait here while I fetch your present?"

"Yes, sweetheart," Réchetthaerielle said. "I thought to spend the morning talking with the Three from Maedwe Na while you found my plums. But they have not heard my song. Do you know where they are?"

"The fish tell me they feel the Arkhanfeie near. Perhaps the Three attend him." Baeriboelle gathered up the petals in her watery hands and lifted them to her crystalline face, breathing in the bouquet with a sweet smile, and then scattering them back to the pool with a splash of her fingers. "There are men coming. Did you know?"

"Yes."

Baeri's sparkling, clear eyes regarded Réchetthaerielle with a merry comprehension. "You have seen them," she laughed. Baeri had seen men many times, too, and had teasingly caressed their legs as they had waded through Ripar Flowan, causing them to yelp and jump and run. "What have you taken from them?"

Réche looked at her friend for a moment without responding, and then said in a low voice, "I have not taken ... I have given."

"The fruit!" Baeri cried, aghast. "Does the Arkhanfeie know?"

"No," Réche said, her face darkening. "Not yet. Perhaps."

"Oh, Réchetthaerielle, what have you done?" she whispered, and struggled to look solemn for a moment. Then the sun shone brightly again through her face, and she smiled again, laughed again, almost as if she had forgotten all about the men. "Thank you for the flowers!" she said. "Wait here, and I will be back with your plums."

Kenyan felt the bright glow of moonlight intensify before his face, the light falling on his skin like rain, and he opened his eyes slowly. She was there—the beautiful shining countenance he had longed to see again, fear and wonder still alight in her eyes, and perhaps something more.

"Don't run," he whispered, and the soft radiance of her face flickered briefly, perhaps signifying hesitance or alarm, but she did not run.

"Thank you for the fruit," Kenyan whispered, and for an instant a smile danced across her features, and her eyes flared with some emotion Kenyan did not recognize. The soft light emanating from her skin, pale as a ghost, turned slightly golden as he continued to gaze upon her. His breath was very shallow in his chest.

"Do you have a name?" he asked, and even as he said the words, he wondered if she had a voice, and what it would sound like. The girl's lips parted, and she hesitated again. Kenyan was suddenly struck by how very lovely her mouth was, and then she was gone, a familiar burst of blinding white light.

Chapter Twenty-Seven

Biaulabonelle was one of the Three of Maedwe Na, along with her sisters Caümagauderelle and Brisàflourelle. Biaula was gifted with far sight—not far in the sense of being able to see things at a great physical distance, but rather the ability to see things backward and forward through time with a clarity uncommon among the nymphs of the meadows. Because of this gift the Arkhanfeie occasionally sought her counsel; though, to be certain, it was clouded by the limitations of the limniads' perceptions. Biaula could *see*, but the significance of the things she saw was difficult for her to comprehend.

Her sister Caüma was placid and serene. She had scarcely any of Biaula's ability to foresee, but Architaedeus Himself had graced her with the ability to trust His purposes without question. While this made her a source of much stability and comfort in Maedwe Na, it also served to make her counsel of little practical value. The grace of the third sister, Brisà, was that she was exceptionally loving and gentle. When Brisà appeared in the meadow, birds would light upon her arms and sing gaily; chipmunks would come to her and rest against her feet. All three of the sisters were fair of face, for thus did Architaedeus create the Feie.

The Three cared for the lands of Maedwe Na, loving the grasses, the blooms, the earth itself, as Réchetthaerielle loved Maedwe Feorr. The limniads tended the meadows—these four caring for the eastern part of the Feielanns, and other sisters tending other fields of Architaedeus' planting. Naiads (like Baeriboelle) cared for the rivers and brooks and ponds and the creatures therein. Dryads tended the lives of the trees in the great forests, and oreads cared for the lives of the stones and jewels hidden under the earth. The Arkhanfeie, who had a name that none knew save Architaedeus, was set above them to order and rule.

Right now the Arkhanfeie stood facing grimly toward the east, toward where the clumsy, uncaring, lumbering men trampled his grass as they plodded westward into the heart of the Feielanns. Men were coming, this he knew (as he knew most things that occurred within his borders), but he had not received this information from Réchetthaerielle. *O Réchetthaerielle, why does your heart betray you?* he thought to himself. *Why does your heart betray the Feie?*

The Arkhanfeie knew (as he knew most things that concerned his realm) that one day humankind would overrun the borders even of the Feielanns, for they were ever expanding, ever conquering, ever spoiling. What he did not know was when that day would come, for that information Sovereign Architaedeus had not revealed. The Blessed One had commanded the Arkhanfeie millennia ago to hold the Feielanns, to hold the Feielanns as a treasure, to hold until the day that He commanded to cease holding. And that command had not yet come, nor did the Arkhanfeie feel the end of his days approaching, and so it was his intent to hold yet longer.

Blessed One, teach me to know the number of my days, so that I may rule your holdings with wisdom, he breathed into the wind. No whispered answer was carried back by the breeze, and so the Arkhanfeie understood that his course was his own to determine.

"Biaulabonelle, what do you see?" he asked.

Biaula laughed, delighted to be able to use her gift for the Arkhanfeie, and asked him, "Where shall I look?"

"Set your gaze to the east, beyond Maedwe Na if you are able, and look forward into days yet to come. Tell me what you see."

Caüma drew up beside them, laying her hand upon the Arkhanfeie's arm as softly as a butterfly lighting upon a flower, and murmured, "Why does your heart trouble you, dear one? Whatever Biaula may see, Architaedeus has already seen—seen and purposed."

"True as your voice is," he replied solemnly, "my way is hidden from me." He smiled a grim smile toward Caümagauderelle, telling her that he did not disdain her words, and she smiled and rested her head upon his shoulder.

"I see men," Biaula whispered. "Two men."

Brisà knelt before the Arkhanfeie and pled with him. "My lord, do you remember the love that Blessed Architaedeus has given you for the Feielanns? The love that encompasses tree and rill? Grass, seed, stalk, and gem? Your own people? Even your Brisà?"

The Arkhanfeie looked gently down to Brisàflourelle, and said, "Yes, dear one, I do remember my love."

"Then," Brisà continued as a pale golden tear formed in her eye, "have you not love also for man, who will walk these sacred fields when we have long since returned to the Blessed?" She held his gaze steadily, solemnly—an extraordinary feat for a nymph.

The Arkhanfeie's face darkened, and he frowned. "Brisàflourelle … what do you know?"

Clouds began to creep across the sky, blotting out the sun's light, rending the warmth of the early summer's afternoon with a chilly slash of wind.

"I see darkness," whispered Biaulabonelle.

Brisà said, trembling, almost inaudible, "I feel that the men … are loved."

"Great darkness," Biaula continued.

197

"Loved?" Anger flared in the Arkhanfeie's eyes. "By whom?"

"I think—I think Réchetthaerielle loves the men," Brisà said, her eyes wide and sad.

"Réchetthaerielle?" the Arkhanfeie said severely, but he knew as he said it that he had already suspected as much. "What is this darkness that you see?" he demanded of Biaula.

The nymph with the far sight giggled nervously, and said, "I don't know."

He said somewhat stiffly (though maintaining a sort of dignified patience), "Is the darkness of my making, or Architaedeus'? Does it signify only a passing storm, or the end of all things?"

Biaula began to cry, and said, "I don't know!"

The Arkhanfeie closed his eyes with a stern grimace, and struggled to sustain his composure. "Do not fear, little one. I am not angry with you."

All three of the nymphs were jittery by now, disquieted and skittish. The clouds continued to darken above the Arkhanfeie's head, and the air continued to cool unnaturally, unnervingly. Suddenly a white bolt of lightning flashed across the heavens, and the three frightened sisters disappeared as well to haunts more comfortable, white sparks of light mimicking the argent fury of the thunderbolt.

The Arkhanfeie, a furrow of frustration wrinkling his noble brow, said, "I shall see."

※

Gumnbote watched the gathering storm, and said to Kenyan, "That ain't normal. Is it?"

"Doesn't seem so," Kenyan said, the cloud of concern in his pale gray eyes mirroring the storm clouds in the distance.

The two men saw the flash of lightning from across the river, and jumped involuntarily. "Seems angry somehow, don't it?" Gumnbote murmured.

The next instant, they were face-to-face with the Arkhanfeie, and the storm which had appeared to be miles away a moment before was suddenly all around them. The wind whipped Kenyan's hair, and dust and grit lashed him across the face. Gumnbote dropped immediately to his knees before his old adversary, bleating out a fearful cry. Kenyan also dropped to one knee before the awesome presence facing him, and bowed his head in what he hoped was a respectful manner.

The Arkhanfeie, clothed in jewels, clothed in living green, clothed in fury, looked sternly at Gumnbote, recognizing him immediately, and barked, "You were banished, and yet you have returned. Your doom is upon you."

"Yes, Your Majesty," Gumnbote blubbered, and began to sob.

The Arkhanfeie turned his gaze to Kenyan, looked again more deeply, and remarked, "You, o man, bear a faint gleam of *pouaeimus*. Why have you come trespassing upon my Feielanns?"

"I don't understand *pouaeimus*, m'Lord. I just came with my friend. We hoped—"

"I weary of men and their ways," the Arkhanfeie interrupted crossly. "You have come to the land of the Feie, which you understand not. You have traveled with this benighted, deficient companion, whom apparently you know not. You bear *pouaeimus*, which you comprehend not—you know not even your own nature!"

"Forgive me, m'Lord. It's true that I'm not much of a man. I'm sorry for that, but I'm all that I am, and I can't change it," Kenyan babbled, terrified.

"Please be silent," the Arkhanfeie said, his tone perhaps softening somewhat. "You are more than you know." He paused to consider for a moment, as the wind continued to whip angrily and huge drops of rain splattered upon the ground next to them. "If you were journeying alone across the Feielanns, I would grant you safe passage, and command the daughters of Architaedeus to bless you."

The Arkhanfeie turned his face upward into the threatening blackness of the clouds, as if listening for something. "But … you have come, admittedly, with this … *friend* of yours: twice a trespasser, twice a transgressor. Once banished, twice damned."

"Forgive us, please!" Kenyan pled. "We only sought—"

"You shall share his doom," the Arkhanfeie judged, remembering what it was that Biaula had foreseen. "The darkness that once bound this encroacher, this intruder, shall wrap itself around him again as a cloak, and no weight of pity shall be sufficient to release him. But you, o man, since you share the bonds of affection with him, shall help him bear this burden. He shall not be alone in the dark night of his soul; nor shall you be."

The darkness of the clouds intensified, extending down to the horizon on all sides of the men, and Kenyan's view of the Arkhanfeie himself grew dim, except for the bright glow of his face. Even though Kenyan could not see the Arkhanfeie's lips move, he heard his deep voice from somewhere within his chest. "To show you that I am not completely without pity, I will allow you one more time to see that which you most greatly desire. Perhaps the memory of it will comfort you in the coming night."

Kenyan thought to himself in a fit of panic, *The thing that I most desire to see?* Flashing through his darting mind in an instant came the notion of Lanadine and the love he had borne for her, the love for which he had suffered, but no vision of her appeared to him. In less time than it took to realize it, he thought of Solonsee and his generous friendship, but he did not see that smiling face either. The home of his childhood? … but no. His father? His dear mother? And just before the darkness became complete around him, he saw in his mind's eye a face, beautiful beyond measure, softly glowing with moonlight, a look of awe-filled wonder flowing from her eyes as she gazed back at him, and he recognized the nymph from the night, the fairy who had brought him gifts of fruit, and he suddenly realized that *that* was the thing that he most wished to see again, out of all the sights he had ever beheld. And as the whole world became black, and he was urged toward terror by the blackness itself, he found to his gentle surprise that he was content.

Chapter Twenty-Eight

The blackness was like nothing Kenyan had every experienced. He blinked his eyes deliberately, trying to be able to tell whether they were open or closed, but he couldn't discern any difference. He turned his head from side to side, hoping to see any light in any direction, anything that appeared to be something other than blackest black, but again, he could not tell. No sun, no moon, no star, no fire, no torch, no dawn. Nothing but black. Kenyan suddenly realized that he would quickly lose track of time altogether, and wondered how soon it would be before he lost his sanity, and wondered why it mattered.

"Gummy?" he whispered. Silence.

He tried again, and detected a note of panic in his voice, as if it were coming from somewhere besides his own throat. "Gumnbote?"

"Are you talkin' to me?" The voice came from close by and a little behind Kenyan, and he turned his face in that direction, staring blindly through the nothingness to where he thought the voice might have come from.

"Yes, it's me—Kenyan," Kenyan said, whispering again. Somehow it seemed more appropriate to whisper here in the darkness, though for all Kenyan knew, the sun might be blazing brightly overhead, and the blackness be a blindness of his own, not the world's.

"Can you see anything?" Gumnbote asked.

"No. Nothing."

"Is this what the world's like, or are we blind?"

Kenyan, worried, said, "Don't you remember?"

"Don't I remember what?" Gumnbote's voice challenged.

"Anything. Do you remember me?" Kenyan asked. "Your friend. Kenyan."

A moment of silence passed, before the disembodied voice said hollowly, "No, I fear I don't. And, try as I might, I can't seem to recall my own name neither."

"You are known to me as Gumnbote. And I am your friend, Kenyan."

"Aye. You said that."

Kenyan sadly had no answer for that, so he sat in dark silence for a moment until the silence and the darkness grew too great for him to bear.

"Gummy."

"Aye."

A pause.

"What do we do now?" Another pause.

"I guess ... I don't know."

Réchetthaerielle cowered against her anticipation of the Arkhanfeie's anger, and sought to hide herself from his approach by spending a precious bit of her *aeterpradistum* and leaping ahead in the future by the span of a week. With her hands full of ripe plums, she had seen the black storm raging, and knew what it had to have meant.

An instant later, after she had blazed like a flaming arrow through the space of six days and one, she stopped, breathless, finding herself in the same spot near the river, the plums lying in a brown heap between her feet, spoiled.

The Arkhanfeie waited there for her, and when she saw him, she fell to the earth before him and wept.

He regarded the nymph's quaking back patiently; she was clothed in a diaphanous, silky substance, colored by the pale yellows and greens of her springtime fields, with the flowers of Blue-as-Sky decorating her tangled flaxen hair. Whatever force of rage that had once burned in his rigid breast toward this simple, sensitive limniad, this Réchetthaerielle, dissipated as the sound of her sobbing reached his ears.

"Do not fear, little one, tender of the garden of Maedwe Feorr," he said softly. "It was wise for you to run to this seventh day, for the anger I might have borne you has been blown away by the breezes of your sky, and the hardness of my heart has been softened by the showers from your clouds as I waited for you." He knelt down and began stroking her hair, her shoulders, as she continued to cry. After a few minutes of that, the Arkhanfeie began to grow mildly annoyed again— why would she not stop her weeping?

"The Three suspected," he began again, "that you had feelings for these men … that were *unseemly*." His voice rose sharply on that last word, and he was a bit surprised at his own sense of being affronted. "They said that you bore love for them." The word *love* caused a foul taste in his mouth, which caused him a moment of disquiet. Architaedeus the Blessed had commanded love, had *created* love … why was now the idea of love an insult to the Arkhanfeie? He concluded quickly that there must be a love that was right, and a love that was wrong; what else could explain it? For he was the Arkhanfeie, and he was not given to capricious judgments; he had been gifted and burdened with the order of the Feielanns, and the Blessed had surely equipped him for the task.

"The Three said that I love him?" came a small voice, muffled by the ground.

"They said that you loved—" the Arkhanfeie realized that she had not said *them*, but *him*. "Which one do you love?"

Réchetthaerielle stayed silent … but at least she had stopped crying for the moment.

"Rise, and give answer."

She obeyed reluctantly, drying her tears with the back of her hand. "I am sorry, my Prince."

"Which one do you love?" he repeated testily.

"I have not said that I do love," she replied with a hint of trembling fire, "but if I did, could you wonder which one it was?"

"You have seen the man with *pouaeimus* in his soul." The Arkhanfeie mulled this, and remarked, "You have looked deeply into his essence. How can this be, since it was my command for you to avoid mankind, to hide yourself from them?"

She looked at him bravely, sadly, silently, with fresh golden tears welling up in her eyes again.

"Have you no answer for me, little one?" the Arkhanfeie said with regret.

"I have done what I have done, and I will bear my disgrace," she said through lips that quivered, as the tears spilled down her cheeks again.

"Even," said the Arkhanfeie, "if I should be forced to give Maedwe Feorr to another?"

The fulgurating stab of fear surged like a white-hot bolt of fire through Réchetthaerielle's breast, and she swooned, nearly collapsing upon the ground, her knees unable to support even the ethereal weight of her nymph's frame. She reached out blindly to steady herself, and felt the Arkhanfeie's strong arms supporting her. Lose Maedwe Feorr ... could she possibly bear it? What would become of her? Would she be forced to wander, a lonely spirit with no home? Or would her days simply come to an abrupt end, her *aeterpradistum* poured out on the earth of Maedwe Feorr like water from a jar? Like tears from a jar?

"I see you understand the gravity of your disobedience," the Arkhanfeie said sympathetically. He bore the nymph no malice; the limniads were gifted to tend the gardens Architaedeus had sown, but were not burdened with any particular wisdom beyond their love of the growing, living land. Réchetthaerielle probably had not understood the disaster that she had courted; how could she have?

She steadied herself against the Arkhanfeie's arms, and made herself stand again. "Have you made his eyes dark?" she asked him timidly, and the Arkhanfeie was surprised rather at her boldness, that she should even wonder about the human, when the threat of her own doom was nearly upon her.

"I have," he replied sternly, and though he felt no need to explain his judgment to this foolish, reckless nymph, he found the words coming from his mouth nonetheless. "He was admittedly the companion and friend of the accursed one who had flouted my mercy. He is sharing the reward for his companion's disrespect."

"I understand," Réchetthaerielle said, and looked into the eyes of her master for a moment before dropping her gaze in submission. "Is he near?"

"They are," said the Arkhanfeie, refusing to reduce their discussion to only the one man.

"May I—may I feed him?" she said in a voice barely loud enough to hear.

Such audacity from a nymph! The Arkhanfeie was fairly stunned. He said in a severe tone, "Réchetthaerielle! Your guardianship of Maedwe Feorr hangs in the balance! Have you no place left for prudence?"

"My Prince," she pled, "that is why I asked your permission, instead of merely feeding him without your leave." Her eyes flicked upward to meet his gaze again, and then again she dropped her eyes in humility. "May I speak?"

He stared at her, his brow furrowed with frustration, the living jewels of his crown flaring red as ruby. "You may speak."

"The Blessed One has given you the authority to chase men from the Feielanns if you feel them to be a threat, and to blind them with darkness if they will not understand … but he has not granted you leave to kill them." She spoke passionately—the words had taxed all of her wisdom, and she had spent many days formulating the thought that poured forth now. "At least, that is what I think I understand." She swallowed, blinked, and met his gaze again, and held it. "May I feed him?"

The Arkhanfeie gazed at her in fury, angry with her for her insight, but loving her still, because—even though he was angry—it was in him to love. The wind whipped around him and the clouds darkened again as they had a week earlier, as he silently cursed her for her lack of understanding and blessed her for her tenderness, and suddenly, in a burst of blinding light, he was gone, and the sun was shining brightly overhead in a calm blue sky. And the voice of the Arkhanfeie lingered on the breeze just long enough for Réchetthaerielle to hear: "Yes."

It had been seven days since Kenyan had eaten anything besides what he dared to pull up from the earth next to him—grasses moist with dew, roots still clinging to earth. Since he could not see what he was harvesting, he did not know whether his fingers were feeling wildflowers or poisonous weeds. But poison or no, he felt that he would surely starve if he did not eat, and what difference did it make then whether he died of starvation or poison? But still he grew weaker, for the nutrition offered by the grasses of the field where he sat back-to-back with Gumnbote was not the nutrition of meat, of fruit and vegetable. He was listless and sad, and contemplated his coming end with bleak resignation, figuring that he had been mostly a failure all of his days, and that now he was passing into eternal darkness in the least significant way he could. He had not helped Gumnbote discover himself; Gummy had even lost what little he had left. He had not become a knight in Ordric's court, and could not really say that he even cared anymore. He had not married, though admittedly his prospects for that had been bleak enough anyway.

But he felt no resentment toward God, or even the Arkhanfeie for that matter. He recalled moments that he had spent under the oak trees, listening to the birds, and a faint bittersweet smile creased his face. He remembered his adventure with Mott the dwarf, and laughed silently at his own foolishness. He remembered Solonsee's friendship, and thanked God that he had known him. And he still could see, just faintly in his mind's

209

eye, the face of the beautiful fairy, and felt grateful that he had seen such a sight—such a sight!—and wondered what he might possibly see should God open his eyes again on the other side of death.

So he waited patiently for that death to come, leaning against Gumnbote's back, arms linked so that they should not lose each other. From time to time he would speak softly to Gumnbote, reassuring him that he was there, and that he would not leave him, and that he was his friend.

Réchetthaerielle walked toward the two men lying against each other in the afternoon sun. The man with the shining soul stared blindly in the direction of Ripar Flowan; perhaps he could hear faintly the sounds of Baeriboelle splashing in the water. Réchetthaerielle remembered how tentatively, how timidly, she had first approached the man in the darkness of midnight, for fear that he might somehow see her. Now she approached him boldly in the golden sunlight, with no fear that he could see her, and she was sad.

She knelt down beside the man, sorry for his weakness, paused to make sure that he still breathed. He did, and she released her own breath. From someplace within his stupor, he felt the delicate breath of the fairy upon his own face, and recognized it as being something other than the breeze.

"Who's there?" he croaked, a dry rasp. "Are you there?"

She almost flashed away, but wrapped her courage about her like it was Maedwe Feorr itself, and said in a light, piping voice, "I am here."

"I knew it was you," Kenyan whispered. "I would know your voice anywhere, for it is as bright and beautiful as your face." He struggled to smile in the direction of the voice, but was unable to lift his head.

"You are weak," she whispered back. "I will feed you."

"It might be too late for that ... I am spent, I fear. Though I thank you for thinking of it," Kenyan said.

She hesitated for a moment, because it would be very costly to her. But she decided, paused, decided again, and she did not flinch at the price she would pay. "I will feed you four days ago," she said, and she was gone. Kenyan thought, *What a strange thing to say*, and *Don't go*, and then thought nothing.

It had been three days since Kenyan had eaten anything besides what he dared to pull up from the earth next to him—grasses moist with dew, roots still clinging to earth. Since he could not see what he was harvesting, he did not know whether his fingers were feeling wildflowers or poisonous weeds. But poison or no, he felt that he would surely starve if he did not eat, and what difference did it make then whether he died of starvation or poison? But still he grew weaker, for the nutrition offered by the grasses of the field where he sat back-to-back with Gumnbote was not the nutrition of meat, of fruit and vegetable. He was listless and sad....

Réchetthaerielle pressed the plums into his hands, and said, "These will strengthen you until I return with something more. They are a bit overripe, but they will give you life. Eat, and I will be back soon."

Kenyan sat up, stunned—it was the fairy! He felt the fruit in his hands, and realized she was gone already. "Gummy," he said, "Sit up. We have food."

Chapter Twenty-Nine

Réchetthaerielle sat cross-legged in the sun-washed meadow, the breeze tossing her long pale hair and ruffling the translucent chemise that she wore to cover her body's nakedness. In her lap rested a small mound of fruits and nuts, from which she occasionally handed a piece to Kenyan, who in turn passed slightly more than half to Gumnbote, who ate moodily, silently.

Kenyan had quite recovered his strength, though not his vision. He spoke only a few tentative words to the fairy, fearing that he might frighten her off again, not knowing that she sat at ease in the center of her own realm, and was growing more and more comfortable in the presence of the man with the shining soul.

Remembering his question from days before (which she had never answered), she said in a soft treble voice, "I do have a name."

Kenyan said, as respectfully as he could, "I have longed to know it. May I?"

"I am called Réchetthaerielle."

"Thank you," Kenyan replied, and repeated her name softly to himself, which made her smile with delight. "I am called Kenyan."

She giggled. "What a funny, small name! Is there more?"

"Not that I know of," he grinned. "It always seemed enough for me, since I'm a smallish kind of man in many ways."

"You are small? I do not understand."

Kenyan was happy to finally be able to converse with the girl, and he didn't wish to confuse her or frighten her away again, so he explained as gently as he could. "I know that I seem tall of stature, but I am awkward and foolish in many ways. Among my own people, I'm considered to be uncommonly ugly, and I've been a failure at just about everything I've tried."

"Ugly!" she exclaimed, astonished. She had not heard, or did not care about, his assertion that he had been a failure. "What could that possibly mean? Have they not looked at you deeply?"

"No, not so much, I guess," he reflected.

She fell silent then, wondering at what kind of hideous, cruel people would look at the man with the shining soul and name him Ugly?

He felt her silence keenly, and after a few unsteady moments asked, "Are you still there?"

"The people of the Feie," she said slowly, "look at each other deeply, and the beauty of the soul is more precious to us than the fairness of our forms." She struggled to express herself. "Our forms may change ... but our souls are our souls."

Kenyan thought he understood about the fairies' forms changing, from the stories he had heard from Jairrus and Poll and Gumnbote. "I would know more of your people, if you would tell me," he offered.

"I will sing to you of my people, and then you may ask what you will," she said, and then in a clear soprano tone she began:

> *We saw the world's first morning dance*
> *across the blood-red sky.*
> *We saw the hands of Architaedeus*
> *teach the birds to fly.*

We saw the sons of Adam born—
the sons of Adam die.
And through it all, we sang and laughed,
and over all, we cry.

He gave the garden of the Feie
the morn the earth was born.
And when, by sin, man broke His heart,
the world was rent and torn.
But since no law did break the Feie,
the Feielanns were restored.
And through it all, we sang and laughed,
and over all, we mourn.

    Ah-h-h, the delights of the world He gave!
    Ah-h-h, the joys of the Feie!
    Oh-h-h, the beauties of the earth He gave!
    Oh-h-h, how blest are we!

For love of Architaedeus,
our service we supply.
The Feielanns are His garden blest,
of earth, of water, sky—
We shall secure the land He gave,
until He calls us nigh.
And through it all, we sing and laugh—
    through it all, we sing and laugh—
    through it all we sing and laugh,
and after all, we die.

The waiflike melody, to Kenyan's ears, was an impossible contradiction of joy and sorrow, of beauty and of pain, and was lovely and poignant almost beyond his ability to hear. He tried to speak, but choked on his words. His blind eyes blinked back salty tears, until finally he cleared his throat and said, "Thank you."

"You have heard my song," she said. "Not all are able."

Gumnbote said irritably, "I heard it too. All about death and blood it was."

Kenyan, still blinking, said softly to his friend, "But about joy, too. Did you hear it?"

Gumnbote grumbled something unintelligible and refused to say more.

Returning his attention to Réchetthaerielle, Kenyan asked, "Have you been alive ... forever?"

"No," she said, laughing gaily. "Only Architaedeus has lived forever. I had a beginning, and I shall have an end."

"But ... how long have you been alive?" Kenyan wondered.

"Oh, for many days," she replied carelessly, and that seemed to be the correct answer. "The Feie were created for the bright springtime of the world, but it is said that our bloom will fade and fail when comes the withering heat of autumn."

"Oh!" Kenyan said, truly regretful. "I'm very sorry."

"It is our *phaemerpradistum*," she said simply, as if that explained it.

Kenyan, not wishing to talk about the fairy's end—whenever that might be—tried to change the subject slightly. "Have you always lived here? In the Feielanns?"

"My home is Maedwe Feorr, which is only a small piece of the Feielanns. I am bound to Maedwe Feorr. This is how the nature of the Feie differs from the nature of Man." She tried to explain the concept that she only barely understood herself. "You—man—may move from place to place. You may enter Maedwe Feorr, and you may leave it. But you are bound to time. It only moves in one direction for you, one moment after another after another.

"The Feie are bound to the land. We must not leave our appointed place, at our gravest peril." She trembled involuntarily, again wondering how she had escaped wrath for leaving Maedwe Feorr that one time. "But we are not bound to time in the same way that you are. We may choose to linger in a moment, if it is lovely to us. Or we may choose to move swiftly through moments that are unpleasant or fearful. Sometimes, at great cost, we may even go backward through time, though it is very hard. It would be as if you tried to walk up Ripar Flowan with the water crashing against you going the other direction. You might be able to go a few steps, but it would quickly exhaust you." Réchetthaerielle seemed to be nearly exhausted herself with this outpouring of words. There had been entire years go by in her past where she spoke only a rare word of greeting to Baeri or one of the Three. But she felt compelled to explain herself to this man, so that he could … *know* her. Kenyan. "I am lingering in this moment."

Kenyan blushed and smiled, grateful, and wondered what he had done to deserve such an honor. "May I ask you something else?"

"You may," she replied, smiling back at him though he could not see.

"Your skin … how does it glow?"

"I do not know," she said plainly. "How does yours *not*?"

217

"I, ah—I don't know," said Kenyan, and he laughed, and then so did she.

Chapter Thirty

Time passed, and nothing changed. Kenyan slept, and he woke, and he slept and he woke, and nothing changed. Kenyan had been sitting in the dark for many days now, he reckoned. And Gumnbote was not particularly companionable; many times now he did not even respond when Kenyan attempted conversation with him. And, to be fair, Kenyan was growing somewhat morose himself. It wasn't that the days were unpleasant, really … it's just that nothing ever *happened*.

The hours he spent talking with Réchetthaerielle were enjoyable enough in their way, he acknowledged, but not so much now as at first. She did seem willing to spend most of his waking hours attending him— bringing him food, singing to him, relating the history of her people, and listening to Kenyan's stories too. Sometimes she would help him walk around in a circle, lightly holding his arm to keep him from stumbling. But without the ability to see her … he found that he was becoming frustrated and bored. He was sorry that his gratitude toward the fairy who had saved his life ran so shallow as that. But without some kind of a sense of purpose to his life … he felt as if a slow burn of impotent anger had been kindled in his belly, and would not abate. It made his head hurt. So he determinedly unfurrowed his brow … but after a few moments more, he found his forehead creased with irritation again.

Was this the sum of his life? To sleep. To sit blindly in the dark. To eat. To ask Réchetthaerielle to leave him alone for a few moments so he could squat and relieve himself. To share an unsatisfying, grunting exchange with Gumnbote, who did not even enjoy the pleasure of the invisible fairy's conversation, since she virtually ignored him. Was this the sum of his life? To be sure, he had never hoped for too much more than this … but he had at least hoped, somehow, to be *useful*, to someone, someplace, sometime. Was this all? To be a kept thing ... a pet? Was this—?

Réchetthaerielle said to him, her soft voice tight with concern, "Dear one, your face is pained." Kenyan frowned grimly, but did not reply. She tried again: "I am unfamiliar with your needs ... what more do you desire than to sit in the glorious summer of Maedwe Feorr, fed to the full, and sung the songs of the Feie?"

Kenyan knew she was doing all that she could to bless him, and he regretted his own recalcitrance. "I am sorry, m'Lady. But the summer or the winter of your land—it's all the same to me. Here in the Arkhanfeie's darkness, it's always clammy and cold." He determined to tell her the truth about what he was feeling. If she left him, he would doubtless die ... but at least that would be *something*. "I have enjoyed very much hearing the sound of your voice. But without seeing the beauty of your face as well, I am ... lessened. I am sorrowful. Whatever the limitations of a man's sight may be, it is nonetheless very precious to him. Whatever the failings of a man's freedom may be, it is to him as dear as his life's breath."

"The Arkhanfeie has judged this to be your doom," she said tentatively, defensively.

"I meant the Arkhanfeie no harm by coming to your land. I showed him no disrespect. I even came bearing a gift for the Arkhanfeie, but he refused to so much as hear me!"

A tremulous note of alarm sounded in Réchetthaerielle's voice. "He is the Arkhanfeie."

"Yes, he's the Arkhanfeie. But he's not—he's not Architaedeus, is he? Is the Arkhanfeie infallible?"

There was no answer from the fairy, and Kenyan did not know whether she was angry, or thinking, or gone. After a moment, he said, "Réchetthaerielle?"

She whispered, "I will think about what you have said. I must leave you for a time."

Caümagauderelle heard the song of her sister Réchetthaerielle carried on the wind from across Ripar Flowan, and gracefully made her way toward the sound. It was not far, either in miles or in moments, and she was eager to see her sister, whom the Arkhanfeie had called foolish, and find out something of what that folly might be. When she arrived at Flowan's burbling waters, she found Réche kneeling at the far bank, speaking earnestly with Baeriboelle the naiad. When Baeri saw Caümagauderelle, she waved merrily, sending a prismatic arc of water through the air in her direction; then she laughed and disappeared back into her waters. Réchetthaerielle stood and waited for Caüma to approach.

"Réchetthaerielle, my sister: Sweet is your voice to me," Caüma greeted.

"My eyes are full now that they behold you," Réche replied.

Caüma smiled placidly and asked, "What means your call, dear one?"

"I have come to drink deeply from your wisdom, sweetheart, if you would grant me to drink."

"Such little wisdom as I possess is yours for the asking. What is it your heart seeks?"

"The will of Architaedeus," Réche said. "Is the will of Architaedeus always accomplished, or no?"

Caüma paused a moment before answering, as if listening for an answer to some prayer unuttered, wearing a faint smile shadowed by a hint of mystery. Then she said, "The depths of Architaedeus are deeper far than the wisdom of a limniad can plumb. But since you ask me straightaway, I will answer you in like: My heart would say ... Yes. The will of Architaedeus is as solid as the mountains, as constant as the sky. What He has determined, He shall perform." Caüma laughed abruptly, a girlish giggle, embarrassed and flattered that she had been asked to speak of things of such import. "My heart does not often deceive me, dearest, for the Holy One has granted me the grace to trust. I pray for your sake that it has not deceived me this time."

"Thank you, my sister," Réchetthaerielle said. "May I ask more?"

"The music of your voice is ever a delight to my ears."

"If a matter comes to pass, should we take that to mean that it was the will of the Blessed One?"

Caüma cocked her head quizzically, as if she had never thought of it from that angle before. She said slowly, "If the will of Architaedeus is always accomplished ... then if something is accomplished at all, it must be the will of Architaedeus. How strange." She lifted her hands to the skies, and said, "And yet, the thought fills me with calm. Earthquakes. Floods. The coming of Man. Death itself. Are these in the hands of the Blessed, or of blind chance, or of some other power malicious in nature?" She laughed again, and her eyes twinkled gaily at Réchetthaerielle. "You are taxing me, sweet one. But again, my heart cries that the glory belongs to the Blessed

One, and not to any lesser, created thing. Shall not Architaedeus serve the bitter with the sweet? His wisdom is all, and over all, and in all, and through all."

Réchetthaerielle nodded solemnly, eagerly. "That is also what my heart tells me, though the ears of my heart have been confused by other noises of late. One more question, sweetheart?"

Caüma smiled and nodded.

"If I were to try and do something about which I am unsure ... about which I cannot tell dark from light ... could my folly thwart the will of the Blessed?"

Caümagauderelle nodded again, solemnly. "And there is the heart of your question. Can you defy the will of the Holy One? Perhaps not ... perhaps not. But if you *do* attempt it—even if the outcome was never in question ... what would be the price to your own soul?"

Réche knelt on the edge of the riverbank and felt the smooth cold waters lapping up at her knees. The path before her remained as dark as it had been before ... but Caüma had helped as best as she could. "Thank you, my sister," Réche said thoughtfully. "I must offer prayers, and see if the Blessed will give light to my path."

"My darling," Caüma said, "I will not be dishonest with you. When I heard your call this morning, I was keen to see with what manner of deception you had betrayed yourself. To see if you were as foolish as I had heard." Caüma smiled an apology, and Réche waited patiently for her to continue. "But you have asked questions of depth, and humility, and substance. Perhaps the path you contemplate is indeed according to Architaedeus' design. Perhaps." She drew in a breath, and smiled graciously. "I must also tell you that others of our people are not so sure of Architaedeus' unqualified sovereignty as I am, or as you are. If you had asked one of my sisters their counsel—or if you had asked the Arkhanfeie—but you knew that, did you not?" Réche did not speak. "So this is the sum of the counsel I offer to you now: Submit yourself to Architaedeus' judgment, and appeal to His mercy, and then try whatever your heart permits … and be ever listening for His voice, whether it be for reward or rebuke."

"Thank you, my sister," Réchetthaerielle said, bowing her head. "I will remember your words."

"Gummy."

No answer.

"Gumnbote." Kenyan reached out across the invisible expanse to touch his companion. Yes, he was still there. "Gummy, are you awake?"

"It's Kenyan, ain't it?" Gumnbote said weakly. "Why'n't you just let me go ahead an' die?"

Dismayed, Kenyan sought for words, but they all seemed feeble, inadequate. "You mustn't talk like that, friend. I believe we may be saved yet."

"What's the point?" Gumnbote asked reasonably, and Kenyan had no answer for that. What *was* the point, anyway?

"Still," Kenyan said hesitantly, "if you have no desire to live for yourself … won't you try to live for me?"

"What do you mean?" Gummy sounded slightly more interested, and Kenyan grasped that faint thread of hope.

"I have been near despair myself," Kenyan said softly, "and one of the only reasons I could think of for that despair was that I no longer had any purpose—any usefulness. I thought maybe it was the same with you."

Gumnbote said nothing, but he was listening to Kenyan's words, and considering them.

Kenyan continued, "If you need purpose, my friend, then won't you please hold on ... for me?" A pause. "*I* need you, Gumnbote."

Gummy thought of saying, *Why should you need me? You have your fairy*. But he held his tongue, and considered the possibility that what Kenyan said was true. He couldn't remember much beyond the blackness of his present world, but nothing suggested to him the idea that Kenyan was false. "What do you need me for?" he asked grudgingly.

"I have begun telling Réchetthaerielle about our disillusionment," he whispered. "It is in my heart that she may make an appeal to the Arkhanfeie on our behalf."

"Then you might's well give up right now," Gumnbote darkly declared. "If you're lookin' to *him* for mercy, you might's well just let me die."

"Just hold on a bit longer," Kenyan pled. "Will you?" He waited for his friend's response. "Please?"

"Hmmp," Gumnbote grunted, and Kenyan took that for a *yes*.

Chapter Thirty-One

Réchetthaerielle jostled the man with the shining soul, who was asleep. "Awake, O Prince. Awake, Kenyan."

He blinked, unseeing, not knowing whether it was night or day. "Is it you?" he asked, and immediately felt foolish for asking.

"Yes," Réchetthaerielle answered, unaware of his sense of inanity. "It is time. You must rise, you and your sister." Kenyan took that to mean Gumnbote, and didn't bother trying to correct her.

"What is it time for? The Arkhanfeie?"

"No!" Réche said with a note of horror in her voice. She almost lost heart then, but steadied herself and continued. "It is time for you to leave the Feielanns."

"Leave? But ... how?"

"I will make myself bright enough so that you should be able to see me, unless your darkness is very dark. It is not important for you to know how." She thought of the ordeal that lay before her, and shuddered involuntarily. "I will go before you, and when you see me, you must follow. I will lead you on a safe path, for your eyes will long be dim."

Kenyan reached over and shook Gumnbote, rousing him. His mind was full of questions, but they didn't seem to make any difference. His only choice was to obey, or disobey. If he desired his own freedom, then, well, his decision was already made.

In short order Kenyan had raised his companion to his feet, and the two men were standing with arms linked, Gumnbote fearfully saying, "What's going on?"

"It's Réchetthaerielle. She said we will be able to see."

A moment passed, and Gumnbote said, "I don't see nothin'."

Another moment passed, with Kenyan staring intently into the blackness until his eyes ached. "Neither do I," he whispered.

For what felt like an interminable length of time, Kenyan and Gumnbote clung to each other and glared frantically, painfully, into the blackness, until tears ran down their cheeks and their tenuous hope began to fail.

But then, Kenyan saw a bright prick of light, tiny as a pinhole in the fabric of the night. It pierced the darkness like the point of a tiny sword, causing a faint gray glow to stain the black world like a wound. "There," Kenyan whispered, and pointed.

"Where?" Gumnbote hissed. "I don't see it!"

The little gray splotch of light was more beautiful than anything Kenyan could remember having seen before; it was as if Kenyan had never seen *anything* in his life before. He stared at the infinitesimal point of white light at the heart of the gray, cherishing it, loving it, yearning to follow. But he lingered a moment, out of respect for Gumnbote. "We'll wait until you can see it too … then we'll follow it together."

But after a few more tense, drawn-out moments passed, Gumnbote said desperately, "I can't see it!" Cursing aloud, he said, "Just go on without me, and leave me to my damnation!"

Pained, Kenyan said, "No. No, I won't." Taking his companion's arm in both of his hands, he said, "Come with me; trust me. If you can't see the light … I can. I'll lead you there."

Gumnbote cursed again, but followed Kenyan's halting steps.

They shambled along slowly, occasionally tripping over a rock or stumbling when a foot would get snared in a tangle of weeds. Kenyan would experience a moment of panic when they fell, losing his bearings until he could rise to his knees, crane his neck and locate the light again. "There she is," he would whisper to Gumnbote, for he soon realized that the lantern he followed through the darkness was none other than Réchetthaerielle herself. Kenyan had no idea where she was leading them, whether east or west, toward mount or vale; even as Gumnbote had to trust him to follow the light, he also had to trust the light itself that it would lead them along the promised safe path.

They lurched along their faltering way for some hours, Kenyan reckoned. After weeks of almost complete inactivity, it was quite exhausting for the men, even though their pace was no faster than that which a man would normally walk.

Suddenly the bobbing lamp that led them flickered, faded, flickered again, and went black. Kenyan stopped abruptly, and Gumnbote, who had been walking with him silently, almost patiently, said, "What?"

"I've lost her," Kenyan said. "It's all black again."

"Well, let's sit," Gumnbote said, breathing heavily. "I'm done in."

"All right," Kenyan agreed regretfully, wondering where Réche had gone. His eyes scanned the gloom, hoping to see a spot where it appeared the least bit faded … but all was utterly dark. He slowly lowered himself to the ground, still searching the darkness for … anything.

A faint voice sounded in his ear, fluttering, febrile, exhausted. "I must rest. Forgive … I am spent."

Réchetthaerielle! Kenyan longed to say some words of comfort, of gratitude, of encouragement. But he could hear her fatigued breathing immediately slow to the heavy pace of inexorable slumber, and he realized that she lay unconscious on the ground next to him, something she had never done before, as far as he knew. He knelt over her protectively, as if warding away any dangers of the dark that should try and trouble her sleep. With fists clenched, he defended the vulnerable nymph in his blindness, understanding that she had spent herself for him, and willing to the uttermost to be spent for her, too, should the need arise. It did not, and after a time, his head slumped, his fists relaxed, he rested back on his haunches, and he slept too.

Réchetthaerielle awoke to the brightness of the late-afternoon sun bathing her face with its delicious golden rays. She blinked a few times, clearing the fog of slumber from her eyes, then saw Kenyan sitting next to her, a protective, vigilant look upon his noble face. She smiled as she looked up from the grass at his concerned countenance; he seemed to be guarding Réchetthaerielle, even as she guarded Maedwe Feorr.

"Do you watch over me?" she asked him, and was surprised at the weakness of her own voice.

"You've awakened," he said, blushing. "I feared for you."

"Have I slept long?" she asked. "I do not often sleep. It is very pleasant, though, is it not?"

Kenyan ignored her questions and asked instead, "What did you have to do in order to let me see you? I feared that I had lost you. That it may have cost you … all."

She tried to laugh, but found that she was unable to muster the strength it required. "Do not fret. I'm not sure I could explain it to you so that you could understand. I shall just say that, in a way ... I was attempting to hold back the river."

"M'Lady, if the cost is too dear for you, Gumnbote and I can sit right here until the end of our days, and we won't speak a word of complaint again."

"Thank you, Prince Kenyan," she smiled. "The virtue of your spirit shines again like brightest silver." For a bittersweet moment, Kenyan thought she was going to accept his offer, but then she said faintly, "After I rest a bit more, and perhaps eat a bite or two, we may proceed again. Two more days of travel like yesterday, and you will be free."

"We can wait a few days for you to recover your strength," Kenyan offered, but the steady rhythm of her breathing answered him that she had fallen back asleep.

It was dark when Réchetthaerielle woke again. She felt quite refreshed, and lay back on the grass of her meadow, gazing happily at Architaedeus' star-filled sky. The sounds of whispering came from nearby; the men were hungry. "It is time to go, Kenyan and Kenyan's friend. I will lead you to a place where you can find food."

Before Kenyan could reply, she had left them. A moment later, he heard her cry from the distance, "This way," and the ebony curtain of his world parted, allowing in a small window of living light. This time, Kenyan could just make out Réchetthaerielle's face in the center of the

231

luminous circle, which made him all the more eager to rise and follow. Not only could he see light, he could also make out a shape ... and it was a shape that his heart cherished.

"Can you see her?" he asked Gummy.

"No."

"Then come with me. I won't let you go."

The next several hours passed much the same as they had the night before: Kenyan leading blind Gumnbote through the impenetrable darkness, following the only thing he could see—the brightly glowing face of fair Réchetthaerielle. Sometimes one or the other of the men stumbled, but each time Kenyan said, "Don't fear. I see her still."

The duration of the march was, Kenyan thought, somewhat less than the first time. Whether it was because he was physically stronger after the previous day's exercise or that Réchetthaerielle was unable to continue for as long, he was unsure, though he feared the latter. When the dipping, bobbing lamp that he followed started to gutter and fade, he was tempted to run toward her while his quickly fading sight remained, but he dared not leave Gumnbote.

The two weary men squatted on the ground awaiting the return of the fairy, but soon Gumnbote was snoring, and still Kenyan waited. No voice came to whisper in his ear that she had returned, that she needed rest, that Kenyan's deliverance was now only a day away. Kenyan fretted and fumed, wondering where she was and hoping she was safe, and discovering the truth that he cared less for his own deliverance than for Réchetthaerielle's wellbeing.

As the hours dragged on with no hint of her approach, Kenyan felt sick with worry. It seemed to him as if his bowels were being twisted into the knots his father had taught him when he was a boy living on Pembicote by the Great Sea.

He prayed, or at least tried to. *God ... Architaedeus. I mean no disrespect, but it seems like You're both the same person, though You go by two names. If either one of You are listening, I'm trying to get a word through to the God of the Feielanns, or perhaps the God of the whole world. Please, I beg You—spare Réchetthaerielle. If there's anything I can do to help her, please show me how. She was just trying to show me mercy ... please have mercy on her.*

Feeling unsatisfied and impotent, he concluded. But as he waited still in the darkness, listening intently for any irregular sound, he found his heart repeating the same plea several times. *Please have mercy on Réchetthaerielle.*

As dawn broke upon Maedwe Feorr, Kenyan noticed the blackened sky growing less intensely black, fading just slightly to perhaps a deep charcoal gray. He saw murky shapes making grotesque designs on the blackness—the limbs of trees waving in the wind, perhaps? At first he thought his fevered mind was playing tricks on him, but the longer he stared, the more he was able to discern that what he saw was, though bleary and insubstantial, at least some kind of honest representation of what was actually there. He felt just a brief surge of gratitude—*I can see again*—that was quickly replaced by an anguished sense of burden—*I must find her.*

He jostled Gumnbote's shoulder; he could just make him out, lying nearby on the ground. "Gummy, I need to leave you."

233

"What?"

"I can see."

"I know you can."

"No—I mean I can see other things, not just Réchetthaerielle."

Gumnbote quickly assimilated that bit of knowledge, and said, "Well, that's grand. But you're not leavin' me!"

"I need to find Réchetthaerielle," Kenyan pled.

"Well an' good. Just take me with you."

"I'll come back for you, I promise."

"Stop a bit, and think this through: You can see *now*, but what if you get half a mile away, and you can't no more? Then how'd we ever find each other again?"

Kenyan stopped, and grudgingly admitted, "I take your point. Well, if you're coming, let's go now."

Gumnbote lurched to his feet. "Be with you in a shake, if you'll hold your peace just a second more. Let me hold my own piece, and drain my pouch a pint or so."

"Well," Kenyan began, but there was nothing to say to that.

※

He started off in the direction he thought he had last seen her, leading Gummy by the arm. Soon he saw a gray form lying on the gray earth, a bleak absence of movement nearly hidden among the waving gray grasses. She was face down, and still.

Kenyan knelt at her side, tears pouring unbidden from his gradually healing eyes, and he laid his hand softly upon her delicately curved back. He waited, and a tremor of anxiety shook his spine. He waited … and she breathed. She breathed still! He stroked her hair and her shoulders, and wept as she slept.

Chapter Thirty-Two

"Prince Kenyan," she whispered as she looked up at his face, a dark shape backlit by the afternoon sun. "My dreams have been full of dark foreboding. The anger of elves ... the careless violence of men—"

"Don't speak," Kenyan said. "I have berries if you're hungry, and water for your thirst."

"You do?" she said, surprised. "How?"

Kenyan laid his fingers against her brow, and she did not flinch. He brushed some wisps of flaxen hair from her forehead, and said, "The healing that you began when you were a lamp to my eyes ... your kind God Architaedeus has continued. It is still imperfect ... but I see more today than I did yesterday, or the day before."

"Have I been asleep so long?" she asked in astonishment.

"So long as that," he affirmed with a whisper.

She weakly tried to raise her head, but the effort made her neck tremble, so she rested it against the cool earth again. She lay silently for a few peaceful moments, studying the silhouette of Kenyan's face, knew that he was gazing back upon her, and said with a frail smile, "Is the form of my face still pleasant to your eyes?"

Kenyan pursed his lips, wondering how she knew what he had been thinking, and said in a hoarse voice, "Yes." From behind Kenyan's back, Réchetthaerielle heard Gumnbote snort—she had forgotten about him.

"Does your friend see, too?" she asked.

"No, I don't," Gumnbote said tartly, and Kenyan smiled apologetically at the girl.

By that evening, Réche was able to sit with her legs crossed, and eat berries from Kenyan's hand. He brought water to her on a broad flat leaf, and she drank a sip.

He noticed her slender, bare legs—how could he not? He had never seen such a sight before. Except for children and harlots, the women of Hagenspan covered themselves from neck to ankle. The fairy did not seem to be immodest, though … just innocent. He blushed with shame for the stirring that was awakened in his belly, and was momentarily thankful that Gumnbote was blind. For her part, Réchetthaerielle seemed not to notice his discomfiture.

She said, "Tomorrow I will be strong again. And though the thought gives me sorrow … it will be time for you to leave the Feielanns."

"Leave," Kenyan repeated dully. He hesitated, and said, "I have a mind to stay here with you, if you would grant it."

"No, dear one," she said softly. "The Arkhanfeie would be very angry."

A gloom fell upon Kenyan then, as he recognized the truth behind her words. "But won't he be angry with you?"

"Perhaps." She smiled sadly. "Perhaps not so much."

"If I mustn't stay with you … I mean stay in the Feielanns … could you possibly … come with me?" Kenyan asked, although he was fairly certain he knew how she would respond.

Réchetthaerielle remembered something she had heard Kenyan tell Gumnbote many days before, and said, "I will not leave Maedwe Feorr. Maedwe Feorr is my mother."

Kenyan said, as a hot tear blurted from his eye, "I had to ask."

"I am honored that you had to ask," she replied solemnly. "But I am a limniad of the Feie, and you are a man. You must go and do the things that men do, and I must stay and tend Maedwe Feorr."

Kenyan felt as if his heart was being torn from his chest, and he exulted in the magnificence of the pain—the glory, the agony. He supposed that this must be something like love. He knew he had never experienced it before—that the exalted feelings he had supposed he held for Lanadine were as common as lust, as dry as dust, compared to this splendid misery.

"I'll not forget you, no matter where I go," he said brokenly.

"And I will hold you in my heart until my final breath," she answered. "If a limniad could possibly give her heart to a man … I would knit mine to yours, O Prince Kenyan." She touched his fingers with hers. "But this, I believe, is not to be."

A day later, Kenyan and Gumnbote were both safely beyond the borders of Maedwe Feorr, headed more or less back toward the east where they had come from. Kenyan had said goodbye to Réchetthaerielle … but that was too hard for him to think about at the moment. For now, it was enough just to try and decide what to do next.

Gumnbote seemed rather cheerful to be back beyond the reach of the Arkhanfeie, though he still was as blind as he had been. To be up and walking, and to be headed *somewhere*—these seemed to be fine things to

Gumnbote at the moment. "So," he said to Kenyan, "how's about if we take stock of our position?"

"All right," Kenyan said without much interest.

"All right, indeed," Gumnbote said enthusiastically. "Let's see—we started out with a cart." He held up a finger. "That's gone. We had provisions." He extended another digit. "They're gone. We had a fine magic stick that you kept sneakin' looks at. Do we still have that?"

In spite of his disillusionment with his present circumstances, Kenyan allowed a small smile. "Nope. Gone."

"Ah, that's good," Gumnbote said, holding up three fingers. "'Twould just weight us down, believe me. Now, let me think some more. What'd we start out to accomplish?"

"We were hoping to recover your lost memories."

"Ah! Did we do that?"

"No, it seems you lost most of what you still had."

"Ah, good, good," Gumnbote nodded. "Anything else?"

"We were supposed to get a jewel from the Arkhanfeie's crown."

"Well, we *musta* got that, then, right?"

"No, he struck us blind." Kenyan laughed.

"'Twas only fair, I'm sure. You know," Gummy said confidentially, "if he'da gaven us that jewel, I'm pretty sure we woulda lost it, the way it sounds like we take care o' things."

"I believe you're right," Kenyan agreed.

"Was there anything else we was supposed to do?"

"I believe the king's intent was that we should travel all the way through the Feielanns to the west, and get a letter from my old Lord, Ester."

"Well, we ain't in the Feielanns no more, right? Did we get through?"

Kenyan shook his head, though Gummy could not see. "As near as I can tell, they never even let us in the front door. We only got as far as the stoop."

"Aye, that sounds like us, all right." Gumnbote nodded happily. "So!"

"So," agreed Kenyan.

Gumnbote chewed on a blade of grass thoughtfully for a moment, and said, "Well, then, where does that leave us? Does your king want us back?"

"No, I don't believe he wanted to see me again without one of the Arkhanfeie's jewels."

"So ... we can't go back," Gummy deduced. "Why'n't we go on, then?"

"On?"

"Ain't there no way around the Feielanns?"

"Well ... yes, there's a road to the north."

"Does it go back to your Lord Esty?"

Kenyan corrected, "Est*er*. Actually, yes, it does."

"Well, then," Gumnbote decided, "if you ain't got a better idear, let's get on to your westerlands, and fetch that letter. It ain't in the right order, p'raps—puttin' the mule behind the cart, so t' speak—but at least it's somethin'. A place to start."

"It's a good idea. We'll start out first thing in the morning," Kenyan said, noticing that the sun was casting long shadows from the west.

"Night 'r day, no difference t' me," Gummy said, tapping his own head. "Always dark in here."

"Yes, but if I'm going to lead you there, I'd better be able to see," Kenyan said wryly.

"Aye, I s'pose it's so. Though—not to be unkind—I'd be surprised if you ain't got us streck deef before mornin' hits, based on our past string o' successes."

Kenyan laughed, and said, "Maybe so! Maybe so."

Kenyan lay on his back looking at the twinkling stars, which he could just make out through the milky gray haze that was his sense of vision. He could see more clearly now than even an hour earlier, and he breathed a brief prayer of thanks to God, or to Architaedeus, for the gift. He wondered if his earlier prayer— mercy for Réchetthaerielle—had been the occasion for the relief of his blindness. Perhaps she would have perished if he had not found her. Who knew?

The thought of Réchetthaerielle wounded him again, a bittersweet piercing to his heart. He rolled over and faced westward, toward where he knew Maedwe Feorr lay covered by the night's dark mantle. Straining his eyes, he sought to see the firefly-flash of light that he knew now to be the passing of one of the fairies through a moment of time. He longed to see the little wink of light that might represent, somewhere, sometime, Réchetthaerielle. He even tried not to blink his eyes, lest he should miss that moment of revelation. But he saw nothing.

He drew in a slow breath and released it deliberately, a regretful sigh. He remembered.

Réchetthaerielle had accompanied the two men to the eastern border of Maedwe Feorr, and as they had walked, she had allowed Kenyan the privilege of holding her hand. Kenyan didn't know whether holding hands had any particular significance in the culture of the Feielanns ... but it did to him. As he had walked beside her, his heart had been heavy, even though in a sense he was also ridiculously happy, and they had traveled mostly in silence. He felt as if, finally, at this precise moment in time, he was exactly where he would choose to spend every moment that was left to him, if the choice was his. And he felt as if he was leaving this moment behind, right now, and that it would never be captured again.

They arrived at the unmarked border of Maedwe Feorr, and Kenyan felt Réche pull back on his hand; she would go no further. He turned to her, and saw to his amazement that her face was wet with tears.

"Is this where we must part?" Kenyan asked in a voice tight with regret.

She closed her eyes and nodded.

Kenyan gazed at her for a long moment. "I do not wish to leave you."

She looked into his eyes, frankly, openly. "That wish is also with me. But sometimes, I think, our small wishes are ignored by the One Who rules according to His own wisdom."

243

Kenyan knew that this moment was about to escape him, becoming part of the great tapestry of things that had gone before, and he determined to be very bold about how he would spend it. "I have a request, if you will." She nodded, a sad pout magnifying the fullness of her lips.

"You have said that you do not find me ugly," he began.

She said earnestly, "You are the most beautiful man that I have ever seen."

Kenyan smiled, a small, foolish grin, and his cheeks felt warm. Stuttering, he said, "I, ah—may I, ah … may I kiss you?"

Réchetthaerielle looked a bit startled, and said, "What means a kiss to your people?"

"It's, ah, when a man and a woman, um, touch their lips together," Kenyan explained. This was going badly.

"I know what a kiss is," she said pertly. She had shared kisses with the Three, and with Baeri, but it seemed that Kenyan was asking for something more. "My question was intended to mean, when people of your kind do kiss, what does it mean to them?"

"Oh." Kenyan felt the sting of humiliation again, and was glad that Gumnbote was pretending to ignore them. "It would mean, um … it would mean that I, ah, that I have feel—"

Gumnbote, who was not ignoring them, said, "It would mean that he thinks he loves you, fairy lass."

"I see," Réchetthaerielle said. "Do you think that you love me, Prince Kenyan?"

Crimson-faced, Kenyan saw nothing for it but to tell the truth. "Yes."

"Then you may kiss me."

Kenyan, who towered over the slight frame of the nymph, bent over her upturned face, and touched his lips to hers. He rested his hands lightly on her shoulders, and the moment stretched on, soft and moist and warm. Finally, he straightened again, releasing her lips with a faint, regretful *pop*. "Thank you," he said hoarsely, unsteadily. "Each moment I have spent with you surpasses the one just past."

"I am enlarged," she said sorrowfully. "I am diminished. You have made my heart greater than it was," she said, "but now I am sending half of it away with you, to the wilderness beyond, and I shall not have it again."

"You are not diminished," Kenyan answered, "nor shall your heart be. For I will be leaving half of my heart here with you."

She clung to him then, and Kenyan thought, *This embrace is sweeter even than the kiss.*

Finally she released him, and said, "You must go now. Go east until you can no longer see me, and then you may go whatever way your heart leads you—only do not return to the Feielanns. I will sit in the grass and watch you go."

So Kenyan and Gumnbote had gone. Every so often, Kenyan would turn back to the west and see the beautiful flaxen-haired girl perched at the edge of her meadow, a child sitting in the grass, a queen seated upon her throne, each time smaller than the last time he had looked. Finally, when she was just a blurred spot on the horizon, he waved wildly, and shouted, "Goodbye, Réchetthaerielle!" He stared for a moment. Was she waving back, or was it the wind tossing her gossamer hair, or was it just some trick of his still-weakened eyesight?

"Goodbye," he whispered, and then he turned and left.

As Kenyan lay now in the natural darkness of night, searching wistfully for any spark of light on the horizon, he touched his lips softly with his fingertips, trying to remember the press of Réchetthaerielle's lips against his, but it was too late. It was gone.

Chapter Thirty-Three

The weeks passed, and summertime became harvest-time, and Kenyan walked the westward-leading road that led from Ruric's Keep to Raussi to Sarbo to Ester, the same road he had taken eastward so many months before. But this time, he led blind Gumnbote by the hand, and they appeared for all the world like two miserable beggars shambling along from morning to night, stopping only to forage for fruit or grain, or to relieve themselves, or to halt for the night and sleep on the earth. Hot meals were unknown to them, or the taste of meat or bread, except for those rare occasions when they were shown goodwill by the few folk that they met along the path.

Gumnbote and Kenyan grew to be loyal friends. If Gumnbote had been a bad man once, as Kenyan had occasionally conjectured, he was not so now. As time went by, it was often the blind man who tried to cheer the sighted man, rather than the other way around. Sometimes when Kenyan would present him with a particularly succulent piece of fruit, Gummy would say, "This'n's almost as good as one of 'em what your fairy lass used to bring us." And that would set Kenyan to suffering again the great emptiness of his soul: the absence of Réchetthaerielle. For his heart was ever toward her, and he thought that, if he had days enough left in his sojourn, he would return to the Feielanns at last to see her one more time, even if the Arkhanfeie should require his very life.

※

There was a dry rustle of leaves in the air when they came upon the village of Raussi. The first thing Kenyan noticed, to his surprise, was the wooden frame of the livery stable stretching high into the sky, looking remarkably intact. It was only upon closer inspection that he saw the charred, blackened boards from the fire he had helped to start, boards which had been reused by the builders when they could be saved, and interspersed with new blonde lumber. A tall, white-haired man, as tall as Kenyan, leaned against the front wall, idling away the afternoon.

"Are you the livery-master?" Kenyan asked him as he led Gumnbote up to the stable.

"Bilkinwreath," the man said, raising a suspicious eyebrow at the strangers' approach.

"If you could extend a bit of courtesy to two weary travelers, we would be blessed indeed to bed down in your livery tonight." Kenyan was unaccustomed to begging, and the words tasted foul in his mouth, but the idea of sleeping on sweet hay with a roof overhead was very appealing to him.

"Don't know," said Bilkinwreath with a doubtful frown. "I ain't been overly happy when I chanced to give favors to strangers. Last year one of 'em burnt me right out."

Kenyan hoped the flames rising in his cheeks would not betray him, and said, "Yes, I noticed you'd suffered a fire," and nodded toward the charred boards. "Was a dwarf, what I let spend a night," the liveryman said. "Name was Mott, or Knot, or somethin' like that. Little stump of a feller." He spat on the street. "Nowtimes, whenever I see a dwarf, I chase 'em right off."

Since the only dwarf Kenyan had ever met was Mott, he asked politely, "Do you get lots of dwarfs in Raussi?"

248

"Some. They come down from the mountains to the north, where they dig for stuff. There don't seem to be many of 'em left."

"Oh."

The three men stood outside the stable, Kenyan and the liveryman looking around at things and avoiding the unanswered question that Kenyan had asked, which lurked invisibly between them, ugly as a dwarf.

Bilkinwreath finally spoke. "Your friend, here—can he talk?"

Gumnbote replied, "Aye. But I can't see."

Bilkinwreath was intrigued. "Oh! Blind, are you? Hmm." He didn't seem to be able to think of anything else to say, and Kenyan wasn't being very helpful either, so Gumnbote decided to try his hand at securing their lodging for the night.

"You know, the gods take it as a kindness when you give help to a blind man."

"You don't say," Bilkinwreath commented. "That does seem likely."

"And if you'd bring us a hot meal besides, I'd be obliged to tell your fortune," Gumnbote continued. "Seein' as how I can't see with my eyes, the gods've gave me the second sight."

"You don't say! The second sight!"

Gumnbote solemnly nodded, as Kenyan looked on uneasily. Kenyan had no knowledge of Gummy's "second sight," and it seemed to him that whenever he was cavalier about the truth, bad things were likely to result.

"Well, all right, then," Bilkinwreath said. "I'll have my wife put out a platter o' stew for you, if my fortune's good. Will you tell it now?"

"Aye," Gumnbote said. "Come close." Bilkinwreath did, and Gumnbote made a great show of feeling the lines and calluses of his hands, and his grizzled, pointed face. "Now spit in my hands," he said, and the white-haired man did so. Gummy rubbed his hands together, and then put them up to his own face, sniffing. Then he wiped his hands on his tattered shirt, and made as if he were staring off into the distance, swaying slightly and humming distractedly.

He stopped his humming abruptly, and blinked a few times. "Well, you've got a fine future ahead o' you," Gumnbote said with an impressed look upon his features. "I see grandchildren bouncin' on your knees."

"Yes, yes—I got three!" Bilkinwreath said, excited.

"There'll be more," Gummy promised. "I see prosperous days ahead for the livery."

"Thanks be t' the heavens!" Bilkinwreath said happily.

"And," Gummy said, "what's the leading man of your city here called?"

"Why, that's the Majire o' Raussi."

"I see that, one day, you—Bilkinwreath—will be the Majire o' Raussi!" Gumnbote concluded triumphantly, hoping that this would be enough of a fortune to obtain their dinner.

"Why, I already am now!" the liveryman laughed. "Well, that's not bad, not bad, young feller. Better'n some coulda done! You boys can spend the night in the barn, all right, and I'll have Maudie come around with th' stew."

※

The first traces of snow were pirouetting drunkenly through the air when Kenyan and Gumnbote passed the raspberry patch where Kenyan had held the weeping boy Jace in his arms—how long ago now? More than a year, anyway. Kenyan wondered if the boy would be happy to see him again.

He said to Gummy, "About an hour's walk, and we'll be at Ange's house."

"And then I guess we'll know if I'm the missin' man 'r not, fin'ly," Gumnbote said nervously, and he tried to smooth back his hair a bit. He had taken to hoping that he was in fact the husband who had disappeared from the little family, and he hoped too that they would be glad to have him back. Then, whether his memory was actually restored or not, at least Kenyan could tell King Ordric that Gummy had gotten back what he'd lost.

"Well," Kenyan said, wanting to keep his friend's self-conscious anxiety in check, "even if you're not, I'm sure it's a place where we'll be able to get a meal without having to tell someone's fortune." He remembered sitting in a circle on the floor next to Powder's bed, sharing a pot of bean porridge, and he smiled faintly.

When the two men came around the final bend in the road before reaching Ange's house, Kenyan expected to see hens in the dooryard, a column of smoke coming from the chimney, maybe Jace chopping firewood at the side of the hut. He was rather looking forward to seeing his old cat, Patch, purring in Powder's lap again. What he saw was … not that. There were no signs of life around the cold, empty house … no clucking hens, no wisp of smoke, no human activity at all. Gumnbote felt his friend's pace slow, felt his disappointment, and said, "What?"

"They, ah … they look to be gone."

"Oh," Gumnbote said, and his own disappointment suddenly threatened to overwhelm him. He had been privately harboring the hope that, even if he was *not* Ange's lost husband, perhaps she would take pity on him, and he might somehow end up with a wife and a family of his own. That is, if the missing husband had not returned. Now ... now ... oh, well.

A cold wind was whistling along the channel carved out by the road among the trees, and Kenyan realized that winter would soon be upon them in earnest. If nobody was living in Ange's house, the pragmatic thing to do would be to winter there anyway, and then push on the rest of the way come spring. He said to Gumnbote, "We should go inside and ... see."

"Well, *you* can see, anyway. Tell me what you do," Gumnbote said, a halfhearted attempt at a joke.

"Sorry," Kenyan said. He felt no sense of levity, only a grim sense of loss, of bereavement. He led Gummy to the doorway, and had him sit and wait while he looked around. The cookpot was still hanging on its peg above the fireplace, but it was draped with cobwebs, and the little wooden table was covered with dust. In the shadows sat Powder's bed, musty blankets still there in a crumpled heap. Kenyan sighed deeply, and wearily pushed open the back door, looking out over the stoop where he had slept that night so long ago.

He stepped out into the back yard, which was overgrown and brown. He looked around the small plot, recalling the morning Jace had walked out behind the now-empty cowpen in search of breakfast eggs. Continuing his perusal of the disorderly tract, searching for some clue as to why or where the family had gone, he spied something out by the edge of the trees that caused his heart to leap up into his throat, and he thought he understood.

Several minutes later, he stepped back through the kitchen, his legs feeling like leaden weights just barely capable of supporting him. He made his way to the front stoop and invited Gumnbote in, helping him to his feet. "There won't be any problem with us using the house for awhile, I think."

"What'd you find?"

Kenyan breathed, swallowed, tried to speak, took another breath, and tried again. "There are ... what appear to be two ... graves, out by the trees. One small. One big."

Gumnbote paused to digest this information, his heart a frightened bird in the cage of his chest. "How small?"

"Must be ... Powder."

Gumnbote bowed his head respectfully, sorrowfully, a bit surprised at the intensity of his reaction. "How—how big?"

"It'd have to be Ange."

Gumnbote felt staggered, and he reached out an arm to steady himself against his companion. Through Kenyan's tales of the little family, he had begun to think of them in some way as his own, for, even if they were not precisely his, they were the only family in the world that he actually knew anything about. Now they were lost, and he felt the grief almost as keenly as if he had been the one who'd had to turn the spade. "What—what about the boys?"

"I don't know, though it seems that they probably had to be the ones who did the burying. Probably went on to seek their fortunes ... somewhere."

"Is there somethin' here I can sit down on? I'm feelin' a mite weakly."

"Yes," and Kenyan led him over to sit at the edge of Powder's bed. Gumnbote hung his head between his hands, and several silent tears made furrows in his grimy face. Kenyan walked out among the trees and began gathering fallen twigs to use as kindling for a fire.

The winter was long and for the most part uneventful. But when snowdrifts were piled up against the walls of the hut and the wind shrieked its mournful wail through the cracks and holes of the wretched little dwelling, it was hard not to hear the ghostly cries of Ange, of Powder, as if they were asking where they were, or why was it so dark and cold, or who these men were that were living in their rightful place. And even though the hut was relatively comfortable—for it was warm around the fireplace, and Kenyan kept the fire constantly stoked—the men were always hungry. For drink, they had melted snow. For food, they had not much at all—just what Kenyan could forage from among the trees near the house, which was nuts and not much else.

Toward spring, part of the hut's thatched roof caved in, which made them extremely miserable until Kenyan was able to patch it with pine boughs. But even though Kenyan repaired the roof to the best of his meager ability, the spectral voice of the wind became even more insistent, more plaintive, than it had already been. And when the ghostly wail was at its loudest, it also made the fire gutter and spark, as if it were being stirred by some invisible hand. This unnerved Kenyan, even though he told himself that it was just the wind, and Gumnbote, who could not see the tricks the ghosts played with the fire, could nevertheless sense their increased animosity, as well as his companion's increased skittishness. Long before spring arrived, the men were ready to leave.

Chapter Thirty-Four

The winter was long and bitter in the Feielanns, too, and Réchetthaerielle suffered much from the cold. In past years she would have leaped across the frigid days, lingering only long enough to ensure that all was secure in Maedwe Feorr.

But since the days when she had lit the way for Kenyan's escape, she felt different—paler, somehow, almost hollow in a way. She feared to exercise her *vitapradistum*—the gift Architaedeus had given the Feie which allowed them freedom from the strict passage of time—for concern that her life's essence might be running low, and that the exertion required to bypass the winter should drain her of all.

So she endured, experiencing each bitter, lonely moment in the tiresome tyranny of the winter. She wondered how men could bear such tedium ... one moment after another after another, without the choice to lengthen that which was sweet, or shorten that which was disagreeable. The gray-shrouded, snow-filled days were made even more monotonous because Réchetthaerielle had no one to share them with. The Three were gone, off to some future sun-filled springtime, and it seemed that Baeri was gone too, for the waters of Ripar Flowan were still, frozen into a furious sculpture of crystal.

For weeks, in the summer just past, Réchetthaerielle had talked every day with Kenyan—the most ebullient outpouring of words from her lips that had occurred in all the long ages of her dominion. And now that she had learned to enjoy the art of speech, there was no one to share it with. No one, for months ... months of which she must experience each agonizing, listless moment.

For Réchetthaerielle could feel herself fading. She could feel herself waning, like the last silvery crescent of the moon before a night of darkness. She had lost Kenyan, her chosen Prince. She had spent much of her life's essence, her vitality, in order to lose him—an irony she could not understand, but could feel the mockery of. She had lost the trust of the Arkhanfeie, which also stung her deeply. The only thing she had not squandered, she felt, was Maedwe Feorr itself ... but if she was fading like it felt like she was fading ... Maedwe Feorr would soon be losing her.

She knelt in the snow, her head bowed, and watched with curiosity as the tears dropped from her face, melting little tunnels in the snow as if they were so many rabbits disappearing into their holes. She had nothing better to do.

When Kenyan and Gumnbote staggered into the town of Sarbo, they were nearly starved, and nearly drowned as well. The river called Sarbo's Run had swelled with the melting of the northern snows, and the two weakened men had had some difficulty fording the treacherous, sleety waters. But finally they had made it across—soaked, shivering, sprained, panting—and they limped into the mud-caked village, leaning on each other for support. Kenyan observed, somewhat to his relief, that the two warships, the nefs of Sarbo, were nowhere to be seen.

There were some fishwives tromping about, slogging back and forth from their huts to the river and back, but not many; the streets were too muddy even for them. None of the prettier women of the town, either of harlots or brides, were to be seen, and neither could a man be found, for the ships were at sea, and all able hands were aboard.

Gummy said hoarsely through chattering teeth, "I feel like I'm startin' to slip. I need to get some food an' some rest, or—"

Kenyan spied the sign for Pelly's Grog House, and pointed his friend in that direction. "I know where there's food, if they'll give us some. We'll ask, anyway."

Gumnbote grunted his acquiescence, and groaned, "I don't want to sound like a nitpicker. But I'm blind. I don't think I can take any more river crossin's."

"I'm sorry." Kenyan half-carried him the rest of the way to the Grog House's door. "Maybe you won't have to cross any more rivers at that."

Kenyan shoved open the heavy wooden door with his foot, and called out, "Master Pelly! Are you about?"

"He ain't here," chirped a hidden voice, the voice of a child. "It's jist me, an' I'm cleanin' the cookpots."

"Is there any way we can get something to eat?" Kenyan asked.

"I don't know," said the child doubtfully. "Hang on." In the doorway that led from the public room back to wherever it was that the child had been washing the dishes, there appeared the shadowy silhouette of a small boy. The next instant, the boy cried, "Pa!" and came hurtling from the shadows to cast himself into Gumnbote's quaking arms. It was Jem.

Kenyan could do nothing but look on as the little boy sobbed— whether for joy or for sorrow, he could not tell. At one moment Jem buried his face in his father's ragged tunic, and the next, he was angrily pounding his small fists against Gumnbote's chest. Then he wrapped his arms around Gumnbote's neck and cried, kissing his father's bearded cheeks. "Oh, Pa!" the boy snuffled against Gummy's neck. "It's been mighty hard."

"I'm sorry, young feller," Gummy replied, holding him as securely as his weakened arms would allow. "I'm surely sorry."

"It's Jem," Kenyan told him softly, and Gumnbote repeated, "Jem," stroking the back of the boy's head.

"Where've you been gone to for so long?" Jem asked plaintively.

"I been cruelly used by the fairy folk, I fear," Gummy explained. "I'm blind, for one."

"Oh, Pa," the boy said sorrowfully, and lifted his face to look into his father's eyes. He stroked Gummy's cheeks, and said, "Did you know Ma died?"

"Yes, I expect I did." Gummy smiled sadly in the direction of his son's voice. "I shed a tear or two about that, I'll tell you."

"Me, too."

Kenyan asked, "Is your brother … is he all right?"

"I remember you," Jem told him. "You gave a cat to Powder."

Kenyan nodded, smiling gently.

"Jace is off to sea, ridin' on Old Delicious' boat."

Kenyan was unsure how to react to that piece of news, so he just nodded again, and said, "Is he well?"

"Yes, he's strong, all right," Jem replied. "He don't never smile too much, though."

At that moment, Pelly, the proprietor of the Grog House, came stomping through the kitchen, shouting, "Boy! Where are ye?"

"It's my Pa!" Jem shouted back. "He's come!"

Pelly stepped into the room, all full of bluster and conceit. When the nefs were gone to sea, there was no one in Sarbo more esteemed than Pelly. He didn't look very happy to see Gumnbote, or Kenyan either. He said sternly to Jem, "There's still pots to be scrubbed."

Jem scrambled out of his father's arms, and ran to Pelly. Before he disappeared into the scullery, he said, "You'll still be here later, won't you, Pa?"

"I will, Jem," Gumnbote promised, and the boy scampered back to his labors.

Pelly gave the two travelers a sharp look of appraisal. "Ye look like a pair o' drown'd cats."

"That's quite close to the truth," Kenyan said ruefully.

Pelly suddenly recognized Kenyan. "Ye're that feller what gave Old Delicious his red hoss."

Kenyan said, with just a hint of defiance, "Yes, I am."

Pelly chuckled. "Well, I guess ye got the short end o' *that* deal. For when the boys come t' Sarbo—meanin' Jem an' Jace—damned if that cat didn't come back with 'em. So Old Delicious ended up with th' cat *and* th' hoss, and you ended up with a extry-big fistful o' nothin'!"

Kenyan said nothing in reply, just grimaced slightly.

Gumnbote was beginning to tremble again with weakness, and said, "If you please, sir, can you spare some bread an' meat?"

"Well," Pelly frowned. "Jist because ye're Jemmy's father don't mean ye're entitled t' free bread an' board, ye know. Though I ain't a hard man." He scratched his belly, which was very rotund. "Is there anywhat that ye can do?"

259

"Well," said Gumnbote, "I been known to tell a fortune 'r two."

"Hmm." Pelly thought quickly, calculating the possibility of a fortune-teller helping him to separate some of the citizens of Sarbo from a piece or two of their gold. "That might come in handy at that. Mayhap we can strike a bargain." Clapping his hands once sharply, he decided. "Well, sit yeselfs down, an' I'll set out some cold pork for ye, an' a loaf. Beer?"

"Please," said both Kenyan and Gumnbote in unison. Kenyan put his arm around his friend, and helped him to a bench.

As they gorged on pork and crusty brown bread, and sipped cautiously at their beer (it had been many months since either of them had tasted strong drink), Kenyan suddenly realized that he was going to be soon parting from Gumnbote. The thought filled him with sadness, for they had been companions for nearly a year, and had suffered and endured many hardships together.

But with this new turn of events, a question presented itself to Kenyan as well: If he was going to be on his own now ... where should he go next? His tentative plan had been to head back to Beedlesgate and retrieve another letter from Lord Ester ... but did he even care about that anymore? He had thought that he would try and pursue his quest, and indeed, he had completed the first stipulation, after a fashion. Gumnbote had received back what was left of his own. But did Kenyan even care about becoming a knight anymore? It seemed like an entire lifetime ago that he had.

Suddenly his heart was overwhelmed by a renewed longing to see Réchetthaerielle again. Mightn't he just go back to Maedwe Feorr and spend what was left of his days in the presence of the one that he most cherished? A disquieting bolt of fear shot through him—what if she had already forgotten him? But then he comforted himself with her own words: *You have made my heart greater than it was, but now I am sending half of it away with you.* Her love for him was true, he hoped. It *must* be, he decided, remembering how great a sacrifice she had made for his freedom.

And even if he went and got the letter from Lord Ester, fulfilling two of the three provisions of his quest … how would he ever presume to get a jewel from the crown of the Arkhanfeie? The very notion of that seemed so ludicrous that he almost laughed aloud.

"Whatcha thinkin'?" Gumnbote asked.

"I, ah … I was just wondering what I should do next."

"What do you mean?"

"Well … I figured I'd be leaving you here with Jem … but I won't be staying in Sarbo."

"Oh," Gummy said. "I hadn't thought of that." He was silent for a moment, chewing a wedge of bread reflectively. "Of course, it's clear what you've got to do."

It is? Kenyan thought, but he said, "Are you telling my fortune?"

Gumnbote chuckled, and said, "You might say."

"Well?"

"I know you have it in your heart to go back and see that fairy lass. I know you've been thinkin' about her all winter long." Gummy waited for a response, but when Kenyan remained silent, he continued. "But you should go on to your old lord first, and get that letter."

"Why do you say that?"

"Think about it. Your fairy girl don't seem to ever get any older, accordin' to what I was hearin'."

"I didn't think you were listening."

"I was listenin'. So no matter how long you wait to go back to the Feielanns, she won't have aged a day, nor will she have forgot you, unless I miss my guess."

"That might be," Kenyan said thoughtfully, "but what about me? *I'll* be getting older."

Gumnbote smiled wryly. "The way I figger it, it don't matter how old you're goin' to be when you get back, neither, for once the Arkhanfeie finds out you're back, you won't have more than a couple o' minutes left to look upon your lass anyways."

Kenyan again had nothing to say in response to that, but he asked, "Why then would I want the letter from Lord Ester?"

"Well, why not?" Gumnbote asked reasonably. "Think about your quest, what the king sent you on. You got me back to my boys, though I'll need a good bit of time to figger out what it means to be their father, that's for sure. That's part one of your quest, and it's answered better now than it woulda been if we had got my mem'ries back, but not the boys." Kenyan nodded slowly in agreement.

"Well, if you get that letter, then you got two parts of your quest licked." He took a swig of beer, giving him a moment to compose his next thought. "You know, your friend Sir Pease seemed to think you were livin' some kind of a charmed life—mebbe you are at that. Say that somehow you *did* get a gem from the Arkhanfeie. Wouldn't it be nice to have that letter, so's the quest was complete? Even if you never did anythin' about it, at least you'd have the choice, if you wanted to."

"Well ... you've given me something to think about," Kenyan admitted, grudgingly impressed with Gumnbote's flow of logic. "If you season all of your fortunes with as much wisdom, you'll do well indeed."

Gummy smiled, and reached his hand out toward his friend. Kenyan grasped it, held it for a moment ... released it.

The next morning found Kenyan slipping through the muck of the streets of Sarbo as stealthily as he was able. He had no particular facility for stealth, but it mattered little; no one was about this early. There was also a fine, cold drizzle falling which discouraged any early risers from venturing out of doors unless there was greatest necessity, which there wasn't. Still, Kenyan feared that at any moment, he might be confronted by the point of a sword and an angry challenge, and he knew he would be defenseless against either.

He was searching for the home of Audacious Kak, the red-bearded captain who had given him the cat Patch in exchange for Constant, the horse he had received from Lord Ester. Sometime during the night before, in between tankards of grog, it had occurred to Kenyan that, with Kak gone off to sea, it would be a fine thing to steal back the horse that had been stolen from him.

There had not been many patrons in Pelly's last night, just a few men who were too ill or too injured or too old to go out with the nefs, and a few women who were there to amuse them. Gumnbote had told fortunes for anyone who had something to trade for one, and he had split the profits with Pelly, who had feasted Gumnbote and Kenyan and Jem with so much meat that their bellies were stretched painfully tight, and had pressed mug after mug of grog on Kenyan. As drink followed drink, Kenyan became aware of a new courage streaming through his veins, and a new keenness of insight in his brain, and that was when he had thought of Constant.

When morning's throbbing sobriety arrived, Kenyan figured that he probably wouldn't *really* try to steal the horse from the pirate captain, after all ... but he thought he might still creep surreptitiously through the streets and at least see if he could find it.

There were few horses in the town of Sarbo. Horses were a luxury that most of the town, being attuned to the sea instead of the land, simply did not care about. But here and there Kenyan encountered a stable, a pen, a picket, and it didn't take him long at all before he did find Constant, the handsome russet gelding, in a small pen behind a wooden shack that sat a little above its neighbors. Constant nickered a greeting to Kenyan, who fought to dismiss the notion that the horse had recognized him.

He peered back and forth, all around, and again. There was no one near. Kenyan stole quietly toward the horse-pen, and noticed a little wooden shed attached to the fence, probably the place where the horse's tack was stored. He thought he might just try the door of the shed, to see if it would open without making noise. As he stretched out his hand to grasp the wooden latch, a husky voice said from behind him, "Hold, mate."

Kenyan jumped involuntarily, and turned slowly, to the sound of a deep, throaty chuckling. The sight he encountered now was only a portion of what he had feared: the point of a sword—yes. But instead of a face filled with anger, it was an amused face, almost mocking. A woman's face.

"What're ye up to?" the woman asked good-naturedly. She was quite pretty, but very stout. She held the sword unwaveringly, and Kenyan suspected that her apparent stoutness was due largely to muscle, not fat.

He saw nothing to be gained by lying, so he said, "I was going to steal this horse."

"That so?" she said, a deep alto chortle. "I think my husband might not be pleased."

At that moment, a cat sauntered over to the woman, purring audibly, and rubbed its patchwork-colored fur against her ankles. Kenyan thought—but was not certain—that it was the same Patch that he had received in trade for Constant a year ago.

"I'm sorry," Kenyan said.

"Well, hoss-thief," the woman replied softly, still smiling, "shall I slice ye from neck t' navel, and use yer giblets in my stewpot? Or shall I let ye go yer way in peace?"

From her manner, Kenyan thought perhaps that to beg for his freedom might not produce the desired result, though he was also quite certain that he should not ask her to slice him open and eat his giblets. So instead, he waited patiently for her judgment, not taking his eyes from the point of the sword, and said a silent prayer for deliverance.

"Ah, get on wi' ye," she said at last, and lowered the blade.

Kenyan exhaled, and before he realized what he was saying, he blurted, "Can I at least take my cat?"

"*Your* cat?" she said incredulously. And then it was as if the light of understanding dawned on her face. "Wait. Ye're the one what Kak got that hoss *from*, ain't ye?"

Kenyan nodded. It hadn't occurred to him that she would take him for a common thief, though now that he thought of it, why would she think that he was anything but?

She raised the point of the sword back up again, aiming it toward his belly, and wondered what to do next. After a moment of contemplation, she suddenly giggled, and said, "Ye're goin' to have t' scamper out o' Sarbo Town, ye know. It won't do fer ye to be caught here, ever again." Kenyan nodded earnestly.

The woman handed him the sword, and said, "This may come in handy to ye, somewheres down the road."

"Thank you," Kenyan said slowly, baffled at this turn of events.

"Which'd ye rather have?" she asked, and when Kenyan just looked at her, bewildered, she repeated the question. "Which'd ye rather have—the cat, 'r the hoss?"

Kenyan found his voice at last, and stammered, "The horse, if you please."

"Pretty talk!" she said with approval. "Now, I'll saddle 'im up for ye, and then ye'd best *scoot!*"

Chapter Thirty-Five

The riding lessons that Sir Pease had urged upon him during his days at Ruric's Keep had made Kenyan a substantially improved horseman from the last time that he had sat upon Constant's sturdy back, and both Kenyan and the horse seemed to realize it.

He fled the town of Sarbo without stopping to say goodbye to Gumnbote or Jem, which caused him to experience a pang of regret. But he could hardly pull up in front of Pelly's Grog House on Audacious Kak's fine red horse without someone from the town voicing an objection! So, with a mud-spraying splatter of hoofbeats, Kenyan sped out of Sarbo, past the startled, shouting guard stationed at the western edge of the village, and followed the westward road to Ester.

He gazed off toward the horizon in front of him, or at least such of it as he could see; the sky was filled with a silvery mist, almost like the spray that rose from the coast as it crashed on the jagged rocks below Kell's Lookout. A sudden melancholy filled him, a longing to see the Great Sea once more. If he had time, perhaps, he could cross over to the isle of Pembicote and visit his boyhood home one last time. One last time, before going to spend the remainder of his days in the landlocked wilds of the Feielanns.

Constant galloped along the road for a couple of hours, Kenyan's elbows flapping like a bird's, but it became apparent after awhile that he was not being followed. So he slowed the horse to a more comfortable gait, and rode on through the midday. The sun broke through the clouds, and God's multicolored bow lay across the steel-gray sky.

Early in the afternoon Kenyan turned from the road and led Constant through the dripping trees to the small grove of oaks where he had spent so many pleasant hours of solitude during his days as a guard at Beedlesgate. He found his old spot where he used to sit upon the grass with his back against a tree; it looked comfortable, homey, but yet somehow changed, as if somehow he had grown taller and was seeing the familiar sights, but from a different angle.

His whole world had been changed. He knew that he would never see an open meadow again without thinking of Réchetthaerielle, and then he wondered if there had been hidden fairies surrounding him all the time as he had sat in this wood watching the birds and squirrels.

On a whim, he spoke. "Are there any dryads about?" There was no sound but the dripping of the raindrops through the golden springtime leaves. "I would know you, if you would," he said, and listened for a response. "I've met the Arkhanfeie." Still nothing. "I've befriended a limniad—perhaps you know her? Réchetthaerielle. Of Maedwe Feorr."

He waited a moment more, the only new sound being Constant pulling up the clearing's fresh young grass, and then the sound of his chewing. Then one more voice was added to the quiet chorus: the rumbling of Kenyan's own belly. He had not eaten since last night's feast at Pelly's, and now he was hungry again. He felt a moment of envy toward the horse, but cheered himself that he was not far now from Beedlesgate, and perhaps Lord Ester's table. Or at least a bowl of stew with the guards.

"Well, goodbye," he said aloud. "I would be your friend."

After spending another moment listening to the soft patter of the rain, he led Constant back to the road.

It was early evening when Kenyan arrived at Beedlesgate, pulling back on Constant's reins and halting so the guard could identify him and grant access to the castle grounds.

"Well, if it ain't Ragshag!" Creel said, slapping his thigh and laughing. "We figgered you'd been kilt six different ways by now!" He reached up to grasp Kenyan's hand, and he appeared to be genuinely pleased to see him.

Kenyan was a little suspicious; Creel had never been particularly cozy with him when they had been guards together. "Heya, Creel," he said cautiously. "You've got guard duty, eh?"

"Ayeah," he said sheepishly. "Two weeks straight. You don't need to know about that."

"You look well," Kenyan ventured.

"Well, thanks. If you don't mind me sayin' so, you don't look all that good yourself."

Smiling ruefully, Kenyan replied, "I've had a hard few days, and that came after a lean winter, too."

"Well, hop on down. Food we got aplenty, and a soft bed too, if you need one."

Kenyan clambered down from Constant's back, and asked, "Are any of the other boys around?"

"Slater's out at Kell's. Parry, Tiria, Danna, Peliah, Aoemer—they're all around someplace. Solonsee's got guard duty indoors, outside Lord Ester's study."

"How about Henry?" Kenyan asked.

"Oh, I forgot all about him," Creel laughed. "'Twas just a short while after you left. Lord Ester gave him a sweet job overseein' his cattleherds, and he off an' married that girl Marlina. They've got a wee one now, a fat little boy baby."

"Well, what do you know about that?" Kenyan said, beaming.

"I'm thinkin' about gettin' married myself," Creel said a little self-consciously, and Kenyan decided that perhaps that was the cause of his increased cordiality. "I think you might remember her. It's Lanadine's old maidservant, Millie."

Kenyan shook Creel's hand enthusiastically. "Congratulations!" Without thinking, he blurted, "You've done so much better than I thought you could have done!"

Creel laughed heartily, with no apparent bitterness. "I've did better than *I* ever thought I could've, too!"

Since Lanadine's name had been mentioned, Kenyan thought it proper to ask of her. "Solonsee told me that Lanadine had run away, or been kidnapped, or something. Has she returned?"

"No, and *that's* a fine tale all by itself. But here comes Captain Barner—I should look busy. If no one tells you about Lanadine before tomorrow, I will."

"It's good to see you again, Creel," Kenyan said. "Would you please give my regards to Millie?"

Creel nodded and said sheepishly, "I'm sorry, that when I seen you just now, I called you Ragshag. It's just, uh, that I ain't seen you for more'n a year, and, to tell you truthful, I couldn't come up with your name."

"That's all right. It's Kenyan."

"Of course it is. Welcome back, Kenyan."

※

Kenyan dropped Constant off at the lord's stables and chatted for a moment with Bellings the stable-master, but shortly excused himself and headed inside the castle, making his way toward Lord Ester's private study.

"Kenyan!" Solonsee said, in a kind of subdued shout of greeting. "Glad to see you alive!"

"Thank you," Kenyan grinned. "It was a chancy thing a few times, to be sure."

They clasped hands earnestly, almost—but not quite—hugging each other.

"You've endured, though," Solonsee said approvingly. "But you've lost weight."

"And I wasn't that fat to begin with!" Kenyan laughed.

"When Lord Ester goes to dinner for the night, I'll be relieved of guard duty here," Solonsee said. "And then you and I can share a bite, and you can tell me of the adventures you've had."

"Gladly," Kenyan agreed. "But I've really come to see Lord Ester. Is he available now?"

"Not a chance! You look like you've been drug through the mud by a pack of angry dogs. And, truth to tell, your smell's not that good either. Get yourself cleaned up and have a good meal. Have a peaceful sleep tonight, and I'll get you in to see Lord Ester tomorrow. You can't wear *that* in to see the lord, either," Solonsee said, indicating Kenyan's torn, filthy garment. "I'll bet we have something around here that you could change into."

Kenyan, recognizing the wisdom of his friend's sentiments, decided to go and bathe, and join Solonsee afterward for a meal with the guards.

Later, sitting on the edge of a borrowed cot in the guards' barracks, he chatted with Captain Barner, Solonsee, and another guard named Peliah. After having shared some stories of his days at Ruric's Keep—but saying very little about his quest for the king—Kenyan asked Solonsee, "So, last time I saw you, you were searching for Lanadine. But Creel said that she hasn't returned, and that there's a tale to be heard. What happened to her?"

Solonsee stole a look at Barner, but before he could speak, Peliah did. "You haven't heard? She's the bloody queen o' the pirates!"

"What?" Kenyan asked, stupefied.

Captain Barner gave Peliah a look of reproof, and said quietly, "Speak lightly, lad. She's still Lord Ester's daughter."

Solonsee added, "We don't really know all that much. Just rumors, mostly."

"Well, what are the rumors?"

Barner said, "See that you don't mention it to Lord Ester." When Kenyan nodded his assent, the captain continued, "All we've heard is this. She ended up a captive of Black Sarbo. There's some conflict as to whether she ran away, or was taken. But there's little doubt that Sarbo intended to make her his … bride." He spat the word with a sardonic scowl.

"But you remember Lanadine," Solonsee interjected. "For all her faults, she was a lass with high spirits."

"Aye," said Peliah, and another look from Barner stopped him from further comment.

"As the story goes, she absolutely refused Sarbo—said she would kill herself first, or else kill him—unless he would put away all of his other wives, and cleave to her alone."

Solonsee added, "Well, you've seen Lanadine, of course. It wasn't long before old Sarbo dismissed all of his wives, and made her his, ah, his queen. We've even got a couple of his old wives working here in the kitchen now."

Kenyan just stared at them, stunned. *Queen of the pirates?*

Peliah said, with a defiant look at his captain, "They say she don't stay on land when the ships go to sea, like all of his old wives did. They say she goes right to battle with 'em, and that she's twice as treacherous an' cruel as old Sarbo ever was on his own."

Kenyan, dazed, tried to take in this mystifying information, tried to think of something to say in response. "I, ah—I don't have anything to say," he said.

It's best that way," Captain Barner gently affirmed.

Chapter Thirty-Six

Lord Ester was dozing at his desk. The droning of flies at his windowsill— flies which had been apparently resurrected by the warmth of the springtime sun beaming into the lord's cloister—was a soporific to Ester, a kind of buzzing lullaby. He heard snoring, his own, and it startled him, waking him. Or had that been a knock at his door? He picked up a scroll and pretended he had been studying it, and called out, "Yes?"

Solonsee entered and said, "If you please, Lord Ester, Kenyan has returned from King Ordric, and requests an audience."

Kenyan? The name sounded familiar, but he couldn't immediately place it. He couldn't remember sending anyone by that name to Ordric recently. "Help me, Solonsee. Kenyan is…?"

"You disciplined him at Lanadine's request, and sent him to the king."

"Ah, yes, I remember. Hmm. Back from Ordric? I wonder why."

Solonsee waited patiently for Lord Ester to command him, resisting the urge to say anything that could be interpreted as insolent.

Ester yawned and laid the scroll back down on his desk. It seemed that there had been something commendable about the young man who had offended his daughter, but he couldn't recall what it was. Well, no need to keep him waiting, he supposed. "Yes, thank you, Solonsee. You may send him in."

"Thank you, my Lord."

Kenyan entered a moment later, briefly kneeling before Lord Ester's desk, and then rising to his feet. Ester, who now recognized Kenyan's face—even though the lad seemed to be somewhat thinner—said, "Welcome, Kenyan. Please draw up a chair, and tell me how it goes with you. Do you bring greetings from the king?"

"Yes, I do," Kenyan said, "though it has been many months since I have seen His Majesty."

"Months? Ruric's Keep is but a fortnight away, on horseback."

"Much of my journey has been afoot," Kenyan replied. "And I was not sent from the king to you directly. I have been on the king's quest."

"Indeed? A quest," Ester said, impressed. "I had not thought that he would—forgive me, Kenyan. I was just about to say something uncomplimentary."

"No need to apologize, m'Lord. If there's anyone who's aware of my deficiencies, it's me," Kenyan said, a small, sheepish smile playing at the corners of his mouth.

"Enough said about that," Ester declared. "You must have pleased the king somehow, if he gave you a charge. What was it, if I might inquire about the king's business?"

Kenyan said, "You may. The king promised me a knighthood, if I should complete three tasks for him."

"Hmm, yes. A knighthood, eh? Quite impressive. Much more so than being a guard in Ester's court, yes?"

Kenyan looked closely to try and determine whether Lord Ester seemed angry or resentful, but he appeared to be in a good humor.

The lord continued, "Well, how stands your quest? Have you completed the tasks?"

"One of them, yes. And the second—which I can complete with your aid— is why I am here now. The third, I fear, is likely beyond my reach."

"Well, well—we shall have to hold counsel about the third to determine whether it is possible for you or not—but first, the second." He chuckled, thinking that he had accidentally made a small joke, and Kenyan smiled encouragingly. "What is it that you have come for?"

"Your Lordship will perhaps recall that you sent a letter of introduction with me to the king?"

"All right," Ester said cautiously. He had forgotten, but it sounded familiar, now that it had been mentioned.

"Well," Kenyan said, searching for the right words, "I was ... unable to deliver that letter."

"No?"

"I am afraid that I lost it ... when I met with some unsavory companions. It was stolen from me."

Ester, who was starting to recall the letter he had written, asked, "But why would anyone want such a thing?"

"I believe that their intent was only to mock me."

"I see," said Ester, almost feeling a small pang of regret for the dismissive way he had represented Kenyan in his note to the king.

"And so, m'Lord, one of the provisions of my quest was that I would obtain another letter from you, and present it to the king."

"A whimsical and imprudent demand, but it does sound like something the king would require. To be truly a king's quest, there must be something both noble and foolish about it, it would seem."

"Yes, m'Lord."

"I wonder—how did you ever gain access to the king without my letter?"

"That is a lengthy tale, m'Lord, but I would gladly relate it if you wish."

"Well, perhaps at dinner, then," Lord Ester granted. "You will join me at table tonight?"

"It would be my honor, m'Lord."

"Yes, of course. So," Ester said, "you need a new letter recommending you to the king. I shall draft one this afternoon. But about the third provision of your quest...?"

"M'Lord. The king required me to obtain a jewel from the crown of ... another ruler in Hagenspan."

"Another ruler? Who?"

"He is called the Arkhanfeie."

"Bosh!" the lord said, with a wave of his hand. "I have heard the word before. Children's tales! The king has indeed given you a task you cannot complete."

Kenyan did not wish to dispute the existence of the Arkhanfeie with Lord Ester, seeing no real benefit that could result from that argument, so he simply said, "Yes, m'Lord."

"It seems he favors you but little, after all. Unless—" another thought occurred to him— "unless you were planning on taking a jewel from some other source, and presenting it to the king as being from this Arkhanfeie?"

"Oh, no, m'Lord! I would not lie to the king," Kenyan replied hastily, though in fact that thought had occurred to him quite early on in the quest.

"No, I suppose not," agreed Ester. "He would have you hung by your thumbs for your impudence." He stroked his beard thoughtfully. "Then what is your intention? Do you plan on wandering the earth like a vagabond for the rest of your days?"

Kenyan ducked his head guiltily. "In a sense—yes. The king does not wish me to return to him without a jewel from the Arkhanfeie's crown, so ... yes."

Lord Ester drummed his fingers upon his desk while Kenyan waited, did it again, and then said, "I have another proposal for you to consider, ah, Kenyan—if you wish."

"M'Lord?"

"Lanadine no longer lives here at Beedlesgate. I don't know if you've heard that. You could come back and fulfill your service to me here. I might even find something more rewarding for you than guard duty."

"M'Lord is most generous," Kenyan said sincerely, but secretly he was beginning to regret his decision to come back to Ester for the letter. He drew in a breath, steeled his nerves, and said, "Lord Ester ... I must ask you, most respectfully, if you would please release me from my oath of service."

"Release you? But why? Do you wish to roam like a wild beast? You certainly don't think to find this prince of the fairies and steal a gem for Ordric, do you?"

Kenyan felt helpless to explain himself. "M'Lord, I do seek a jewel ... but not that one." Feeling that he needed to add something more, he blurted, "While I was in the wilderness ... I discovered a treasure."

"A treasure?" Even though Lord Ester was beginning to grow annoyed with Kenyan, his interest was piqued now; his love for bangles and baubles and glittering things was well known. "Tell me."

"I am certain that, to a great man such as Your Lordship, the thing that I have found would be worth less than the least of any one of your amusements," Kenyan explained hastily, feeling just a bit desperate now. "But for a lowly man like me, the treasure I found was incomparable—worth more to me than all the king's riches."

Lord Ester, who had briefly been tempted to throw Kenyan in the stockade if he didn't reveal what this treasure was, suddenly understood, and snorted with derision. "By God!" he said, "You have found a woman!"

Kenyan's cheeks turned crimson. He wasn't sure if a limniad was precisely a woman, but in essence, Lord Ester was correct. "Yes, m'Lord."

"Didn't I tell you once never to trust a woman?" Ester said with a bawdy laugh.

"Yes, m'Lord," Kenyan replied meekly, though he thought that if Lord Ester had ever known somebody like Réchetthaerielle, he would feel differently.

"Well, this is a bit of damnable foolishness that is common to all men, isn't it? But the cool workings of logic seldom prevail when the loins are set ablaze. By God. Well, if you've found a woman that will have you—no offense intended—go! Go while you still think you want to."

"Thank you, m'Lord," Kenyan said, a surge of relief coursing through him like the Ripar Flowan.

"Do you still want that letter?"

"Well, yes ... if it's not too much of a bother for Your Lordship."

"I'll bring it with me to dinner," Ester said, and stifled a yawn. He was unused to extending this much time or courtesy to the likes of a guard who had been dishonored, and now that he had solved the riddle of the treasure, he was quickly wearying of the conversation. "I suppose you won't be staying very long, then?"

Kenyan had not considered how long he might be lodging at Beedlesgate, but he was suddenly filled with the desire to be reunited with Réchetthaerielle. So he said, "If you please, m'Lord—if you'll give me your blessing, I'll leave with the morning light."

"Blessing. Blessing," he waved dismissively. "Be gone, now. I have writing to do."

Black Sarbo had told his young bride about the first time he had seen her, from his hiding place behind the curtain in the secret passageway to her father's study. His intent at the time he told her—during the tumultuous "courtship" when Lanadine had demanded he put away his other wives—had been to show how earnestly his lusty pirate's blood pounded through his veins for her and her alone ... even while he was begging for the privilege of keeping his other wives. But Lanadine's interest in that particular story, as much as it appealed to her vanity, was not in Sarbo's declaration of his passion for her. It was in the fact that there was a secret passageway to her father's study.

Sarbo did not use the hidden entrance anymore. Since he had appropriated Lanadine for himself, Lord Ester bore him no goodwill, and even though Sarbo feared no man, he was canny enough not to court trouble needlessly. But after much pestering from his raven-haired bride, Sarbo had finally revealed the place where the passageway began—the mouth of a cave, hidden by overgrown bushes and shadows, leading to a tunnel which in turn led to Ester's private den. Sarbo had thought that it was a miracle the cave wasn't well known, but Lord Ester, who had the power to command where his guards should, and should not, go, had managed to keep the shadowed corridor a secret.

Lanadine sometimes, whenever a fit of homesickness or a caprice of mischief came over her, crept through the tunnel and hid herself behind the heavy draperies that separated her from the homely comforts of her father's world. She would listen to him debate with other lords, or dispense justice to his servants and hirelings, or sometimes just snore. Once or twice, she had come to the curtains and discovered the study empty, and had slipped into her father's den, sat in his chair, caressed his belongings, and stolen a souvenir for herself. It amused her to think about the furor that would ensue when the trinket was discovered to be missing— how it would be searched for, who would be blamed, what punishments might be apportioned.

On this day, Lanadine had just crept into the dank bower to listen to the sound of her father's voice, feeling that she would like, just once, to be able to have him hear her, too—to know that she was there. It wasn't that she wanted to go home; she relished her position as Sarbo's queen, which she figured was better than she could have done by marrying some second son of a minor lord. But from time to time, she asked herself why she should not have *both*—her old life and her new. Was she not Lanadine?

From behind the curtain, she could hear the muffled sounds of her father talking with someone. The voice of the other sounded vaguely familiar, but she couldn't immediately place it. Then she heard that voice say, "M'Lord, I do seek a jewel ... but not that one," and her ears perked up. She had inherited her father's love for sparkling things. Then she heard him say, "While I was in the wilderness ... I discovered a treasure," and she thought, *A treasure!*

Wide-eyed and holding her breath, she took a chance then and peered around the edge of the drape, and over her father's shoulder she saw ... Goblin-beak! The ugly guard, the one who had tried to kiss her that time, once, a lifetime ago. The one who had bored her with his bird talk and humiliated her in front of her father's guests, and then had caused Solonsee and Fat Henry to scorn her in front of all of the castle community. She blazed with remembered fury, as if she were experiencing the shame afresh, as if she could still see the mocking laughter in the eyes of the people of Beedlesgate.

The contemptible fool was just saying, "—treasure I found was incomparable—worth more to me than all the king's riches," and Lanadine decided instantly that whatever treasure the repulsive wretch had found should be forfeited to her—Lanadine—in recompense for his transgression against her dignity.

She heard her father say, "By God! You have found a woman!" and almost forgot herself, almost laughed aloud. Goblin-beak, with a woman? What woman in all of Hagenspan would deign to give herself to him, unless she'd plucked out her own eyes first?

No, she told herself, wondering if her father was a fool too. *The ugly man had found a treasure of some kind, all right. And it would be hers.* For a moment she faltered, wondering how she would be able to make that happen. And then a grim smile flickered across her face. *I'll make Sarbo get it for me.*

Chapter Thirty-Seven

The sun was shining, its warm face unmasked by cloud, the caress of its rays eagerly welcomed by the thawing earth. A few small, lumpy piles of snow remained in the places where the winter winds had swept it into shadowy drifts, but anyplace where the sun's golden shafts reached was moist and fresh, the grasses greening, the trees budding. Ice-cold water ran joyously through the brooks and streams that had once been frozen solid—the blood of Hagenspan reborn, coursing through her veins again.

Sparrows flitted among the bushes at the sides of the road, cheerily chirping greetings to Kenyan and the dappled horse he rode. (When Bellings, the stablemaster of Beedlesgate, had offered to outfit Constant for Kenyan's departure, he had demurred, judging that trying to sneak the red horse through the town of Sarbo one more time might be too risky—even if he *did* have a charmed life. So Kenyan chose a horse instead that was not likely to be much of a temptation to the bandits, should he happen to be detained by them again. And, remembering blind Gumnbote's imagined love for a dappled horse, he picked a knobby-kneed gray nag with long yellow teeth and faint white speckles on its flanks. He thought that, if the horse should make it all the way to Maedwe Feorr, the fairies' golden fields would make it a suitable home.) Kenyan listened with delight to the birds' chattered songs, remembering his former days with fondness, and thinking—a bit wistfully—that if things did not go well with the Arkhanfeie, his days of listening to the songs of birds might be drawing to a quick, dark end.

But still the thought of Réchetthaerielle drew him on. Sometimes he despaired of the notion that she could still be waiting for his return, longing to see him again, loving him. But he asked himself, what did that really matter after all? For he knew that he loved her, and if the last sight his eyes should behold would be her face one final time, then he could count that a life well lived.

He wondered again about old King Hagen. What had motivated that venerable explorer during the twenty years he had roamed the wilderness of the land that now bore his name? Surely Hagen had not known that he would one day be called a king. He probably had expected to die in the wilderness, alone and unremembered. So what had driven him during those days, if not the desire to see things which no other man had seen, to discover treasures that were hitherto unknown?

Well, Kenyan reflected, he had found a treasure, too. He had found a prize that was worth more to him than any honor King Ordric could possibly confer. His eyes had seen that beautiful thing which, according to Réchetthaerielle, no man had ever seen before. In some small way, that made Kenyan more like the great Hagen than like, say, Aoemer. And if Kenyan was the only one in the world who ever knew that fact, well, what did it matter?

He was drawing near Sarbo's town now, and becoming apprehensive. The sudden fear filled him that the last sight he might ever see should not be Réchetthaerielle's lovely face, but rather the point of Audacious Kak's blade dripping with his own blood. An involuntary shudder shook him, and he drew back on his reins. Perhaps there was some way to skirt around the village instead of going straight through? But if there was, Kenyan did not know it, and to try and discover it might be just as ruinous as to forge straight ahead. *I need to think*, thought Kenyan. *No ... I need to pray.*

He dismounted, still gripping the reins to the dappled horse, and dropped to one knee. The mud quickly soaked through his trousers, a cold, wet, brown stain upon the clean new clothes that Solonsee had just given him, but Kenyan understood that a stained knee was a small price to pay in order to prove his humility to God. He prayed aloud, little more than a mumble, hoping that his voice could still be heard when he was so far away from the Feielanns.

"O God Architaedeus. Um. Your kindness to me has been, uh, much appreciated, so far. Thank You indeed. I, um, I find that I don't really know what to do next. Please, ah … please, if I've found favor, somehow, in Your eyes, then please lead me on the rest of the way back to the Feielanns. I'd like to see Your daughter again—Réchetthaerielle, You know—before I die. O God," he sighed dejectedly, "this sounds a bit simple-minded to say it out loud, I fear. But I expect You know my heart already. That's what I'd like, if it's all right with You, Your Lordship. If You please."

Kenyan suddenly wished that he knew more about Architaedeus. Was there some sacrifice he could make in order to secure God's favor? Were there some words that he was supposed to say to gain God's ear? But there was no way for him to know, and no time left to learn, he figured, so he hoped that his own simplicity and honesty would suffice, and he hoped that God was somewhat more merciful than he feared.

Sarbo watched the man kneeling in the mud, and for a fleeting, almost disappointed second, thought that he had led him to the treasure already. But then he realized that the man was praying, and nearly spat with disgust.

He had followed the man on foot, jogging along the easily discernible trail left by that decrepit bag of stew meat that he rode upon. Lanadine had told him the man's name, but he had forgotten it already, so he had named him Lumpkin—it seemed a fitting moniker for the ungainly dolt, who was the most remarkably foolish-looking man that Sarbo had ever seen.

When Lanadine had come to his cabin aboard the *Sea Witch* (which was the name of Sarbo's nef) demanding that he get Lumpkin's treasure for her, he had initially been surly and foul, cursing her by all the gods and demons he could think of. Why chase a man across land for a landlubber's treasure, when it was the sea who had made him richer than the king? —the sea who had treated him more sweetly than a mother?

But after a cold, sullen night's reflection, he had grudgingly become convinced to do as she asked—Lanadine would give him nothing but trouble until he did, and nothing but misery if he did not. By the time dawn broke, he was almost eager to go. It would be a holiday for him! He could, perhaps, visit some of his old wives that Lanadine had sent away; he could spend a few weeks, maybe, away from the sound of Lanadine's voice. Oh, there was no doubt that she was the most beautiful wife he had ever taken, and her bold cruelty and treachery demanded that she rightly be his queen … but a few weeks away from his queen might be a happy, sporting time indeed. And then, if Lumpkin really did have a treasure to be gained, so much the better! It would be Sarbo's. Or, perhaps, if the treasure were not quite so impressive as Lanadine imagined, he would go ahead and give it to her.

He saw the man stand up and lean against his horse. Apparently he had prayed enough, if that's what it was he was doing. He waited impatiently for Lumpkin to mount up and move on, but it seemed that, instead, the idiot was going to stop and have a meal. Sarbo watched as he led his horse off to the side of the path, and draped the reins over some branches. Almost snarling aloud at the man, he squatted alongside the path and thought murderous thoughts as he watched him sit on a stump and eat. A grumble of complaint began to sound from his own belly, and Sarbo balled his hand into a fist and pressed it against himself until the murmuring stopped.

When he saw Lumpkin fold his hands across his chest and close his eyes, it was nearly all he could do to keep himself from striding up to him, sword in hand, and angrily demand that he lead him to the treasure, *now*— but instead, he decided to sneak past him and on into his own town. He needed to eat, provision himself for a journey, and get a horse. It wouldn't do for him to follow Lumpkin afoot all the way to the treasure. Besides, he'd need some way to get the treasure back to his town; he could ride one horse, and use Lumpkin's horse to carry the booty.

"Who goes?" sounded a challenge from the hidden outpost at the western edge of the town of Sarbo.

"Do ye need t' ask?" Sarbo snarled.

"Oh, it's *you*, Cap'n!" said the guard, an old sailor who was no longer a steady hand at sea. Perplexed, the old salt blurted, "Where's the *Sea Witch*?"

"Docked at Ester, if it's any o' yer concern," Sarbo said testily. "I got other business."

"Aye, Cap'n," came the hurried reply.

Before Sarbo stomped off to find his meat and his supplies, he turned and said, "There'll be a man followin' me after a bit, ridin' a dapply-gray horse. Let 'im pass."

"Aye, Cap'n."

Chapter Thirty-Eight

Kenyan waited by the roadside, dozing fitfully until dusk, and then made his way into Sarbo on foot, trailing the horse behind him. To his great and grateful amazement, he was not detained or disturbed in any way. He slogged through the muddy main street of the town, and though several of the townspeople viewed him with resentment or suspicion, they did not greet him or challenge him, only stood aside to let him pass. This, Kenyan decided, was clearly an answer to his prayers, and he determined to pray more often.

For the next several days, Kenyan traveled eastward, past landmarks that were now familiar to him: the spot where he'd met Jairrus and Poll, Ange's house where he and Gumnbote had wintered, the town of Raussi, the thicket where Mott had left him his little rabbit-fur cloak. At last he came to the spot on the road where he had led Gumnbote on their way north from Maedwe Feorr, and he turned off the road and headed into the wilderness. Another day's travel, and he came to the place where he had last seen Réchetthaerielle, sitting in the grasses at the border of the Feielanns, and waving her sad goodbye.

He made camp there, eating the last of his bread and bacon over a small fire. He wondered if Réchetthaerielle, wherever she was, could see the fire, could tell that he was coming. The sense of her nearness was so real to Kenyan that he longed to run into Maedwe Feorr, shouting her name, crying out that he had returned ... had returned for *her*. But instead, he sat on the ground, his eyes searching fruitlessly for little winks of light, chewing his food nervously. He prayed.

※

Black Sarbo had missed the spot where Lumpkin had turned off the road and headed south; he was not an experienced tracker. He had continued eastward toward Ruric's Keep for almost an entire day before he was sure that Lumpkin was no longer in front of him, and it had taken two more curse-filled days for him to backtrack and find the place where the man had left the road. Even then, it was only the merest chance that enabled him to find the trace; the dappled horse had left a trail of droppings just a few feet off the road, pointing like an arrow to the south.

Sarbo looked resentfully toward the tangled wilderness where Lumpkin had disappeared, and felt a humiliating wave of fear breaking suddenly over him, with a shudder and a cold sweat. Fearless at sea, and undaunted among men, there was nevertheless something about all of this vast *otherness* that caused Sarbo a moment's panic. Cursing himself for a woman, he left the road and stepped deliberately into the terrifying wild.

After turning loose the gray horse, Kenyan had wandered Maedwe Feorr for three days, searching without success for Réchetthaerielle. Bewildered and despondent, he got as far eastward as the Ripar Flowan and then turned back and headed in the other direction again. Once more, the similarity of his quest to that of ancient King Hagen—though on a much smaller scale, of course—occurred to him. Hagen had spent twenty years crisscrossing Hagenspan, and Kenyan, if he must, was prepared to wander back and forth across Maedwe Feorr for twenty years too, until he discovered what had become of Réchetthaerielle. Maedwe Feorr would become his Hagenspan; Maedwe Feorr would become his mother.

From time to time he called out her name. At first he feared that he would be heard by the Arkhanfeie, but as each one of his cries vanished into the air unanswered, he no longer dreaded even the Arkhanfeie. To be answered by anyone would be, at least, something.

Kenyan walked for a day again, back to what he considered to be the western border of Feorr. As he walked, he prayed. He called out her name. He wept. He despaired.

He remembered the time the Arkhanfeie had offered him the gift, before he sent him into blackness, of seeing one last time the thing that he most longed to see. He wondered if he was being punished again by the Arkhanfeie, but now in a more insidious way: now he could see everything *except* the thing that he most wanted to see.

He turned back toward the west, chose a slightly different course, and began walking, searching, calling.

Sarbo spotted Lumpkin off in the distance, apparently wandering aimlessly. He looked lost. Had the damnable fool forgotten where he had hid the treasure? Or had someone else found it, and taken it?

Muttering a black oath, Sarbo cursed the man's mother and his grandmother. He considered for a moment changing his plan; he could walk up to the man, greeting him with feigned friendliness, and ask if he could help him. Then, if Lumpkin should describe what it was they were looking for, perhaps Sarbo could find it first and just take it away himself, unless it be very large. And if Lumpkin found the boodle first, well … then it would be: slit his gullet with the edge of Sarbo's blade singing a quick *snick-snack*, which had been the plan all along anyway.

Just as Sarbo was readying a plausible story as to how he should have happened across Lumpkin's path in the middle of this vast empty place, he saw that the other man suddenly stopped his aimless wandering and began jogging eagerly toward a grayish lump in the distance. The treasure! He must have found it after all!

Sarbo placed his hand on the haft of his sword and smiled. Now that he had passed out of the thickets and into the open meadow, he felt as if he could breathe more easily again. The sky above was almost as wide and generous as it was when he fearlessly rode the waves, and even though the tall grasses around his feet still reached out to grab his ankles like scores of flaxen serpents, he felt as if his courage had been restored. He felt like a man again. He was *Sarbo*. He watched as Lumpkin arrived at his goal, and began striding in that direction.

Kenyan had not found Réchetthaerielle, but he had found something that comforted him a little, though admittedly, it was a very small comfort. It was the cart that he and Gumnbote had pulled into Maedwe Feorr, so long ago. How long ago? —Kenyan had lost track of the days.

But surprisingly, the cart remained nearly as intact as it had been the day Kenyan had lost it. Grasses had grown between the spokes of the wheels, and the wood showed signs of having been weathered by rain and snow. Whatever had remained of food had apparently been eaten by mice, but of the hard goods stowed on it, none were touched. Apparently the

Arkhanfeie cared nothing for the things of men. Or perhaps Réchetthaerielle had kept it as it was as a memorial to Kenyan. He shook his head. Maybe nobody had even noticed that it was still there.

Reaching into a corner of the cart darkened by shadow, he felt the velvety folds covering the elfin rune-stick. He felt a brief surge of relief, though he had no idea why. He had intended to make the stick a gift for the Arkhanfeie, who had apparently not even cared about it enough to take it after Kenyan had gone. What possible good could it be for Kenyan now? Nevertheless, he was grateful to have it again ... whatever it was. Gently he unwrapped the stick and looked at it again; the gnarled rod still did not reveal any of its mysteries to Kenyan's eyes.

"What've ye got there, Pallie?" said a voice behind his back, and Kenyan, startled, jumped involuntarily, dropping the stick back into the cart. He knew immediately that the voice did not belong to the Arkhanfeie.

Chapter Thirty-Nine

When Kenyan had first returned to Maedwe Feorr, the Arkhanfeie and Réchetthaerielle had hidden themselves among the field's waving grasses. If Kenyan had looked directly at them, which he nearly had, twice, he would have seen nothing but grass being gently blown by the wind.

It had nearly made Réchetthaerielle's heart burst to hear Kenyan, her Prince, calling out her name, weeping and forlorn. When he had turned in her direction, she had breathlessly thought—hoped—that he could see her, hidden though she was, and she had nearly defied the Arkhanfeie and revealed herself to him. But to do that would surely have invited the Arkhanfeie's wrath, which would have been troublesome enough for her, and disastrous for Kenyan, whom she loved.

She and the Arkhanfeie had held a hushed debate, but again, if Kenyan had heard it, he would have recognized no words, only the whisper of the wind.

The Arkhanfeie was saying, "It is only for my great love of you, foolish one, that I am not banishing your man to the darkness from which he could not return."

"Thank you," Réche said, and then tremulously continued, "I think, dear one, that you would not do that, even if you loved me but little. You have seen his soul, and how brightly it shines."

"Do not presume to understand more than you do," he replied sternly, a faint rumble of thunder. "This disobedience of yours threatened to unmake all of the Feielanns!" He glared at her, and sharp words came unbidden from his lips. "You see so little. You tend Maedwe Feorr, and think that it is the whole world. What do you know of the forests, where the great trees have lived for ages, many of them with their own dryad who tends to nothing but their care? What do you know of the oreads, who live in the hills of rock and stone, creating gems precious and beautiful to delight the eye of Architaedeus? What do you know about the waters—?

"Baeriboelle is my sister," Réche said defensively.

"And what do you know of her?" he demanded. "When she is not laughing and splashing and bringing you fruit—" he scowled at her knowingly, "—do you know how she spends her days? Do you know what tasks the Blessed One has appointed her? Do you know that she cares for not just the waters, but also the fishes, the insects, the frogs? Do you know what gives her joy? What gives her sorrow? Do you know the number of her days, and what will become of Ripar Flowan when she is no more?"

Réchetthaerielle, ashamed, said, "No."

"You are the guardian of Maedwe Feorr," he said sternly, "and while that is a great honor and a great burden, little one, you must understand that you are one of the least of the Feie." He said this without unkindness. "Your meadow is small and uncomplicated, so much so that it only requires one limniad—you—to watch over it. On your eastern border is nothing. On your west lies Maedwe Na, which is tended by The Three. But deeper in," he continued, "—deeper in, where the waters and the forests and the mounts and the meadows all converge, there lies the great city of the Feie, where there are scores of our people, each with their tasks, each with their burdens, each with their joys. Each one loved and blessed by Architaedeus. Each, whose moments have been written in His book. And your lassitude in obedience threatens not just you, not just Maedwe Feorr, but all of them. All of *us*."

"May I speak?" Réche asked.

The Arkhanfeie nodded, but the severity did not leave his eyes.

"If all of the moments of the Feie," she began tentatively, "are written in the book of Blessed Architaedeus … then how could the choices of the least of the limniads change one mark of His writing?"

His eyes blazed. "How little you know! How poorly do you understand!" the Arkhanfeie raged, but he offered no further explanation. "It makes me almost to know how these bloody creatures, these *men*, can kill each other so lightly!" Clouds gathered above the meadow, clouds dark and heavy with rain. "For I would kill him if I could, this man of shining soul, in order to save the Feielanns! I would kill!"

"Oh, *no*, my Prince!"

"No, indeed," he snapped. "I shall not. As you have noted before, it has not been given to me to take life away from men, who value it less than we. But though I may not take life, I may take light; I may send him into darkness." He considered for a moment. "I believe I shall."

"Let it not be, dear one," Réchetthaerielle pleaded. "He has done no wrong, except that he loves me, whom you also said you love. Please, beloved Arkhanfeie, show mercy!"

"Mercy!" he stormed. "Mercy! Faugh! Would *he* show mercy, if he knew that his very presence could unravel all that we hold dear?'"

"But *how*?" Réche cried. "He is only a man, one man, and his very spirit shines forth that he is kindly and good! I don't understand!"

"That is your problem! You don't understand, and so you think that it cannot be so! Réchetthaerielle, there are many things in this world that surpass your knowledge, but that doesn't mean that they cease to be!"

"I know it," she said sadly, "but still I beg you—mercy!"

"Mercy," he said bitterly. "But wait! See. Another man follows your man into the Feielanns!"

"Another?" Réche said, flustered.

"We will watch them and see what will be," the Arkhanfeie judged. "And then we shall make our decision, whether for mercy, or for darkness."

※

"What've ye got there, Pallie?" Black Sarbo demanded.

Kenyan turned to face the man who spoke to him. He saw a swarthy, mocking face, burned by the wind and the sun, framed by long, tangled hair and a braided black beard, and he deduced immediately that it was Sarbo, though he had never heard of Sarbo doing anything at all on land before, except for resting from his seafaring labors. "What—what are you doing *here*?" he blurted.

"I admit, it's a bit out o' my usual ha'nts," Sarbo sneered, "but I believe it was me what asked a question first of *you*."

"I, ah—I don't have anything," Kenyan said truthfully.

"Damnation!" Black Sarbo cursed, and drew his sword. "I don't mean t' be short wi' ye, Pallie, seein' as how this is to be yer last moment on earth an' all. But I've took about all that a man can take! I've followed ye afoot, I've followed ye ahorse, I've followed ye day an' night on dry, dusty roads, when my throat was parched an' my cursed soul cried out for the sea!" His voice was rising as he gathered his rage. "The *sea*, by damn, not some blasted goblin-infested forest, nor a road so dry that my own spit was dust!" He slashed his blade through the empty air in a fit of exasperation, and uttered a strangled, frenzied cry. "Now I *will* have yer treasure, by

300

damn, or I'll lop yer head off'n yer shoulders, an' lug *that* home as a present for the witch!"

"Treasure?" said Kenyan weakly.

"Aaagh!" Sarbo shouted. "Do ye have a treasure or not?"

"I do have a treasure," Kenyan said helplessly, certain that his life was quickly going to come to an end. "But it's not what you think it is."

"Well, what *is* it?" Sarbo bellowed.

"My treasure ... is the one that I love. A girl. Réchetthae—"

Black Sarbo swung his blade viciously through the air, striking Kenyan on the neck and severing his head from his body. His torso stood still for a second before crumpling to the earth, and his head thudded to the ground several paces away, a surprised look upon his homely face, his last word unfinished in his mouth, his lips still formed to speak Réchetthaerielle's name.

As Kenyan's blood soaked into the earth of Maedwe Feorr, Sarbo stepped over his body and began inspecting the contents of the cart. He picked up the runestick, glanced at it, comprehending nothing of its nature, and tossed it on the ground. He rummaged through the rest of the meager storehouse of Kenyan's belongings, and felt a moment of pity for the man, when he realized how worthless all of his treasures were.

"Poor Lumpkin," Sarbo said aloud. "To have lived yer life with a face like that, and to have accumulated so much *nothin'*. I've did ye a favor by cuttin' it short."

301

Chapter Forty

When Réchetthaerielle saw the dark, wild man draw his blade and begin swinging it about so contemptuously, so threateningly, she nearly burst from her hiding place to try and help Kenyan, her Prince, though she did not know what she could have done to protect him. But any thought of revealing herself was aborted by the harsh command of the Arkhanfeie.

"Stop!" he hissed. "Do not go to him!"

"But—"

"We shall allow the affairs of men to be determined by their own hands," he ordered. "Men are Men, and Feie are Feie. Let them set their own course, and we shall hold our own place."

"I do have a treasure," Kenyan was just saying, "but it's not what you think it is."

"Well, what *is* it?" the vile, dark man screamed.

"My treasure … is the one that I love. A girl. Réchetthae—"

Réchetthaerielle heard her name being uttered by the lips she had once kissed, and watched in horror as the voice she loved was silenced. "No!" she whispered, and then she cried, "No!"

"Hold your place," the Arkhanfeie commanded her curtly.

Réchetthaerielle's slight chest heaved, and then she drew in a deep, quavering breath.

"Stop!" said the Arkhanfeie.

In a wink of light, bright as a star, she was gone.

The Arkhanfeie continued to watch grimly as the evil man scattered Kenyan's belongings on the ground, and then realized that this frayed thread of time was ceasing to exist.

Réchetthaerielle fought her way backward through the buffeting, deafening onrush of time moving forward. It was much harder to do this time than anytime she had ever done it before; indeed, she had not known whether she would be able to exercise her *vitapradistum* at all anymore. Since the day when she had offered herself as a lamp to light Kenyan's way out of his darkness, she had felt empty, drained, and she feared that to spend herself at all might be to spend herself *in* all. If she could make it back only as far as a day … then she could lead Prince Kenyan to safety, before the dark, angry man could discover him and follow him. But her strength was fading. She felt as if she could not move, felt the onslaught of time pounding her like a thunderstorm, felt herself slipping.

She prayed; prayed that she had made it back far enough to save him, prayed that her strength would not fail before she could help.

"What've ye got there, Pallie?" Black Sarbo demanded.

Kenyan turned to face the man who spoke to him. He saw a swarthy, mocking face, burned by the wind and the sun, framed by long, tangled hair and a braided black beard, and he deduced immediately that it was Sarbo, though he had never heard of Sarbo doing anything at all on land before, except for resting from his seafaring labors. "What—what are you doing *here*?" he blurted.

"I admit, it's a bit out o' my usual ha'nts," Sarbo sneered, "but I believe it was me what asked a question first of *you*."

"I, ah—I don't have anything," Kenyan said truthfully.

"Damnation!" Black Sarbo cursed, and tried to draw his sword.

But suddenly, there was a weight on his arm, wrapping itself around him, hindering him.

Startled, Sarbo shouted in fear, and tried to shake the unexpected presence off from him. The eerie sense of dread he had experienced when he entered this wilderness hadn't been just his imagination after all! There really *were* ghosts in the wilds!

Kenyan saw immediately what it was that hindered his enemy. But he was slow to respond, not understanding what it was that was happening.

"Run!" Réchetthaerielle cried weakly. "Save yourself!"

Sarbo heard the faint, female voice, and looked at his sudden encumbrance with surprise. It was nothing but a girl! A weak, trifling girl, clinging to his arm with all of her faltering strength. He drew back his fist to give her a clout.

Kenyan snatched up the rune-stick from where it lay in the cart, and swung it with all of his might in the direction of Sarbo's face, but the pirate had already delivered his crushing blow to Réchetthaerielle, who crumpled to the ground like a withered autumn leaf.

An instant later, a loud *crack!* echoed through the meadow, as the rune-stick connected with Sarbo's forehead, toppling him into a senseless heap upon Réchetthaerielle's still form. The stout branch that had been carved by the elves splintered and shattered, one end of it landing in the grass near the spot where the Arkhanfeie watched alone.

Kenyan cast the other end of the stick onto the ground behind him, and ran to Réchetthaerielle. He rolled Black Sarbo's bleeding bulk off the nymph's slight frame, and tried to rouse her. But she stared off into the distance, her eyes unseeing as Kenyan's once had been, and her head lolled off at an aberrant angle. Kenyan said her name softly, desperately, and shook her, trying to wake her ... but she was gone.

He laid her gently on the ground and bowed low over her, sobbing jaggedly. His tears cascaded down upon her face, and still she stared, unblinking, unbreathing. He kissed her cheek, kissed her forehead, cursed Sarbo, cursed himself for ever coming back to the Feielanns.

He prayed, desolately, "God! No!" and still she stared, her pale cheeks wet with his tears.

The Arkhanfeie picked up the shard of the rune-stick that had landed at his feet, and studied it gravely. The message upon it, written in a hand that he alone in Hagenspan could have perceived, had been interrupted where it had been shattered by the force of Kenyan's blow, but the Arkhanfeie could make out some of the import of what was inscribed there.

"O man of Réchetthaerielle's affection," he said, "how have you come by this relic?"

Kenyan's head snapped up, and he saw the Arkhanfeie standing above him. "M'Lord!" he cried. "Can you save her?"

"She has spent the last reserves of her strength in order to save *you*," he replied. "She loved you indeed. A nymph could scarcely love more."

"Is it too late, then?" Kenyan wept.

The Arkhanfeie studied him solemnly for the span of a heartbeat, and two. "No, it is not too late yet."

"Then save her!" Kenyan entreated him. "Strike me blind, if you must. Or let Sarbo kill me—I don't care! Just save Réchetthaerielle!"

"And you are willing to spend your life for her sake?" mused the Arkhanfeie. "Could even a man love more than that?"

Kenyan threw himself at the Arkhanfeie's feet and begged. "Do what you will with me, m'Lord, only save her, please. Please!"

"I will do as you have asked," the Arkhanfeie decided grimly. "For I love Réchetthaerielle, too, though not as you do. But … this may not turn out as you expect."

Kenyan didn't understand, but he nodded his agreement anyway, rubbing his cheeks with the back of a hand. The Arkhanfeie disappeared without another word, a dazzling burst of white, and suddenly Kenyan felt as if he were trapped in a dream—in a nightmare—and he struggled to force himself awake. The world grew shadowy and vague, as if black mists were gathering, obscuring what remained of the world's receding light, and instead of waking, his consciousness faded altogether.

Chapter Forty-One

The Arkhanfeie experienced little of the difficulty Réchetthaerielle had suffered while trying to go against the grain of time, for his strength was still as it had been in the full vigor of his youth. He emerged several days earlier, on a bright morning in Maedwe Feorr's late spring, and he spied Réche kneeling in the distance, looking with great tenderness at some small blue flowers near the banks of Ripar Flowan. She seemed sadder than he had noticed before.

"What troubles you, little one?" he asked as he drew near.

"My Prince," she replied, bowing her head. "Forgive me. A dark shadow afflicts me, though I know not what it means. A faint portent of some fate that is past my ability to see, perhaps. Let it not concern my Lord; it is likely nothing. Just the fear of a foolish nymph."

"So," the Arkhanfeie said with a small smile, "does Réchetthaerielle now have the gift of foresight?"

"No, I think not," she said, laughing lightly. "My eyes are glad to see you today, dear Prince. What causes you to walk these far borders of the Feielanns this day?"

The Arkhanfeie grew grave, and said to her, "You must trust me, Réchetthaerielle. What I am about to say will be hard for you to hear, but disobedience is not an option for you. You must trust that I love you, and that what I say is right."

Great fear seized Réchetthaerielle's heart then, and she stood to her feet before the Arkhanfeie, trembling. "What is it, my Lord?"

"Trust me," he repeated.

"At your word," she said weakly, but she was shuddering with apprehension.

"Réchetthaerielle of the Feie, limniad of Maedwe Feorr, I am removing from you the guardianship that you have enjoyed," he pronounced. "No longer shall you be the keeper of this meadow, and your place shall be taken by another."

"Oh, *no*, my Lord!" she cried, and threw herself at his feet. "Please—whatever I have done to dishonor myself, let me—"

"There is more," the Arkhanfeie continued. "According to the authority given me by Architaedeus the Just, I am stripping you of your *vitapradistum*. No longer will you be free to choose your way in time; your master shall it be instead of your servant. Forward shall you go, moment following moment, and you will live out the normal span of the life of a ... *man*, according to the number of days allotted to you by the Holy One."

"No, my Lord!" she pled, desolate. "How can that be?"

"I have never had to do such a thing before, in all the centuries of my stewardship," the Arkhanfeie admitted, "but the power was mine to use, at the proper time."

"But what have I done?" she wept, and even as she said it, her conscience reminded her of the time she left her appointed place in order to see the men. And quickly she thought, *Perhaps this is finally my punishment for defying the Arkhanfeie and becoming Kenyan's lamp.*

"I have told you that you must trust my judgment," the Arkhanfeie said, and he was moved nearly to tears himself to see her sorrow. But he steeled his resolve and continued, "You must leave Maedwe Feorr now; it is no longer your home. Go to the west; there the Three will comfort you. Tarry with them until your way is clear."

"My grief is more than I can bear," she sobbed.

"It feels that way now," the Arkhanfeie agreed, "but it is not. Now go, and do not disobey me again."

"I have always loved you," Réchetthaerielle choked, her tears blinding her.

"And I love you still," the Arkhanfeie said, and finally he wept too. He gathered the young woman Réchetthaerielle into his arms, and held her as their tears mingled, stroking her hair, caressing her shoulders.

※

"What've ye got there, Pallie?" Black Sarbo demanded.

Kenyan turned to face the man who spoke to him. He saw a swarthy, mocking face, burned by the wind and the sun, framed by long, tangled hair and a braided black beard, and he deduced immediately that it was Sarbo, though he had never heard of Sarbo doing anything at all on land before, except for resting from his seafaring labors. "What—what are you doing *here*?" he blurted.

"I admit, it's a bit out o' my usual ha'nts," Sarbo sneered, "but I believe it was me what asked a question first of *you*."

"I, ah—I don't have anything," Kenyan said truthfully.

"Damnation!" Black Sarbo cursed, and drew his sword. "I don't mean t' be short wi' ye, Pallie, seein' as how this is to be yer last moment on earth an' all. But I've took about all that a man can take! I've followed ye afoot, I've followed ye ahorse, I've followed ye day an' night on dry, dusty roads, when my throat was parched an' my cursed soul cried out for the sea!" His voice was rising as he gathered his rage. "The *sea*, by damn, not some blasted goblin-infested forest, nor a road so dry that my own spit was dust!" He slashed his blade through the empty air in a fit of exasperation, and uttered a strangled, frenzied cry. "Now I *will* have yer treasure, by damn, or I'll lop yer head off'n yer shoulders, an' lug *that* home as a present for the witch!"

"Treasure?" said Kenyan weakly.

"Aaagh!" Sarbo shouted. "Do ye have a treasure or not?"

"I do have a treasure," Kenyan said helplessly, certain that his life was quickly going to come to an end. "But it's not what you think it is."

"Well, what *is* it?" Sarbo bellowed.

"My treasure … is the one that I love. A girl. Réchetthae—"

Black Sarbo began to swing his blade viciously through the air, but before the blow could find its mark, the Arkhanfeie grabbed his arm in a grip like a vise.

Startled, Sarbo shouted in fear, and tried to shake the unexpected presence off from him. The eerie sense of dread he had experienced when he entered this wilderness hadn't been just his imagination after all! There really *were* ghosts in the wilds!

Kenyan recognized the Arkhanfeie immediately, and, though he did not understand what was happening, he felt that it would be better if he had some way to defend himself—whether against Sarbo or the Arkhanfeie, he did not know. He groped behind him, felt for the elfin rune-stick, and snatched that up.

Sarbo turned to face his assailant, saw the jewel-encrusted crown of living vines upon the Arkhanfeie's magnificent brow, and thought, *So there is a treasure!*

"Turn me loose!" he shouted, and the Arkhanfeie did so.

"I will give you one chance to leave the Feielanns peaceably," the Arkhanfeie said, "though I expect you will not take it."

"What?" the pirate bellowed. "Do ye know who I *am*?"

"No," the Arkhanfeie said reasonably.

"Why, I'm Black Sarbo, by damn!" he blasted. "Where in hell have ye been keepin' yerself, that ye ain't heard o' Black Sarbo?"

"You have pronounced your own doom," the Arkhanfeie said, his voice calm, and immediately Sarbo's entire world became black.

"What kind o' trickery is this?" shouted Sarbo, and began to swing his sword wildly about him in all directions, roaring curses and blasphemies.

"Come aside with me," said the Arkhanfeie to Kenyan, and stretched out his hand toward him. "What is your name?"

Bewildered but wary, Kenyan told him, and allowed himself to be led out of the range of Sarbo's blind fury.

The Arkhanfeie asked him deferentially, "The sceptre that you bear—may I examine it?"

"Of course," Kenyan said, and cautiously extended the rod in his direction. The Arkhanfeie took the rune-stick from his hands, and studied the carving on it.

"The elves crafted these marks, at the direction of Wise Architaedeus," the Arkhanfeie murmured.

"I see," said Kenyan, though he still could not discern what the markings could possibly mean. "I meant that stick to be a gift for you, if you wanted it," he offered.

"No, Kenyan, I think not. This sceptre belongs to you." The Arkhanfeie handed the rune-stick back to him, peering closely at Kenyan's face, and Kenyan had the impression that he was looking deeper than just at his external features—the way Réchetthaerielle had done. "Would you kneel?"

"Yes, m'Lord, of course," Kenyan said, baffled, but willing to obey anything the Arkhanfeie demanded of him. He dropped to his knees before the prince of the Feie, and bowed his head.

The Arkhanfeie reached up to his own forehead, removed his crown of vine and jewel, and laid it solemnly upon Kenyan's brow. Immediately another vine began growing to replace the one he had removed.

"M'Lord!" Kenyan gasped. "What does this mean?"

"In truth, I do not know," the Arkhanfeie said carefully. "But we shall learn, you and I."

"Is it because of the stick?" Kenyan asked.

"In part. I will tell you the words." He reached for the elfin staff, and read: "*The sun of a long day sets; twilight is at hand. The Chosen of the Blessed bears this rod; in meekness shall he rule. A night of darkness, and Man's day dawns.*"

"I don't understand," Kenyan stammered.

"Nor do I," the Arkhanfeie said solemnly, and—Kenyan thought—a little bit sadly. "But this day has long been foretold. And now it has come. What it means to you, and what it means to me, and what it means to the Feie … we shall see."

"Does this mean … that we are friends, now?" Kenyan asked.

"It may be. That would be my hope."

"And mine, too," Kenyan said, with as much earnestness as he could show. "May I, uh—may I ask you a question?"

"Of course."

"The girl—the fairy, Réchetthaerielle, who used to live in these parts. I've been looking for her for days, and I can't seem to find her." The Arkhanfeie nodded. "Can you tell me—is she well? She's not—" Kenyan almost said the word *dead*, but he feared to even speak the word, as if speaking the word might admit the possibility that she really was. "Is she well?"

"She is well … though she is changed." The Arkhanfeie handed the runestick back to Kenyan, and said, "She waits for you on the other side of the river. Go to her. And I will come to you in time."

"Thank you, m'Lord! Thank you!" Kenyan started to leave, but then halted mid-stride and asked, "How will I find her?"

The Arkhanfeie smiled then, gently—smiled at Kenyan for the first time, like a faint ray of sunlight sneaking past cloud-filled skies. "Look," he said simply. "You will find her."

Chapter Forty-Two

When the Three felt him drawing near, they quickly fled, leaving Réchetthaerielle alone, confused, forlorn. She knew that there must be some reason to flee … but she no longer was able. No longer able to discern the peril, no longer able to retreat from it either. This … *human*ness left her weakened, left her vulnerable.

Turning to the east, she saw a figure approaching. Noticing a glint of sunlight off a jewel on his brow, she immediately thought of the Arkhanfeie, and then just as quickly dismissed the notion; the Arkhanfeie would not be walking so slowly toward her—he would simply arrive.

Then the person in the distance raised his hand to his brow, shielding his eyes from the sun … and he saw her. Breaking into a run, he began coming toward her as swiftly as he could through the tall grasses of Maedwe Na, though it seemed he was quite awkward, and his running speed seemed little different from his walking speed.

Alarmed at the stranger's advance, Réchetthaerielle thought to run, to flee as her sisters had. But then she thought, *They are not my sisters anymore*. Deciding to stay and confront whatever this new menace might be, in this life of hers that seemed to be coming to such a caustic end, she turned to face his approach.

Suddenly there was something about his elbows that seemed familiar, and before she knew that she had realized it, she heard her lips whispering, "Kenyan!" Not knowing whether to be exhilarated or frightened or ashamed, she took a step toward him.

※

Kenyan saw her across the field, and tried to run toward her. Cursing himself for an oaf, he was keenly aware of how bumbling and ungainly he must appear. He clapped his hand to his head to keep his new crown from flying off as he jogged.

She took a step toward him.

And then he was there with her, and she seemed so small and so beautiful and so delicate that he didn't know what to do. He didn't dare to embrace her, for fear that she might break. He didn't dare to kiss her, for how would a man presume such a thing?

So he stood there, panting, unable to keep himself from grinning like an idiot, and said, "Hello."

"What are you … doing here?" she asked, glancing at the Arkhanfeie's crown, which she of course recognized.

"I've come for *you*," he said, delight and fear mingled in his breast.

"Me?" Réchetthaerielle said quietly, unsmiling. "I am nothing. I am dishonored."

"You are the most precious thing in the world to me," Kenyan declared earnestly.

"But … you are in danger," she said, but wondered if she even knew anymore. "The Arkhanfeie—?"

"It's alright," Kenyan assured her. "We're going to be friends, I think."

She looked at his face, tried to look deeply, and then said with sadness, "I can no longer see your soul."

"Oh, it's still there, I promise!" Kenyan blurted. Then he said tentatively, "If you can't see my soul anymore ... does that mean that what you *can* see is ugly to you?"

"Oh, no!" Réchetthaerielle declared. "You are still most beautiful to me."

Kenyan breathed a sigh of relief, scarcely daring to believe her words were true, but forcing himself to trust her. "Then ... if you don't have too much objection ... I'd like to spend all the rest of my days with you, if you don't mind too much. That's what I've come for."

She longed to cry *Yes!* but she wanted to be sure that he knew of her shame; perhaps he was unaware. "I no longer have Maedwe Feorr."

"I'm sorry," Kenyan replied, "but I didn't come for your land—I came for *you*."

"But—do you understand? I no longer have Maedwe Feorr."

"Then I will give you the whole world, if I can find a way." He looked into her eyes, and it seemed that a small spark of hope was rekindled from the ashes of her gray sorrow.

"You will stay with me, truly?" she asked, and it was more than a request for information—it was a plea.

"Yes, I will, if you'll have me."

"Then," she said, as she took his fingers in her hand, "I have no need of the world."

Kenyan and Réchetthaerielle lived together in the great city of the Feie for many years, though it was not a city in the human sense. But Kenyan thought that it was beautiful, for he was surrounded by trees of all kinds, and many of his hours were spent watching the squirrels at play, and listening to the chirping chorus of his friends the birds.

The Arkhanfeie called for a great convocation of all the Feie, to introduce Prince Kenyan and declare the day of his arrival. He announced that he would be relinquishing such authority as still remained, to Kenyan, though the nature of things was changing forever with the dawn of Man's day. And even though he declined all power and honor for himself from that day forward, the Arkhanfeie visited Kenyan often, and was his true friend.

Many of the Feie were resentful toward Kenyan, and some were jealous of Réchetthaerielle, and they no longer held to their old ways. But because their day was nearly over, the amount of mischief they could create was small, and most of them simply fled to the future, running as far forward as they could run, wishing to see wonders.

But many more of the Feie were content to let Kenyan govern them, and they loved Réchetthaerielle like the sister she once was. They served Kenyan and the Feielanns with great joy, for he was ever tender and good toward them.

One day, some years later, Kenyan and Réchetthaerielle journeyed to the great city of men, Ruric's Keep. King Ordric was much advanced in years by that time, but he remembered Kenyan and his quest. Kenyan promised him that he had restored to Gumnbote that which had been lost, and he presented him the letter from Lord Ester, and he gave him a jewel from his own crown. And King Ordric asked him, "You have seen the Arkhanfeie, then? Who is he?" And Kenyan replied, "If you please, Your Majesty—I am." And there was feasting, and giving of gifts, and Ordric named Kenyan a knight, but he allowed him to return to the Feielanns. After that, commerce was much increased between men and the Feie, and men expanded their borders, but the Feie diminished.

Several years more passed, and one spring day Réchetthaerielle presented Kenyan with a gift that surpassed all other gifts he had ever been given: a daughter, whom they named Kaeleie. She was fair of face like her mother, and for that grace Kenyan was exceedingly glad, and grateful to Architaedeus.

More years passed, and more, and more. Kenyan's black hair turned white, and his face, which had once been considered ugly, attained a certain nobility that suited his years and wisdom. Réchetthaerielle grew stooped and wrinkled, but in her husband's eyes, she was always as lovely as she had been the first night he had seen her face, wide-eyed, reflecting the moonlight.

One bitter autumn day, Réchetthaerielle died. Kenyan grieved and mourned, and it seemed to him that his sorrow was the heavier to bear, for the great happiness he had known for so many years. But he committed his soul to Architaedeus, who had blessed him with such delights, and, the following spring, sad Kenyan died too. And while their bodies were lain in the ground, and covered with the earth of Maedwe Feorr where they had first known love, it is certain that their spirits walked together again with joy in the streets of the Blessed.

Kaeleie grew tall and willowy, and married Caronell, the second son of Solonsee of Ester. They also had a daughter, who married one of Lord Ester's grandsons. For each generation that followed in Kenyan's line, there was always one child: sometimes a son, sometimes a daughter. And they all married into nobility, for they were noble themselves, and bore the blood of the Feie.

Chapter Forty-Three

"And that ends the story of Kenyan's Lamp," said Alan Poppleton.

"Tell me some more," begged Owan.

"I think I've told it all," Alan said. *"What else would you like to know?"*

"Ain't there any of them left?"

"Ah! How silly of me. Yes, there is still one alive who is known to be descended from Prince Kenyan and Princess Réchetthaerielle. Can you guess who it is?"

Owan looked at him wide-eyed. "Is it me?"

Alan laughed happily, and tousled the little boy's hair. "No, Owan, I'm afraid not! You have noble-enough blood, but it's not you."

Disappointed, Owan said, "Well, who is it, then?"

"It's old Queen Maygret, King Ruric's wife."

"Oh." Owan thought about that for a moment, and Alan rose from where he sat beside the boy's bed. *"Wait,"* Owan said, not wanting to go to sleep yet. *"Didn't she have no kids?"*

"Well, they say she did have one little boy. But he died when he was very young, I understand. So our friend Kenyan won't have any more descendants, I fear."

"So that boy was the last of the Feies?"

"Well, he was, or Queen Maygret is, depending on how you look at it, I suppose."

"Oh."

"Will that do for tonight, then, young master?"

"Wait! Just ... two more questions, all right?"

"Two more," Alan smiled.

"Thank you, Uncle Alan."

"Indeed."

"Well ... did God mean all along for Kenyan to be the ruler of the Feies ... or did that just happen?"

"Oh," Alan laughed. "I'm afraid that would have been a question more suited for your father than for the likes of me! He studied such things, and thought about them a great deal, but I have no such wisdom ... at least, not yet."

"Did you like him?"

"Your father? Oh, yes, he was a great man. A great man. None better. Until you, perhaps!" Alan smiled again, and began to move toward the doorway.

"Wait!"

"That was two questions, Owan."

"One more!"

"Make it fast."

"Um ... what happened to Black Sarbo?"

Alan laughed. "That, my boy, is a story for another day. All right?"

Owan smiled drowsily back at him. "All right."

"Good night, Owan."

"Good night, Uncle Alan."

The End

also by Robert W. Tompkins

The Hagenspan Chronicles

Book One:

Roarke's Wisdom: The Defense of Blythecairne

Book Two

Roarke's Wisdom: The Courtship of Hollie

Book Three

Roarke's Wisdom: Going Home

Book Four

Roarke's Wisdom: The Last Dragon

Book Six

Owan's Regret: Widows and Successions

Book Seven

Owan's Regret: The Dragon King

Book Eight

Owan's Regret: Into the Wilds

and coming soon:

Book Nine

Owan's Regret: Peace of a Kind

non-fiction:

Disease and Faith

The Last Trumpet

Made in the USA
Charleston, SC
05 August 2016